"What an inventive, wide-ranging intelligence Gene Bell-Villada possesses! The characters in ***The Pianist Who Liked Ayn Rand: A Novella and Thirteen Stories*** *leave lasting impressions. Dickie Dickerson's revenge on the library shusher is a tour de force. Jennifer, braceleted in dollar signs, is the Ayn Rand groupie of your wildest nightmares. Bell-Villada treats us to a variety pack of thought-provoking, challenging writing richly layered by the characters' — and author's — love and knowledge of music. This wry mixture of political and academic satire, cross cultural observation, media mockery, and love story offers the reader a high caloric feast."*

— Mameve Medwed, author of **Mail**

"Readers who appreciate wit, an offbeat perspective, and a biting look at the blind spots in U.S. culture will greatly enjoy this volume. From the comic misperception of a young gringo growing up in Puerto Rico, to the tragic romance of a Chicano pianist with the ideas of Ayn Rand, these stories can help us to see — and laugh at — the dark side of the American dream. I particularly enjoyed 'The Duck Hunter,' an acidly funny takeoff on the film, ***The Deer Hunter****, showing the absurd, desperate way in which America has tried to rewrite its role in Vietnam."*

— Rachel Kranz, Artistic Director,
Theater of Necessity, New York

"This concert of fictive pieces will satisfy readers hungry for satire anchored in an opinioned sensibility. Bell-Villada writes with clarity and picaresque charm on the thorny issues of recent decades, be they familial, ethnic, sexual, artistic or political. Moreover, his authorial presence seems a sort of personified ***élan vital*** *that brings selected pasts with it through many presents, heading, perhaps, for some* ***Weissnichtwo*** *in the future. Don't miss the eerie elegance and violent perversity of 'A Report on a Concert.' Poe's ghost walks again! I have long enjoyed conversing with Bell-Villada's works, but never more than with these true fictions."*

— Patricia Wilcox, poet,
author of A HOUSE BY THE SIDE OF THE ROAD

Other Books by Gene H. Bell-Villada

The Carlos Chadwick Mystery: a Novel of College Life and Political Terror. Amador Publishers, 1990

Borges and His Fiction: A Guide to His Mind and Art. University of North Carolina Press, 1981 [**CHOICE** Magazine Outstanding Academic Book for 1981]

García Marquez: The Man and His Work. University of North Carolina Press, 1991 [New England Council of Latin American Studies Best Book Award, 1990]

Art for Art's Sake and Literary Life: How Politics & Markets Helped Shape the Ideology and Culture of Aestheticism, 1790-1990. University of Nebraska Press, 1996 [Finalist, National Book Critics Circle Award, 1997]

THE PIANIST WHO LIKED AYN RAND

A Novella and 13 Stories

Gene H. Bell-Villada

Printed in the United States of America
        First Printing, 1998
        ISBN: 0-938513-24-9
        Library of Congress Catalog Card # 98-71489

Cover photograph by Clermonts 1991

    "The Prize" originally appeared in **JUSTINA**, published by
Cuadernos de ALDEEU. Reprinted with permission.
    "Our Own Miss Puerto Rico" originally appeared in **CHASQUI**.
Reprinted with permission.
    "The Duck Hunter" originally appeared in **IN THESE TIMES**,
September 19, 1979. Reprinted with permission.
    "Hitler Reconsidered" originally appeared in **THE GHARIAL**, a
magazine at Williams College.
    "A Report on a Concert" originally appeared in **SYRACUSE
SCHOLAR**. Reprinted with permission.

AMADOR PUBLISHERS
P. O. Box 12335
Albuquerque, NM 87195
www.amadorbooks.com

for Estevan Romero

Acknowledgments

With gratitude to Williams College for providing research funds for travel to Philadelphia.

With special thanks to: Marie Barbieri, Monique Bilezikian, Sylvia Coates, Patricia Corkerton, Linda Danielson, Jilliana DeVenuto, Monroe Engel, Tamar Heller, John Hassett, Kitty Kovács (in memoriam, 1946-1989), Steve Kovács, Rachel Kranz, Ron Morin, Theodore Morrison, Jorge Pedraza, Estevan Romero, Robin Mayer Stein, and Patricia Wilcox.

And Audrey.

Publisher's Preface
Harry Willson

Upon first reading, these stories seem extremely minimalist — not about anything much — and I couldn't imagine the "modern reader" staying with them at all. But the irony grew. A prize that amounted to very little, the barely-existent connection to Miss Puerto Rico, the non-existent sculpture entry in a contest, the nastiness of a "friend," exaggerated extrapolations on the meaning of a cigarette. Revenge for being shushed in the library — and one wonders, "Is it worth it?" "A story in which so little happens," is actually a line from one of the stories! I wondered how those readers who want everything imaginable to happen in a bath of extra adrenalin will ever condescend to plow through these stories. But, no, they are about something, after all. They're about how we can become content, or make ourselves think we are content, with very little.

As we proceed the irony becomes delightful and more and more important: war resistance is reduced to the subversive act of growing a mustache — I know some serious activists who would be offended, if they could find this story, but they probably won't, since they don't read "fiction," and don't "get" satire.

The Ayn Rand novella uses the same technique, but this time with a stinging message. Nothing happens, as before - the romances are abortive, as the subtitle tells - and we know why, because Ayn Rand Memorial Up-front Self-centeredness can't be the basis for interesting and pleasurable human interaction. And we live in an age when such an obvious observation does need noting, sad to say.

Hitler will be made respectable next, if we don't change. A satirical mock book-review spells out the kind of thinking which is afoot already. And so many thoughtful people, basically people of goodwill, are completely preoccupied by things that matter so very little that it is a crime and a shame — "The Collection" is a loving evocation of Berkeley in the sixties, a portrait of an eccentric scholarly-artist type, but also an ironic evaluation of "academia," and of all the other private little irrelevant occupations humans can escape into, while the "public thing" goes plumb to hell.

The very last story is the very best — the situation to which all this leads. The islanders quit trying to communicate, and watch someone make a virtue of it. "The rest is silence."

Table of Contents

Part One

Dickie

The Prize

Ever since his parents had stopped talking to each other, he had taken to spending more of his spare time with the radio. The phonograph part of the console took 78 RPM's only, and a lot of their records were cracked, broken, or just gone, so that many of his favorite pieces were now incomplete. The only thing remaining of his Beethoven's First Symphony was sides 1 and 8. This was the worst of all cases, though some others were bad enough. And then the recordings themselves were badly worn from so much use. Most of the albums his mother had bought for him years ago, when he was still in kindergarten. It was right about then that she had commented on how, whenever she'd help tighten his school necktie, or their maid brushed his hair, he'd be humming along with the morning radio concert.

WIPR was its name, abbreviated in turn to WEE-pare by the locals. The government station, it played nine hours of classical music a day, and on LP's too, without interruptions. He always dreaded the return to school at summer's end, wished he could skip class and listen to the daytime programs instead. Piano hour at nine. Concert at midday (with its rousing Schumann *Rhenisch* theme). Chamber music in the afternoon. Come September, he'd complain, even cry. His mother would wipe the tears with a kleenex, button his shirt and say curtly, "Stop it, Dickie, you've got to go to school. Otherwise the government might come after you." That scared him. Then the maid Catalina would say, in Spanish, "Don't be bad, Ricardito. A smart boy like you can't miss school." But at least he got to hear the concerts in the early morning and the evening, and weekends and vacations he could hear them all. He liked it when the throaty, rich voice of the WIPR announcer would enter over a fading Mozart *Jupiter* and

1

begin with, *"Buenos días,"* or would simply say, *"WIPR presenta"* (finale to Beethoven Fifth emerging in the background) *"Concierto de la noche"* (trumpets). Often he wondered if the people at the station could see him sitting there, ear next to speaker, listening and sometimes singing.

For more than six years he had been tuning in regularly to WIPR. His homework he also did by the radio, with Haydn, Mozart, or Brahms providing company during his penmanship or multiplication exercises. The music did no harm and may have helped, since his grades stayed in the 90s, even 100 for Conduct one month. Among the few things he'd heard Dad say to Mom this last year was, "I wish he'd do something *bad* for a change. Doesn't he have friends who cut up some?"

Back at school he'd mentioned the radio concerts to someone sometime, quickly dropping the subject when it drew an empty stare. "What's that?" asked bespectacled Rafael, another kid who got 90s and whom classmates nicknamed "El Profe." Everybody listened to WIPR at night, or so he had thought, but greater still was his surprise when Sister Regina didn't know about Concierto de la Noche. She was from New York. Didn't people from New York listen to classical music? After all, most of the orchestras on his records and on WIPR were from the States. Mom and Dad always reminded him he was a citizen of the States, the greatest country in the world. He'd been born in Río Piedras and had never actually seen the States, but he'd heard its orchestras, New York, Cleveland, Chicago... He imagined everybody in those cities flocking to hear the Symphony Orchestra. I wish there were a great big orchestra just like those right here in San Juan, he fancied now and again.

He couldn't read music, but at least he could follow the descriptive details in Sigmund Spaeth's *Great Concertos* and *Great Symphonies*. He could still recall the excitement he'd felt a couple of years back, when he'd found those two books in his Christmas stocking. He used them just about every day, and since then the glossy front cover had fallen off one, was hanging by a few threads on the other. So many times had he listened to those symphonies and concertos plus countless sonatas, overtures, and suites, that his memory itself was like a record album, he knew them all by heart now. Odd, it was easier to recite a whole symphonic movement than to remember a few lines from his English grammar or his Spaeth books. Why was that? He liked going through those pieces in his mind, singing them under his breath. When it wasn't too noisy around his usual seat in the front of the bus, he'd spend the ride to school silently humming the *Pastorale* or the *Unfinished*. Often he hoped there'd be a flat tire, because he knew they'd be delayed and then he could run an entire symphony through his head. Sometimes it was with a start that he'd hear Alejo the bus driver say in Spanish, "O-kay, here we are," and then he'd see 800 other people on the Colegio grounds, in their maroon or khaki uniforms, standing around and waiting boisterously for the first morning bell.

Dad was coming home later and later in the evenings. The maid also cooked late, but oftentimes it was just Mom and himself eating alone together. Afterwards, Dad would arrive and gulp down his dinner at the big metal desk in the study. Sitting by the phonograph he could see the back side of Dad's graying blond head, could hear the gritty voice speaking into the telephone tube, saying well really, Hudson deserved to fold, so does Packard that's all there is to it, silence, so expand now, push those automatics, well, come on, foreign cars don't rate, they're just a damned fad, Americans make the best cars in the world, silence, we're going to get rid of Mike soon, that old fathead, you hear me? Dickie was singing with the nighttime concert, it was César Franck, the Symphony in D minor, luscious sounds there, especially that second theme:

la-LAAH, la-la-LAAH, la-la-LAAH...

"Come on, Dickie, be quiet, I'm trying to work." The voice was loud though Dad didn't turn around to look at him. Mom said nothing as she sipped her drink on the sofa, reading *Newsweek*. During breakfast from time to time one or the other might say, "Dickie, stop, it's not nice to sing at the table." So he'd stop but still hear the sounds in his head, filling the silence. The music seemed to have a taste in his mouth, he thought.

It was summer now, and he listened to WIPR all day. Dad went out to work on Saturdays and sometimes even on Sundays. Mom was at one of the beach clubs, for bridge. Except when she was cleaning, Catalina stayed mostly at the opposite end of the apartment, in the kitchen or her little bedroom. Standing outside on the balcony he liked gazing down and watching cars go by. Some he heard honk; a few he recognized. The radio he kept at a high volume, drowning out much of the noise, though his parents wouldn't have allowed it if they were at home. The salty-smelling breeze felt nice in his face. Up above, a small airplane was skywriting "Pepsi" for a third time. Toward the right he could see part of the University grounds, with its walkways crisscrossing over carpet-like lawns, snail-sized moms idling their strollers to and fro, the bell tower rising above the trees. He missed those times — was it before he'd started school? — when Mom and Dad and he used to go for late walks on the campus and look at its fountains, or sit on the grass where he'd hear the bells play classical music. He missed those days, but since then he'd heard the originals of those pieces, and the bell tower still played them almost daily, so he'd sing along. At midday or at six they'd play Bach, Mozart, or Offenbach, and he might lower the radio and hum with the bells instead.

Every Friday since Easter WIPR had been holding musical identification contests. For fifteen minutes they would play a mystery piece or portion thereof and wait for a lucky listener to phone in the name of the composer and the title, including key and opus number when applicable. The first caller who had all the facts right received a free gift of a classical album. Dickie recognized many of the pieces. He had heard them broadcast on

WIPR sometime or other, and one he'd actually owned before it fell and shattered. On occasions he had almost called in, but the operator's voice had frightened him off. *"¿Número?"* he would hear and then quickly hang up. Last week their mystery piece had been Mendelssohn's *Calm Sea and Prosperous Voyage* overture; he got up his courage, gave the number to the operator, heard a buzzing sound, and again hung up as soon as he recognized, right there over his parents' telephone, the WIPR announcer's voice.

The mystery piece this time was a Beethoven Contra Danse. He knew it from one of the Little Golden Records he used to like putting on the phonograph, when he was in first grade; later it had cropped up as a filler in an album. Nobody seemed to have recognized the piece so far. He got up, walked over to the upright phone and unhooked the receiver. Hand and voice trembling slightly, he spoke into the tube and did as he had done last week, but this time stayed on when he heard the familiar voice from Concierto de la Tarde.

"Haló, la WIPR."

"That piece you're playing," Dickie said, in Spanish.

"Yes, yes, what's it called?"

"Beethoven. The first Contra Danse. In D major. No opus."

"Very good, sir. You've just won a brand-new classical record from WIPR." The man used the formal *Usted* with him. "We've had nineteen calls already. They all missed. Could you give me your name, address, and telephone number, please?"

"Dickie Dickers... I mean, Richard Dickerson." He paused. "Junior," he added in a breathy voice. "1001 Avenida Muñoz Rivera, apartment 501, Río Piedras. The telephone is..." he had forgotten, now looked at the label, "976-R."

"Fine, Mr. Dickerson. You can come to our offices anytime before six. Do you know where we are located?"

"Yes."

"Well, you should be here for your gift certificate within eight days. By the way is that really your name? You must be North American, no?"

"Yes."

"Ah, but you speak such good Spanish. Well, Mr. Dickerson, congratulations."

"Thank you."

"And thank you for calling. Adiós." He hung up.

"Adiós."

Dickie felt his heart beating fast. He wished Mom and Dad were there so he could tell them. He was even more excited when he heard the announcer's voice saying, "We have a winner. His name is Richard Dickerson, Junior, of Río Piedras."

He ran down the hall to the kitchen, almost slipping on his socks.

"Catalina."

"Tell me, Dickie." She was stirring something in a large pot. He couldn't see what it was.

"I just won a prize."

"Ah, yes? What did you win?"

"Records. I identified a mystery piece on WIPR."

"Ah, how nice. You're so smart, Ricardito." With her free hand she patted him on the head.

Every day Dickie used to see the WIPR offices from the school bus. He liked the building's tall, squarish letters.

"Catalina, tell me how can I get to WIPR? You know, the radio station in Santurce."

"Just take the Parada 20 bus here by the building. It stops right across from them. You used it during the school bus drivers' strike a year ago, remember?"

"Ah, yes," he said, then hurried back down the hall to his bedroom and located his shoes. Rather than wait for the elevator he rushed down the five flights of poorly lit stairway. It was hot and sticky out on the street, the smell of diesel fumes stronger than usual. The large, gray, flatnosed Parada 20 bus showed up in less than a minute. Crowded, it was, some jostling. Behind the driver he caught sight of an empty lateral seat and slid himself in, but kept glancing over his shoulder so as not to miss WIPR.

He had to stand up to pull the bell cord (ding, ding). The bus just barely stopped. He crossed the avenue and in the farthest lane was nearly hit by a screeching something — a taxi, he thought, but wasn't sure. From close up the building actually looked a trifle smaller than it had appeared so many times from the road. *EMPUJE,* the door said. The lobby was air conditioned, delicious sensation, especially on his face. The girl at the desk had short, straight black hair, bright red lipstick, and a flowery blouse. She raised her dark eyes briefly as he walked towards her. Pocket mirror in hand, she was fixing her make-up with a kleenex. He took a deep breath.

She clicked shut the mirror and asked him, business-like, "Tell me, little boy, what do you want?"

"Uh, I just won that...that prize on Concierto de la Tarde."

"Aha. And?"

"...Who do I talk with?"

"Well, actually, I don't know, I started working here just this week. But if you go through that door they'll tell you what you must do."

It was less modern inside than in the lobby. A narrow wood-panelled stairway was the first thing he saw; a lady maybe his mother's age, standing in a little office at the right, was the second.

"Tell me, little boy."

"I'm Dickie...I mean Richard Dickerson. I just won that prize."

The lady shifted to almost-accentless English. "Oh, you're Dickie Dickerson. You know, I think I met your Mom once. Well, look, go up the stairs to the second floor and turn right. Efraín the announcer's there. He'll give you your Record Certificate."

Dickie climbed the stairs slowly, in twos. Coming down there was a frowning, balding, gray-fringed man with a loose-leaf notebook and a Cuban guayabera. One of the announcers? Then Dickie caught sound of the voice he'd just heard on the telephone and saw a little room encased in wood and glass. The door was open just a crack. The fellow in the pink shirt who faced the microphone had a roundish head of thick wavy black hair and a prickly, incipient beard. Dickie opened the door further, noticed the LP record sleeves stacked up on either side of the announcer's hefty, curly-haired arms, and heard him saying, "the Symphony Orchestra of the NBC, under the baton of Arturo Toscanini."

The announcer turned toward Dickie, who was about to identify himself, but the man's left hand suddenly rose up with the "Wait!" signal even as his lips were puckering up. It worked — mouth half-open, Dickie froze. The announcer smiled slightly, then spoke into the microphone. "And now, ladies and gentlemen, we will listen to the Symphony Number 3 in C minor by Camille Saint-Saëns, interpreted by..." The station played that piece a lot, sometimes twice a month, Dickie had noticed.

"Well, tell me what can I do for you, kid?"

"My name is Richard Dickerson. I just won that prize."

The announcer looked at him, paused briefly, and said, "Ah, yes, one minute." The deep voice was unmistakable. He puffed at a cigar that appeared out of nowhere, got up, seemed to bounce around, reached leftwards into an open file, and pulled out a piece of hard paper that looked like a small diploma.

"Yes," he said, and sat back down. The Symphony's agitated first theme was just beginning. The announcer sang vigorously and moved his head in rhythm to Saint-Saëns' rapid-fire melody while printing something on the pretty card. He nodded once, rolled the chair to the right in Dickie's general direction, opened up a green notebook with dark red corners and filled in a couple of its narrow little lines, still singing.

He stood up, took another cigar puff and said, "Look, Richard." He shifted to the informal *tú* now, "this is your Gift Certificate. Take it over to Discolandia a few doors down. They've got your album ready. Okay?"

"Yes."

"Well, congratulations for winning, and have fun with your prize, okay?" After giving Dickie a pat on the shoulder, he sat down again and swivelled toward the microphone.

Dickie looked at the paper, said, "Thank you," turned around, and did another about-face.

The announcer looked up from his notes. "Yes, what's happening?"

"How did you say I get to Discolandia?"

"Turn left when you come out of the station. Go toward San Juan just about half a block. It's there." Brief pause. "All right? Well, have fun. Here, I'll open the door for you."

Dickie went quietly down the stairs, glanced at the lady in the office from the corner of his eye. "'Bye, 'bye, Dickie," he heard her say. "'Bye," he said without looking at her. Outside, in the hall, a blond man in a white shirt and black tie finished off his coffee while listening to the smiling receptionist say something funny. The blond man chuckled, placed the cup onto the saucer held in his other hand. "Adiós," the girl said as Dickie opened the street door. He wasn't sure if she meant it for him.

Discolandia was the biggest record shop he had ever seen, but then he hadn't been to any record shops recently. The mirrors and the *luz fría* (he couldn't remember the long English word for the tube-shaped bulbs just now) made the place look even bigger. So many recordings, all the way up to the ceiling, he wished he could hear every single one. The brassy tune being played was familiar, a fast mambo he had heard resounding every night for at least a year from the bar next door. Sometimes Catalina hummed it. Sister Regina once said that mambo is sinful, he remembered.

One of the clerks was tapping on the cash register and shaking his hips to the beat. He stopped when he saw Dickie.

"Yes, young man?"

Dickie held out the certificate to him.

"Ah, yes." He stroked his moustache. "Ramón, here, another one for the people from WIPR. Could you bring it to me, please?"

Ramón, a lanky mulatto in a pink shirt, clicked his fingers, went into a back room, rolled a ladder and clambered up, and returned with a shiny new record jacket, all within a few seconds. "Another one," he said, handing it to the first clerk and moving on.

"Well, young man, here you are."

Dickie held it in his hand, read and examined it.

"Look, sir."

"Yes, tell me."

"This is an LP, no?"

"Yes, precisely."

"Do you have it in 78s? My record player only takes 78s."

The clerk let out a nervous titter. "Well, you see, uh...I don't know what to say to you but, well...Nobody makes classical 78s anymore. That stuff's no good, really. Look, even that mambo by Pérez Prado is on a 45."

He pointed. Dickie saw the toy-sized disc spinning around a drum-like spindle.

"You don't have a 78 I could take instead?"

"Not in classical, sorry. But look, think about it, someday you'll have an LP phonograph." Dickie recalled Dad saying those same words a couple of summers ago. "You'll be able to play it then. Come, give that to me and I'll put it in a bag for you."

A pink-skinned lady in a leopard blouse entered, leading a small Pekingese. "Good afternoon," she said with a smile.

The clerk handed Dickie the bag and addressed the lady. "Ah, yes, good afternoon, Señora Castillo. Listen, the Kostelanetz album finally arrived today. Would you like to try it out?"

The woman's voice receded as Dickie walked out onto the street again. It was still hot, and he had liked the feel of air conditioning, both at WIPR and at Discolandia. Until now the only air conditioned places he had been to were the theaters, like the one in Río Piedras five blocks from the apartment, where he spent many a Saturday afternoon watching American movies. He stopped a minute, realizing he needed to ask directions for the return bus stop. He peeked into the bag. Kostelanetz conducting. Grand Canyon Suite. He wished it were some other piece. He already owned it, or actually three-fourths of it, since sides 4 and 5, with "On the Trail," had cracked some years ago. It had been a present from his father, in first grade, he remembered, and he liked the piece back then, still did, though less so now, less than Tchaikovsky, and far less than Beethoven or Brahms.

Our Own Miss Puerto Rico

All week long people at the office had been saying, "I wonder who'll be crowned Miss Puerto Rico!" Then they'd chuckle and continue with their work. Meanwhile Dickie, clipboard in hand, would quietly get on with inventory, climbing the long ladder and registering the number of "A" cups and "B" cups currently in stock. Sometimes he'd reach for a rag in order to wipe off the dust that had accumulated over the stacks of pink boxes. One pile of D-40s had sat around for so long you could barely read the "Elegant Form" script sweeping neatly across the uppermost boxtop.

"Dickie, please could you get me some coffee?" shouted Clarisa, the secretary. He rushed down the ladder's steps and over to the coffee room next door.

Little did he know it, but his uncle Fred had instructed them to treat Dickie as if he were just another employee. Occasionally, though, the assistant Paquín would screw up his ruddy face, scratch his late-afternoon stubble, and whisper, "Say, Ricardito, could your father sell me a brand-new Chevy at a discount?" And they'd both giggle.

Dickie trod carefully through the door, Clarisa's white cup a-juggling precariously in its white saucer, and finally reached her typing desk. "Ah, there you are," she said, brushing her blond curls from her eyes. "Thanks, Dickie, you're a good boy." Her long hands showed rosy fingernails. She took a sip directly.

"Say, Dickie," said Gladys' grainier voice behind him, "that looks good. Could you get me one too?" As he sauntered alongside the stacked-up boxes he heard her saying, "It's tomorrow, no? And who's going to win?"

"Who knows? We'll see," Clarisa's distant voice came back.

Three-oh-five, said the table clock in the coffee room. As he entered he recognized one of the sewing-machine girls from the factory, pouring herself some Sanka.

"Hi," she nodded at him, her thin, red lips smiling slightly. He liked the smell of her facial powder. She was his height and maybe three years older.

"Hi," was his soft, almost inaudible reply. She turned around silently. The constant factory hum drowned out the sound of her flowery pink flats shuffling across the room toward the three gray stairs.

As Dickie poured the coffee Paquín ambled in, pulling up and tightening his trousers. "*Hola,* Ricardito," he said, giving him a soft slap on the shoulder.

"*Hola.*"

"When is Mister Brown coming back from Havana?"

"Don't know. Mom talked with him last night."

"Well, the new factory must be taking up lots of time."

Dickie remembered the dinner with Uncle Fred, when the only thing he and Dad had talked about was the new plant being built in Cuba. Mom and Uncle Fred looked so much alike, yet she was so quiet, he thought.

He made his way to Gladys' desk and saw Gabriel and Julián standing about. Julián had a big cigar between his front teeth; Gabriel was unclipping his bow tie. The two usually came by at about this time.

"Thanks, Dickie," said Gladys, in English, pushing back a stray tuft of white hair. She switched to Spanish. "Do you guys want coffee?"

"No, no," said Gabriel, "not after walking around in all this heat." He dropped into a stray chair.

"How'd it go today?" Clarisa asked.

Gabriel shrugged his shoulders; Julián's deep voice said, "Pretty good. González Padín took a few big orders. Everybody there wanted to know if I'd heard anything about ...you know ... *that.*"

"Oh, well, maybe...," Gladys reflected.

Clarisa lit a cigarette. "And in the papers? Nothing?"

Gabriel was rolling up his sleeves. "No. And why, really? It was that Eisenhower guy on the front page this afternoon."

Taking a big smoky puff, Julián shook his head. "Those people up there might actually vote for him again. All he does is play golf. What's with these crazy gringos? Crazy, they all are."

The two secretaries looked over at Dickie leaning gently on the nearby racks, and then giggled. "Careful," a smiling Clarisa said, pointing a finger at Julián.

And Julián spun around on his heels to catch Dickie's eye. "Hey, Dickie, nothing against gringos, you understand. I don't even think of you as one, your Spanish is so good."

Dickie blushed, looked at the floor. Paquín gave him a soft punch on the ear, saying with a smile, "He's a *good* gringo, this Dickie."

The two salesmen picked up their briefcases again, swinging them energetically. Gabriel got up from the folding chair and said, "Well, we'll see what happens."

"Tomorrow!" more than one voice said.

Everybody has a life. The thought often runs through Dickie's mind as he rides the crowded bus from work. The fellow in blue overalls sitting at his side; the blonde lady in high heels facing him from across the aisle there, clutching at her New York Department Store bag; the graying man in a guayabera shirt, standing, briefcase in one hand and the ceiling bar in another. All of them have lives that go on after they've exited the bus and are headed home. And yet he saw them just this once and no more as they each continued having lives. He had ridden as far as Río Piedras and now marvelled at the thought that, having made their way through the doors off in Santurce or Hato Rey, they still lived on somewhere in those places. What were they doing now? he wondered.

Dad was down in Mayagüez again on business, Mom said. She hoped he wouldn't be home too late, she said. Dickie and Mom ate quietly. Catalina had the week off. Beethoven's Second

Symphony was listed in *El Diario* for that night's WIPR evening concert, followed by the *Pastorale*. He always loved that Sixth, loved the many repetitions, could hum along with its first movement's every note. The melodies went on ringing in his mind later as he tucked into bed. He had no idea when it was that he heard the front door's unlocking and shutting, heard Dad's familiar footsteps resounding in the dark stillness.

Mom informed him over breakfast that his dad was asleep, so he'd hear about Mayagüez at suppertime. Now, though, he had to get off to work as he heard his mother's reminder, "Don't forget your lunch box, Dickie."

At first the bus seemed uncrowded but there were no empty seats. He was the only standing passenger, up in front. Sitting together towards the rear he spotted two boys from Colegio Espíritu Santo. They smiled as they conversed. One of them fascinated Dickie with his dark, angular eyebrows and constant frown. Dickie always felt surprised when he'd see Colegio kids elsewhere, and yet they too must have a life, just as everyone else does. They even get together when they're on vacation, something he never did. But then he was American, not Puerto Rican.

The five-block walk from Plaza Colón down to the office never ceased to thrill him, so exciting it was to be out there with all those thousands, each of them headed somewhere in the mornings, and he too was one of those people and moreover was receiving $5 every Friday. Just another reason why he liked working at the office.

Clarisa barely nodded at him from her desk as she paid heed to Gladys exclaiming, "So it happened!" and she in turn replied, "Looks as if it did!" and both of them giggled.

"When is it they're getting married?" Gladys asked.

"October, I think."

Gladys bit a lower lip, then said in English, in a deeper voice, "They're gonna be havin' a hot time!"

Now they both guffawed. Dickie joined in too.

"Well, look," Clarisa remarked, "little Dickie laughs and he doesn't even know about those things!"

"Yes, I do know!" Dickie insisted.

The day's heat and humidity were unbearable. Following delivery of that afternoon's messages he went for a large root beer at the Royal Palm, where there was air-conditioning and it was so cool and relaxing. A discarded *El Imparcial* on a nearby stool and its headline, "LUCY DEL VALLE CHOSEN MISS PUERTO RICO," caught his eye. The woman in the photograph had a wide, laughing smile, short, dark hair coming down in a double twist framing both sides of her forehead, and heavy lipstick. Dickie thought the double twirl made her look a little bit scary. The nuns at the Colegio often warned that the Devil can look just like anybody else, can be nice and offer you candy, can be good-looking too. They often criticized Puerto Rican girls for wearing "a pound of make-up," in their phrase. "This Lucy del Valle," Dickie thought, "looks like a pretty Devil, with all her make-up," something he might say at the office.

Walking down the hall he heard fast, excited chatter, soon making out Gabriel's and Julián's voices. As he reached the left turn and approached the wide door he saw Clarisa and Julián hugging each other, though they weren't even married. Paquín and Julián now shook hands, then also hugged. Puerto Ricans do a lot of hugging, Dickie reflected. His parents and relatives almost never did.

"So," said Gladys, "you must feel proud." She gave Julián a little pat on the shoulder.

His entire face seemed to smile. "Well, I'm proud of Lucy. It's her prize, after all." He puffed on his cigar.

"Next October you're goin' to be *Mister* Puerto Rico," she joked, pronouncing the word *meester* for some reason.

"My God, that's right!" Julián guffawed. "I hadn't thought of it that way."

Gabriel now said to the group, more calmly, "He's got pictures," then turned to him. "You're going to let us see 'em?"

"Let's see, let's see!" said Paquín.

Julián now took out a small yellow envelope from his briefcase and produced from it a pack of black-and-white photographs. Everybody was oohing and aahing as they contemplated Lucy all dressed up for the grand ball at the Escambrón, Lucy with her parents over in Arecibo, Lucy in a short-sleeve white dress standing arm-in-arm with Julián, Lucy posing in her dark bathing suit at El Dorado Beach.

"Look at how the bulge shows in this one," Dickie heard Julián saying softly to the men. He looked up and saw all of them grinning.

"Well, Dickie," asked Gladys, "and what do you think of Lucy?"

He flushed, and stammered, "Uh...mm...oh she's very pretty."

Everyone in the room laughed while Clarisa, her arms crossed over her chest, remarked, "Dickie, what do you know about that stuff?"

"Hey, look," said Paquín, "Dickie's a real macho, ain't that right?" He gave Dickie a little punch on the shoulder.

As he rode home he remembered little else about the events. But he prayed to and thanked God that he hadn't said those things about Lucy and the Devil and her lipstick. He would have been hated, and he didn't want to be hated. God must've been watching over him, it does happen, he'd read so in *The Power of Positive Thinking*. He was wondering about the life a Miss Puerto Rico has. Does she wash dishes? Will she take a crowded bus at five? All those people having lives somewhere. There were passengers carrying *El Imparcial* with Lucy's picture on the front page, and he felt like saying to one of them, any of them, "See her? I know the guy she's going to marry in October." He couldn't wait until he told his mom about what had happened, and about Miss Puerto Rico's future husband, Julián, a Mister Puerto Rico, who worked right at Uncle Fred's office.

The Hidden Shape of Things: a Letter

1001 Avenida Muñoz Rivera
Río Piedras
May 2, 1961

Her Honor the Mayor's Commission on the Arts
Sculpture Contest
City Hall
San Juan

Ladies and Gentlemen:

For a good many years now the most trivial as well as the most transcendent of my thoughts have been thoroughly dominated by a graceful, three-sided shape. And it is this item I submit herewith as my entry to your projected first Biennial Sculpture Contest. I feel most thrilled — let it be said — about the prospects of my statue being prized and then publicly exhibited for all fellow San Juanians to see, admire, and be moved by.

To that end I wish to furnish you a sneak preview of my work. The shape, unique and special, looks like this:

Tilting down to the left there is a long diagonal, cutting across like a hypotenuse and forming with its presumed base an angle of seventy degrees; in lieu of that base there is another potential hypotenuse which, were it in turn to boast a base, would result in an angle of twenty degrees; and finally, on the right, surging upwards with a graceful elegance, a taut energy and — I daresay — a romantic sweep, there is a line consisting of thirteen equidistant and identical waves. Statue is untitled.

Material is granite or brass.

This opus of mine holds full sway over my inner thoughts and keeps me constant company. But it also pullulates in the world outside, for I can commonly picture the lush University lawns, the concrete playgrounds at Colegio Espíritu Santo, or the ever-teeming Plaza Colón as typical sites for its uninterrupted public display. Indeed I sometimes imagine the University bell tower itself or even El Yunque mountain as potential blocks whence the shape might be fashioned, though of course being cognizant that that could be so only in the most extreme circumstances!

It was only some years ago that I found myself drifting into sculpture. Before that it was classical music I had cleaved to as my first love. Day after day I'd make it a point to catch every concert program I could on WIPR, the best radio station in the world. It gave me, still gives me, great pleasure, and I'm grateful, too. It's through WIPR that I first discovered Tchaikovsky, Beethoven, Brahms, and the rest. Back in that distant decade I'd go to the Carnegie Library in San Juan or the branch library here in Río Piedras, and I'd bring home books on their lives and music, and having read them I'd sit there in my room and say to myself, "How wonderful it must be to compose great symphonies and concertos, just like the old masters did!"

There was a time when I had a fairly decent record collection, though there's not much left of it now. 78s, you know... Those things break at nothing, and today I've got mostly vestiges, like sides 4 (cadenza and coda of first movement) and 5 (Intermezzo) of the Schumann Piano Concerto. We still have not acquired an LP player at home since my father doesn't care that much about music, and the violin lessons I'd always hoped for haven't materialized yet either. Of course money is tight — as my father likes to say — and lessons are expensive, as are instruments, and I suppose he's right. He is also right, I guess, when he says I could jolly well have shown some initiative and found a fiddle teacher on my own.

"Look at Mike Todd," he remarked a while back.   "A

bookkeeper at age *fifteen!* And what've you done with *your* life, except squander your weekly allowance on some dull, useless books and *records!?*"

So by the time I was in eighth grade I pretty much had laid to rest my hope of playing in the Symphony under Maestro Somohano. (I still get excited, though, whenever I watch him on the TV, conducting Mozart, number 40.) Then came sculpture. I don't know when exactly it was that I read that article in *Time* magazine on Mr. Brancusi, with pictures of his statues and all. (The three of us read *Time* from cover to cover every week.) But it's what first sent me running to the branch library down the street and got me to browsing through their sculpture books. I spent whole afternoons either there or at home, going volume by volume and leafing through its pages and gazing at statues by Michelangelo and Donatello and Rodin, but most especially those by the great ultra-moderns, Giacometti, Brancusi. How wonderful it must have been to make his "Bird in Space!" If that were all Mr. Brancusi had ever done, his life would have been complete.

And so it was that being a sculptor became an overriding passion of mine. If I recall correctly it was in tenth grade that I first was hit by the idea for this triangular shape and also started checking out possible sites for it. During the school bus ride I could already see the sculpture gracing Hato Rey front yards or the Juliá Clinic's expanse or the Espíritu Santo's elementary-school patio. Nice, to imagine some first-grade types playing at hide-and-seek or running in circles around that three-sided shape of mine. But I could also picture good old Sister Consolata or Miss Franco glancing at it as *my* statue, by he to whom they'd taught addition tables and alphabet songs one time, he whose triangular creation they would not mind having replicas of back in their convent or their living room.

I also like it that discovering sculpture has brought me close to music and the chance of finally being a music maker. Now when I hear a composition I can glimpse just how my statue could express that very piece. I'll sculpt a heroic, monumental version of the shape and say, "That's my interpretation of Beethoven's *Eroica*;" or a quiet, rustic triangle that's been transcribed from his *Pastorale*; or a sad and mournful one that I perform as Tchaikovsky's *Pathetique*. The statue thereby serves me as a musical instrument of my own. And then it helps me understand all of that politics out there too. It has always been so confusing to me, I simply cannot follow what the daily town crier says on TV about wars and subversion and defense of freedom all over the globe, but when I conceive of "the enemy" as hordes of threatening triangles and of "the Allies" as a gathering of beneficent ones, I feel as if the isms have been conveniently clarified for me in my mind.

This shape, then, is my entry for the contest. Granted, it lacks as yet something essential, namely, physical existence, though I can well imagine a day when I shall fashion and refashion the shape many times over in a multitudinous variety of materials, textures, and shades.

Still, all this foolishness surely will elicit from you the vexing question: Why keep my mind so busy making shapes that only it can perceive? Why carry these opuses inside of me, dreaming them by the millions, rather than getting down to the task of crafting one, just one? Indeed, why these mental warm-ups and not the sculpting game itself? Such questions have not spared me, and while I know the answers, the ghosts of doubt assail my conscience.

I'm not a sculptor. Or rather I've never learned to sculpt. My dad — an admirable businessman and a good father who has given me life, plus food and housing, plus my past and present education — doesn't think it's really much worth it.

"Got the money?" he replied when, over dinner a few years ago, I asked him about art lessons. "Stone, metal, and marble," he went on to say, "don't grow on trees. Besides, studios are expensive."

I can certainly see his wanting me not to waste time on something that won't pay, especially now as I prepare myself to head up for the States and work toward my degree in Business

Administration.

Oh, I know, again, I could have shown some private initiative, gotten lessons somehow on my own. I could now. At age eighteen, though, it is somewhat intimidating to pick up a new and far-out physical skill like sculpture. And I don't relish the prospect of getting started in the basics yet not perfecting my craft to the point where I could endow the shape with those very features that make it special. I shudder: would I be able to forge freely an angle that is not $69° \; 59' \; 00''$, nor $70° \; 01' \; 01''$ — but $70° \; 00' \; 00''$ and neither more nor less? Could I mold the most delectable possible thirteen frills? And could I give the statue the right tilt and surface textures? I fear that every attempt, its incidental beauties notwithstanding, would be a failure, a shadowy approximation of the idea that is vividly alive and throbbing in my head.

And let us assume my hands did learn to move the way I wanted them to. Having finally fashioned a shape that meets my standards, I would call in the neighbors, my onetime playmate Federico, his kid sister Maritza, and maybe their mother Doña Matilde, for an assessment. (Dad would be busy; mom doesn't talk.) The statue, I suspect, wouldn't mean much to the three of them. Or it might also mean too much. They'd see it as more as well as less representational than it actually is, whereas in truth it represents merely its own shape while indirectly hinting at lots of other things too.

DOÑA MATILDE: Very nice.

MARITZA: What is it?

ME: It's that.

FEDERICO: Interesting. Let's see what else you've done.

"Well, as it happens," I might consider replying, "the only shape that interests me is this one here. Spheres, cubes, pentagons, or whatever all else just leave me cold. And there's enough good statues of people out there, starting with the pharaohs of Egypt, I think."

So the one single opus I'd ever really wanted to sculpt would be staring them in the face.

ME: It's all I've done.
DOÑA MATILDE: Seems promising.
MARITZA: Too abstract for me.
FEDERICO: You've got to build a portfolio now.
DOÑA MATILDE: Yes, of course, a body of work, how does one say...(*snaps her right-hand fingers*), a repertory, that's it.

And then I decide whether or not to state that the entire portfolio/body of work/repertory is what is standing there before them.

Hardly an encouraging prospect, you will grant. It reminds me of the story Doña Matilde likes to tell about the guy from Mayagüez, a distant cousin of hers who went up to New York and spent eleven years there writing a sixteen-line sonnet, in English at that. The poem, reportedly a masterpiece, was rightly accepted and printed by some hot-shot poetry journal, and was then promptly forgotten as its ever-avid readers turned to the next page. Certainly for a moment or two they had been treated to a top specimen of verse in their Anglo-America-Australo-Canadian language. But the lack of further visible effort relegated our one-poem poet to a niche only slightly above oblivion.

That fellow's fate has influenced me and suggested inaction as a wise enough course. Better that my shape remain in the realm of great potentialities. Her Honor's Commission on the Arts now knows me as the inspired sculptor who has not sculpted any statues thus far, yet could well have been a serious participant in this or subsequent contests.

I like thinking of it this way: somewhere in, say, Canada, or China, there lives a great Spanish poet who, chance would have it, never picked up enough Spanish words, if any. Yet has this at all aggravated the world's suffering, his or his potential public's? In contrast I think of the dozens of possible Cervanteses here on this island who feel the pulse of greatness inside themselves and who, however productive, can't put out a single work commensurate with their inner sense of greatness, can't compose a poem as exciting as the insight whence it sprang. All of them Cervanteses to the core, no doubt, but who cares about the core? whose verdict goes so deep?

As a wise man once put it somewhere: who thinks of apples in terms other than round and red? Certainly, once we get beyond the meat of the matter the core — the black, core-shaped, essential core — the core's the thing. But we all say "red apples" and thus disregard how small a portion of the fruit's total make-up that thin red peel happens to be.

So now I prepare myself to study Business Administration up in El Norte. And there are real advantages to my fingers' not doing sculpting. As things now stand I can put that three-sided shape wherever I please and vary its size and textures in a flash. Were I finally to produce the statue I'd begin to feel uneasy about there being just that one shape in this world. I'd see the thing as frozen in its sameness and hence unsatisfying. And I'd feel compelled to make and accumulate more such shapes.

And so here goes:

Suppose I were to give this vision of mine some tangible existence as a 3' x 5' structure in granite.

Once done with, I'd start pondering the gaps still remaining in this world, and would see no reason for there also not to be

a 9' x 15' in copper,

a 15' x 25' in mahogany with inlaid gold,

or a diminutive 6" x 10" in teak for coffee tables,

in a word, a shape of every imaginable size, beginning with 1" x 1.667" and on to infinity. The permutations ensuing from the 100 elements or whatever-number-it-happens-to-be, and from all compounds natural and synthetic, would be endless. Meanwhile there's talk up in the States of going metric, and here as well, and so my plans would henceforth multiply as I now sculpted statues conceived in millimeters on up rather than in old-fashioned feet and inches.

And as my creation overflowed the galleries and plazas and front yards, I'd feel further compelled to sculpt additional shapes for the rooftops, or desktops, or even the insides of bottles, or as lamps. At some point I'd hire as many talented and able-bodied men I can afford to keep in my employ as loyal sculptors of my shape. And at long last, shapes everywhere! No, wait, somewhere in the Rocky Mountains there sits yet another inchoate mass, waiting to be sculpted into a set of three or four of my triangulate shapes.

This, then, is my entry to Her Honor's first projected Biennial Sculpture Contest. I hope you like it. The competition, I know, is considerable. There may well be entrants whose work is as good as mine and even better, more beautiful and mature, or simply more suitable for public spaces. Luck, I do understand, is in some measure the final arbiter of all things.

Meanwhile I shall continue to pursue the joys of sculpture for their own sake. As a wise Miss Thomson said to the juniors at Assembly last week, we will each of us need both a vocation and an *a*vocation. And I therefore see business as my first, the triangular sculpture as my second. Like the sun, remote and unattainable yet taken for granted, the reason for life yet also a source of some discomfort, the shape shines on.

Very truly yours,
Richard Dickerson, Jr.

Friends

Gerd was probably the only Chilean at the school, and certainly the first one Dickie had ever encountered in the flesh. He was also the first person Dickie could ever talk to about art and music. They usually spoke Spanish together, sometimes even when there were regular American students walking along or seated sipping coffee with them. Occasionally Gerd held Dickie by the arm or shoulder a few seconds as they exited from Dietrich Hall out onto a still-green and sun-filled campus. Continental Americans seldom did this, Dickie had already noticed.

They'd first met in Freshman Composition class, where each of them chose front-row seats, Dickie at the far end, Gerd in the middle. The professor, Mr. McKay, distinctive in his trim red beard, did a quick, staccato roll-call, making the full names sound like single words. He rushed through the list uninterrupted save for varied versions of the syllable, "Here," until he read out "Gerd Peters."

A smooth tenor voice, slightly tinged with a Spanish accent, explained, "Oh, if you please, the first name is 'Gerd.' It rhymes with 'paired.' The last is pronounced 'PAY-ters.' Like the writer."

The professor tightened his wire-rim glasses, looked up from his lectern, and, after a momentary silence, remarked slowly, "Oh, you mean Pater, I suppose."

"Yes, exactly," Peters replied. His dark wavy hair and pencil moustache were features that stood out among the half-dozen crewcuts grouped in mid-classroom.

Toward the end of the next class meeting, Mr. McKay announced a free-floating assignment: to attend a cultural event

26

sometime and write a 500-word review of it by Thanksgiving.

Peters's raised hand showed two large rings. "Professor, I would like to criticize Ormandy's rendition of the Brahms Fourth last night. Would that be possible?" His long-sleeved, dark-colored shirt rustled faintly.

The professor, apparently impressed, smiled. "Why, yes, that'd be fine. I'm a symphony nut myself. What did you find wrong?"

"Much too fast and not sufficiently Romantic. And the trombones were too loud."

McKay nodded once, with a brief grin. "Very interesting; proceed. I'll look forward to it." Then he dismissed the class.

Peters was shutting his attach case. Dickie, filing past, asked where he was from.

"I'm from Chile. And you?"

"From Puerto Rico."

As they strolled toward the College Green they switched to Spanish, chatting in bits and pieces about Wharton and the States, Gerd's two-year stint in the family business and, eventually, about music.

Dickie was curious. "How is it you know that Brahms piece so well?"

"Oh, well, you see, my grandparents came from Germany, and felt it was important to keep the culture alive. Besides, they settled in Valdivia, where there's a pretty large German colony. We all spoke German at home." He pulled out a pack of Viceroys from his shirt pocket and offered one to Dickie, who declined, saying, *"No fumo."*

They stopped in front of the statue. Leaning on a bench, Gerd produced a gold-colored lighter and lit up a cigarette. On the paths around them there was a rush of Madras shirts, plaid skirts, and inscribed jackets as students compared class choices or headed for the library. Dickie caught his first sight of a clump of leaves that had turned bright yellow.

Gerd blew out a puff of smoke. "So anyway we had lots of records, many of them direct from Germany. We weren't the only ones, though. Some kids next door even put together their own string quartet."

"Wow," Dickie responded. He felt a surge of friendly envy. "I've never even seen a symphony orchestra, except on TV. My dad hated classical music; so did most everybody at my school. Maybe even on the whole island."

"My God! You poor guy." Gerd touched Dickie on the elbow. "Well, look, next Thursday, I'm going to the Orchestra concert. Want to come? I'll treat. They'll be playing the *Eroica*."

It had come as a surprise to Dickie when some neighbors at the Quad watched him unpack his dozen-and-a-half LPs, and one of them remarked light-heartedly, "Oh, no, not longhair music!" The judgment was heartily seconded by the three others. For years Dickie had heard the scolding nuns at Espíritu Santo say how wonderful the students were back in the States, how much smarter, more hard-working and respectful than Puerto Ricans. And here he was, enrolled at last as a U.S. student in the greatest country in the world, and the only person he'd met who liked Beethoven and Brahms was a South American, though granted, two weeks were hardly enough to start meeting Americans who shared his tastes.

Still, only yesterday his roommate Shane, whose lankiness and blond hair brought to mind the look of many of the Americans seen hanging around El Condado, had responded to the first bars of Ravel's Quartet on Dickie's portable stereo with, "Dickerson, that stuff eats it! Yowling cats in heat! Turn it off or I'm complaining to the authorities." Dickie laughed, but did lower the volume to a minimum. He had, of course, requested a Wharton freshman as a roommate, but now wondered if he might have had a luckier draw, Gerd, for instance.

"Excuse me, do you have the exact time?" The pretty redhead in brown loafers had presumably seen Gerd's gleaming wristwatch.

He slowly raised his left arm, stared intently, and then his face was suddenly transformed, taking on a partly-longing, partly-rakish grin. He turned to her, peering deeply into her green eyes, while his voice deepened into a mellifluous, almost romantic murmur, "Why yes, my dear, it's three-oh-five. Don't you remember me?"

She seemed slightly bewildered and gave a little jolt, but smiled in return, "Oh, have we met?"

"But of course," he asserted, now looking hurt. "At Hill House last week. How rapidly women forget!" Soon enough Gerd had her in conversation about her small town in western Pennsylvania, her major (education), his international-finance major at Wharton, his mansion in Valdivia, and so forth, and at one point he remarked, "Well, it is now 3:10, time for coffee, no?" And before Dickie knew it the three of them were filing past College Hall and going for coffee at Houston. En route Gerd noted the points of resemblance between College Hall and the Addams Family's home, something everyone else on campus also did though somehow he actually made an old fact sound new.

Abby — that was the coed's name — ordered a cherry coke. Sitting next to Gerd and across from Dickie, she asked, "How come you've got a German name if you're from South America?"

Again gazing into her eyes, Gerd told her what he'd just told Dickie, though with other details about Chile, and more charmingly. She accepted his offer of a Viceroy, which he promptly lit, gently cupping her small hands as he did so.

"Yes, it's a beautiful place, Valdivia," Gerd continued. "Visitors are welcome, by the way. We would love having you there." (He just barely emphasized the word "love.") "You can hear the ocean waves from our guest room. Come see us sometime."

Abby, fascinated, blushed. "Oh, I... I can't go to... to Bolivia. It's too far from home."

The twinkle and smile on Gerd's face became more intense. "Ah, well, you would not need to go to Bolivia. You see, Abby, I'm from Valdivia, which is in Chile. And besides, Bolivia has no coast. It is landlocked."

The blush on her face was redder. "Oh, gosh, I'm sorry, I guess I didn't realize. Geography's always been my worst subject, though."

Gerd graciously consoled her with a tap on the shoulder. "It's all right, don't worry." He trilled the double "r," Spanish-style.

Later in the afternoon, as the two young men headed for the Quad, Gerd wondered with quiet scorn, "My God, these *americanitas,* they're so dumb. And just imagine — she's going to be a teacher!"

Dickie asked him how he'd happened to meet "*esa* Abby" before.

"Never saw her in my life," he answered matter-of-factly. "But I imagined she must've been at the Hill House mixer, so I made it sound as if we'd met."

During the next two weeks, Gerd and Dickie went for coffee almost every school day. Dickie was frankly awed by Gerd's skill at meeting girls, captivating and flirting with them from the outset, and getting dates for both Friday and Saturday. His movie-star looks and manner obviously helped, as well as his not having to wear eye glasses.

Gerd even managed to strike up conversation with three blondes in Greek-lettered sweatshirts the Thursday of the concert.

The two were in their coats and ties, waiting for the 21 bus on Chestnut, when they both remarked, gesturally and monosyllabically, on the three girls strolling in their direction. Gerd walked right up to the shortest; the trio slowed down to a stop. Following an indiscernible initial exchange, Dickie eventually could hear Gerd ask, "So why not come to the Symphony with us?"

She smiled, like the others did, and then replied, "Sorry, can't tonight."

"Well, perhaps next week, then," Gerd added, warmly.

"Yes, perhaps," said the tallest and the prettiest, who wore blue jeans. The three of them giggled as they resumed their walk. Languidly, Gerd watched them recede into the dusk, and commented, now in Spanish, "Mm, look at how that tall one walks. What a wonderful little ass! She sure knows how to shake it."

Following the fast ride downtown, Dickie's excitement doubled as they sauntered down Broad Street, descried the flickering gas lights, and caught sight of the many adults in laces and silk scarves milling about on the Academy front steps. Gerd had reserved two front-row seats up in Amphitheater, where the huge chandelier and ancient-looking ceiling art made for a spectacular view. The sight and sound of the gleaming brass and strings thundering out, live and loud, the opening chords of the *Eroica,* had a young Dickie bedazzled. There's nothing like this in Puerto Rico, he thought to himself.

The delayed return bus came as a relief from the slight autumn chill. "What an incredible scherzo in the Beethoven!" Dickie exclaimed.

"Yeah, it was fine, though I still think of Mengelberg with the Berlin Philharmonic as the best," Gerd replied drily.

Dickie had only heard Mengelberg once on WIPR, doing the Tchaikovsky Fifth, he said.

"My parents owned all of Mengelberg on 78 recordings," Gerd further elucidated. "Now they've got most of it on LPs too."

During intermission Dickie had glanced about the lobby, hoping to see faces from Wharton or Penn. He did not see any and wondered why.

His friend now administered him an affectionate tap on the arm. "Ricardito, what do you expect? These *yanquis*, they're the most uncultured people on earth. They don't know how to live." He paused briefly as the bus slowed down for a stop light. "Still, better here than in Russia or Cuba. We'll need gringo help if that s.o.b. Allende ever gets elected."

"What's that?"

Gerd smiled. "'That' is some communist doctor who wants to be the Castro of Chile."

Dickie reflected momentarily. "Sort of like a Hitler, I suppose."

"No comparison." Gerd was definitive and assuring. "Hitler fought the communists and the Russians. I admire him for that. My parents do, too. So do many people in Valdivia. But Castro? He's a communist and he's letting *in* those Russians. Well, I'm not going to allow it, not where *I've* got buildings."

"Yeah," Dickie responded, somewhat bewildered. "Life seems to be hell in Cuba right now."

Thus far Dickie had only spent two-week periods in the States, and in mid-summers only, which were even hotter and more humid than back home, something that regularly amazed him. The visits always took place either with his mother alone at her parents' in Chicago, or with his father alone at the Dickersons' in St. Louis. (Just this June he had found out it was because Dad couldn't stand Mom's relatives, and vice-versa.) Winter and snow he knew strictly by hearsay and from pictures, and he looked forward to his first snowfall. He felt glad to be finally studying in the States, though less sure as yet about Wharton.

Halfway through one of their many silent suppers eighteen months ago, Dickie had said he would like to study music, or maybe liberal arts. He wanted to read all of the great books.

The sounds of silverware touching on or scraping plates continued. Then, without looking Dickie's way, Mr. Dickerson replied, "Not on *my* money you won't."

From her end of the long table the voice of Dickie's mom came out of its accustomed muteness. "Oh, Rich," she interjected. "Why not let him study what he wants?"

Dickie looked back at Mr. Dickerson, who at last replied, shrugging his shoulders, "Honey, he can. F'r all I care, he can major in underwater Zulu carpet-weaving. But not on *my* hard-earned cash." He glanced briefly at his son. "Got the money, Dickie? Besides, you're too specialized. There's more to life than art and music. Time for you to branch out and be more broad-minded."

Eventually it was decided: the father would pay the costs of some top school up in the States, and the boy would agree to major either in engineering or in business administration. Dickie didn't care that much for math, but he did like the people he had worked with at his father's and uncle's offices during vacations, so why not? — business it'll be, he figured. The summer following junior year his mom brought him college guides and catalogs. They spurred his imagination; he wrote for more, borrowed others from Carnegie Library and the Colegio, and perused the contents with the same zeal he still put into reading books about painters or composers.

On occasion his two Colegio friends dropped by — Leo the math whiz, *el profe* the brain — and they all sat around comparing universities, considering possibilities. The small, intimate, Eastern liberal-arts schools especially appealed to their own small, intimate, Caribbean-island backgrounds. Dickie for a while pinned his hopes on Richards College in rural Massachusetts, his dream college, he thought, though he soon found out to his chagrin that none of the four-year campuses offered business degrees.

Much research suggested to him that the only top university with an undergraduate business program was Penn's Wharton. He applied there, and only there, in the States, but also sent in his application to *la Yupi* next door, figuring that, if Wharton didn't work out, he might as well be a student where he'd gone biking with his two friends the year before, and strolling with his parents long ago, and where the bells chiming Bach and Offenbach still gave him daily pleasure. Penn nonetheless came through, wait-listing him in April and accepting him one Friday afternoon in May.

"*Hola*, Ricardito," Catalina greeted him from the faraway kitchen.

"*Hola*," he answered, loosening his beige necktie and seeing the lone envelope, addressed to him, on the coffee table. He took out a hanky to wipe the sweat from his brow and glasses, and settled down into the sofa to open and read what was a good-news letter. Catalina was the only one home at the time. With an odd mixture of satisfaction, uneasiness, and relief, Dickie walked down the long hall, letter in hand, to tell her about it. The fragrance of spices, wafting about from apartments on six floors, struck him vividly even as his soft voice resonated in the outside courtyard.

"Catalina." He approached the kitchen door.

"Tell me, Dickie." She was bent over the oven, basting a bird.

"It looks like I'll be studying up there," he announced flatly.

Catalina straightened up with a slight effort, put the baster carefully on top of the stove, swept a gray hair aside, and looked up toward him. Now smiling, she remarked, "How nice, Ricardito. I always said you'd abandon us to go to El Norte. We'll miss you here!" She gave his arm a little squeeze and then informed him that his parents would both be late for dinner.

Ambling back into the living room, Dickie realized he should telephone his friends. The three had sworn to celebrate at Chicken Inn with pizzas and beer once they all knew their college destinations. Because Leo had since been accepted at M.I.T. and *el Profe* had chosen to stay for *la Yupi,* only Dickie remained. Sliding into the sofa, he dialed Leo's number and got no answer, then *el Profe*'s and got no answer again. He stretched back onto a cushion and was about to doze off, when a screech and a crash beckoned him to the balcony.

Looking down, he saw a cream-colored Cadillac rammed into a Post Office truck, and also a uniformed mulatto and a portly bald man in a gray suit, standing face-to-face and gesticulating wildly as car horns honked from all sides. Dickie moved to the corner of the balcony and turned his gaze toward the University grounds, saw countless students strolling with their books and companions down the lane of breeze-tossed palm trees. Come September these would no longer be his daily sights, he reflected. Feeling bushed, he went to his room for a nap.

A few taps on the door roused him in the evening darkness.

"*¿Sí?*" he said automatically.

"Suppertime, Dickie," his mother's voice announced. 8:40, read the luminous clock face at his bedside, and when he looked again, 8:50.

Dickie had left his Wharton letter on the coffee table, and as he emerged, still groggy, from his room, he saw his father slipping the sheet back into its envelope.

"Well, not bad, I must say," the man remarked, getting up from the sofa and looking directly at the boy. "Congratulations, son," he added, his arms outstretched, wide open. Dickie went over for a brief hug, their first since Christmas, and he liked it. Mr. Dickerson next stepped back, stood facing him, arms crossed, and observed philosophically, "So now you'll study the real world, 'stead of hiding out in all those books and records."

From her work room in the hallway his mom's voice rang out, "Rich, just let him be. If he likes arty things, well, that's his business."

An ever-drowsy Dickie staggered to the sofa and plopped his body down, his left arm serving him as pillow. He noticed the plates of leftovers and the partly-consumed bird spread out across the dinner table.

Father shouted back. "His *business*? Sorry, hon, but, trouble is, it's no darned business whatsoever. He wouldn't've made so much as a buck from any of that stuff." Mr. Dickerson helped himself to a chunk each of white meat and stuffing. "Let the kid learn sales for a change. After all, it's salesmanship that's made America great." He bit off some turkey.

"Yes, Rich, whatever you say," Mom's answer floated in from down the hall.

Dickie was actually hoping to fit in as many art and music electives as he could, along with the finance and accounting requirements. No reason why he couldn't do both, he felt.

What would strike him on his journey from Philadelphia airport to Penn campus and thereafter was the redoubtable irritability of the redcaps, cabbies, phone operators, university employees, and others who steadfastly addressed him and most everyone else with a cordial, guarded growl. Along with the regnant churlishness, it was a mild shock to him to ride and walk through a campus without seeing so much as a single palm tree, a botanical feature he had spent his life half-thinking of as normal. After San Juan, moreover, so many of the local landmarks he now found himself approaching or traversing or just passing for the first time seemed longer, taller, wider, bulkier than had been suggested by their brochure photos. Meanwhile people here and there were asking him if he was a foreign exchange student, and even at the College Hall offices a cute, petite blonde secretary raised her voice in indignation as she gave him back his filled-out papers with a stern reminder clearly to spell out on them his exact visa status.

Dickie took his orientation tour on his first full day, a cool and breezy autumn afternoon. As the students and adult visitors filed past Houston Hall, he wished he'd worn a sweater, though he noticed that many had on tee-shirts and even Bermudas.

"Hi, I'm Ed Wiggins," their guide introduced himself, a short, stocky fellow with chestnut-colored hair, "and I'm a double major in Psych and Econ." From time to time Ed would stop and consult his tour booklet in order to refresh his memory, especially when describing Furness Library and its interior archways "that have made it one of the crown jewels of architectural design."

Meanwhile Dickie took note of a bright red metal statue, abstract yet suggestive of flames, or maybe of tree branches, standing in broad daylight a few yards away. He was amazed.

"Excuse me," Dickie asked Ed. They were approaching Smith Walk. "Isn't that a Calder?"

Ed gave him a puzzled look. "A what?"

"You know," Dickie said excitedly. "Alexander Calder. The famous American sculptor."

While Ed stopped to look it up in his tour book, Dickie murmured to the middle-aged couple at his left, "Doesn't it look like a Calder to you?"

The silver-haired, fatherly-looking man buttoned his red-and-blue checkered sports coat and looked straight ahead as his rich baritone voice came back, "Dunno."

Finally Ed replied, "Well, so it is. Calder, right. Can't decipher the title, though." He reached over the pamphlet to Dickie and pointed at a word.

"Stabile," said Dickie softly, using Spanish vowel sounds.

Ed giggled a bit. "I guess that's what it is, then!" A few others in the group giggled, too.

On registration day Dickie found out from his advisor, Professor Berman, that the only non-business course he could enroll in as yet was Freshman Comp, something that at any rate he felt he needed, having studied English-as-a-second-language all his life and nothing but. The same Professor Berman smiled sympathetically when informing Dickie that he needed to hold out till junior year for those History and Literature electives, and that Music Appreciation, regrettably, was out, except maybe as an extra credit four years down the road. Dickie did see possibilities in International Business, a mandatory course that met in the General Foods Room and soon sparked within him lively thoughts of maybe being sales rep for classical record firms like RCA or Westminster someday. What he most liked about Wharton, however, was the massive Henry Moore that everyone encountered and passed on first entering Dietrich Hall foyer. By then, however, Dickie had learned not to make remarks to fellow students, or other people, about statues.

Except to Gerd, and one mid-afternoon the two of them stopped a while just to contemplate the reclining bronze, Dickie's friend noting "the gracefulness of the line" and its "toughness and restraint," and Dickie himself nodding, *"Sí, exacto"* and adding, "What a beauty!"

The sound of high heels awoke them from their reverie. A blonde in an upswept hairdo and basic-black dress was approaching slowly and now stood erect at the other end of the statue, her arms clutched around a musical instrument case, her gaze fixed intently on Moore's handiwork.

"Look at those legs," Gerd whispered to Dickie. After a discreet, momentary silence he looked toward the newcomer and, switching to English, addressed her with that mellow voice apparently devised and perfected by him for the express purpose of meeting pretty girls, "Beautiful, is it not?"

She looked back vaguely in his direction, smiling equally vaguely. "Yes, the craft is certainly impressive." It seemed to Dickie that she talked differently, like a teacher or professor, or an actress.

"Have you just come from a viola lesson?" Gerd inquired, with cautious warmth.

There was a brief pause — she seemed slightly taken aback — following which she responded with a somewhat broader smile, "Well, I *am* impressed. Yes, I have, congratulations."

Gerd put his arm around Dickie's waist, when suddenly the two had glided over and jelled into a close threesome, with Gerd, almost as if he were host of Dietrich Hall, affably introducing Dickie and himself. "And your name is...?"

Another pause, she stared at them, and then chimed in, "Kathryn." She spelled it and continued, "Kathryn Cromwell. And no nicknames, please!"

Gerd soon had her discussing this her first year in University Symphony string section.

The day was still warm and sunny as they all three ambled out, Kathryn strolling between them and Gerd radiating charm as, occasionally, gently, he touched her on the elbow and led them to the Green. They ended up on one of the benches, Gerd now in the middle. Over their encounter there loomed Ben Franklin's likeness, capped by a cooing pigeon.

"So tell me, Kathryn, what is your major here?" Gerd offered her a Benson & Hedges, which she politely refused, then lit one himself.

"Oh, I definitely plan to major in applied music," she answered, in an appropriately melodic voice.

"Wow," Dickie blurted out. "First time I've ever met a music major. Wish I could've been one." From his end of the bench he explained to her his father's restrictions.

After exhaling a puff Gerd said sympathetically, "And is that not unfortunate?" as he clenched Dickie's left shoulder. "The world is so unjust at times." He inhaled deeply again.

Dickie asked if the Symphony would be playing a concert soon.

"Yes, next month," she indicated. "We're doing *Pictures at an Exhibition.*"

Gerd tapped off some ashes as he mused, "Ah, yes, Moussorgsky. His music is so natural, so different, so... *Russian.* Which is why he and Tchaikovsky formed part of the 'Five.'"

Dickie frowned, perplexed, and was about to speak when Kathryn queried, "And who were they?"

"Five composers," Gerd explained, "who wished to create a more authentically Russian musical style." (He pronounced it "ess-STYLE.")

"Actually," Dickie now ventured, "I don't think those two belonged to the 'Five.'"

Gerd stiffened, his face snapped toward Dickie, and, after a brief silence, he asked in Spanish, "What do you mean?" The sweetness and urbanity in his voice did not match the oddly tense and hostile look on his eyes and lips.

"Just that," Dickie replied, also in Spanish. "Tchaikovsky and Moussorgsky didn't belong to the 'Five.'" Then, switching back to English, "They were each loners."

Gerd stared at Dickie for a few seconds, ignored the comment and also returned to English, continuing to praise Russian composers and finally requesting and obtaining Kathryn's number at Hill House. Following a bit more three-way talk about this or that, his new-found girl excused herself, said good-bye to them both and, still smiling, went off to a late-afternoon class. Gerd and Dickie remained sitting side-by-side as they observed her walking toward 34th Street, viola case and loose-leaf notebook swinging lightly from her hand.

Dickie remarked in Spanish, "Yeah, she sure has nice legs.

And look how her rear end wiggles."

"Listen here, kid," his friend suddenly lashed out. "Don't go showing off in front of people, you hear?"

Dickie was surprised. "What?"

"Just what I said. If there's anything I can't stand, it's show-offs. And don't you go correcting me." This time his facial expression fit the words.

A nonplussed Dickie had no reply.

"Just what the hell do *you* know about classical music? You, who hadn't even been inside a concert hall till *I* treated you last week. Tell me, Dickie," he asked with a mocking voice, "how many symphony orchestras are there on the little island of Puerto Rico?" The embers burned bright as he inhaled on his cigarette. "Another thing: try humiliating me in front of some girl once again, and I'll make you regret it."

"Frankly, Gerd, I..." Dickie stammered momentarily, "I didn't mean to, I... *disculpa,* but I really thought those two weren't with the 'Five.'"

His friend snapped back, with assured emphasis, "Well, you are very wrong. In fact Tchaikovsky was a leader of the group." He flicked his minimal cigarette butt onto the pavement and tried snuffing it out, though it had fallen just beyond the toe of his shiny-brown wing tip. "And Moussorgsky was a founder."

During the long silence that ensued, Dickie flipped randomly through his Accounting book, and finally suggested, "Look, it's time to study. Shall we go to Furness?"

Gerd bit into a brand-new cigarette, played with his rings. "Not now. I need a siesta." In a single movement he snatched his portfolio from off the ground, got on his feet, took hold of his unlit cigarette and pointed it at Dickie, lips curled in as he muttered, softly yet ominously, "And don't you forget what I just told you."

Dickie turned to watch Gerd's frame receding briskly toward the Quad and notice the sun's low-floating disk in a still-bright sky. He straightened up, the statue base's bits of moss now occupying his gaze. The enveloping light had taken on a late, rose-orange hue.

Trudging again toward the library, he stopped to look once more at the dance-like, metal flames, or tree branches, and wished he could make playful shapes like Calder.

The hush inside Furness was gratifying, and the Shakespeare on the stained-glass windows rekindled in him the hope of identifying the quotes someday. He placed his school stuff at the end of a long table next to the encyclopedias, reached directly for the *Americana* volumes showing letters F and M and T, and took a seat across a ruddy-faced blond couple in Greek tee-shirts, presumably seniors, who were giggling, conspicuously yet inaudibly, at one another.

Moussorgsky was indeed part of the "Five," Dickie read, but Tchaikovsky was not, so he and Gerd had been both right and wrong there. He felt surprised, however, on finding out that the group of "Five," with a founder and a leader, had never actually existed. A Russian journalist of the time, it seems, had invented and applied the label, which subsequently stuck for years to come.

Dickie did not know how he should feel, whether mad, or guilty, or sad or something else, yet recognized that Gerd was the one true friend he had here in the States, and that, due to their friendship, he'd been to the Orchestra concert and even met some pretty girls. Moreover they could talk as people do in Spanish, and about artists and composers, Dickie's first real chance to do so. And then there was Gerd's being age twenty, and his having worked the family parking lots and candy shop down in Valdivia, business experiences Dickie hoped to learn from in the near future.

Dickie opened up the *Principles of Accounting,* but found himself unable to focus on its words. He envied Kathryn, in a friendly way, wishing he too could be in a big group that brings such perfect worlds as *Pictures at an Exhibition* or the *Eroica* into being. Just a flick of the baton from a conductor, any conductor, and Beethoven's opening chords came thundering out. And onward to the two closing chords.

Still, once past childhood, Dick knew, a beginner's finger muscles are too far along for him ever to make orchestra. At age eighteen Dickie was simply too old, that really was that. Same thing for art, for though in his mind's eye he conceived all sorts of abstract sculptures, reluctantly he realized that, what with his lack of training or materials, the Dickerson statues would remain great thoughts and imagined possibilities, and no more.

He lay his head, face down, on the accounting textbook's glossy paper. Soon thereafter he straightened up, leaned back, and noted the sweat mark on the page. Slowly he shut his *Principles,* realizing he too needed to go home and have a siesta. Meanwhile the brush-cut blond glanced over at Dickie, grinned out of the corner of his mouth, and turned to raise a chick-yellow eyebrow at his spray-netted blonde friend. The pair made more giggling gestures as Dickie stood up, gathered his books, and departed. Skirting the Green, he chuckled at the thought that, however late and dark it be, the likeness of Ben Franklin never sleeps, nor dozes off. That's immortality for you, he reflected on approaching the Quad, where, campus legend had it, no three rooms were alike.

In an oft-recurring dream of Dick's, music became a referential tongue, along with English and Spanish. Chords took on fixed meanings, as if they were adjectives or nouns, and symphonies spun out stories about people, like books or TV plays did. (Once awakened, though, Dickie never could bring back the tale he'd just heard. All that remained was the music, solitary and self-contained.) The Beethoven Fourth had been doing precisely that, telling a story, when his deep, brief sleep was cut off by the lively sounds of Shane arriving with two buddies.

Reaching for his glasses, the first thing Dickie saw as his eyelids came unstuck was a pea-green tee-shirt saying cryptically, "FIJI."

From across the room he heard Shane's voice. "Hey, Dicker-son, on your feet." Then the three rang out in chorus, "It's SUPPERTIME!"

Dickie breathed out a single laugh, recognizing the guests though drawing a blank on names. Now the freckle-faced Fiji mused more softly, picking up on what seemed an ongoing conversation of theirs, "Yeah, gotta get myself a piece of ass this weekend. That'd really be bitchin,' I do declare." Dick rubbed his eyes as he sat up in bed, figuring the accent and the vocabulary might perhaps be West Coast.

"Ditto here," remarked the slightly older third guy, leaning, arms folded, against the wall. "Like I say, there's plenty of first-rate pussy here in this place." He was tall, brown-haired, square-jawed, and fairly handsome. "The hell, though, failing that, we c'n always find ourselves a queer and bash 'im!"

Their brief, high-spirited guffaw came punctuated with Shane's mock-Southern tenor interjecting, "Sho' 'nuff, ol' boy."

Three sharp, slow knocks intruded on their merriment. Shane went over to the door; Dickie heard Gerd's voice asking for him.

"Sho' 'nuff," was the reply. Dickie turned to see Shane stretching out his hand, saying loudly, "Seymour Butts, kind sir, how do you do?"

"Dick Bender here," the Fiji announced most seriously, hands in his pockets.

They burst out into laughter once again till Gerd disarmingly shook hands with each of them, after which he said in Spanish, "*Mira,* Dickie, shall we go eat?"

Dickie felt relieved. "Yeah, let's."

As they exited into the hall Gerd patted Dickie on the back and issued a little chuckle. "So you're the guy with the crude roommate. Tell me something, Dickie what *were* those jokes about?"

Dickie explained the puns, whereupon Gerd reflected, "My God, these gringos *are* gross."

Once past the food lines in McClelland, they sat down side by side at a round table for their usual talk of music, classes, and the day's pretty girls. Everything seemed O.K., and indeed, even as they were carving up their respective chocolate cream pie crusts, Gerd's voice took on a quality of deep earnestness while saying to him, "Listen, Dickie, about this afternoon. Don't worry. Everything's O.K."

There was a prolonged silence. At a neighboring table, the subject was football and cheerleaders. Gerd stared at a Viceroy, opened and shut his lighter more than once, ignited a flame and further added, "I won't go holding some grudge against you simply because of what happened out on the Green. I'm not that kind of guy."

Following a long-drawn puff, he clarified. "I take things like ethics very seriously. Ever since childhood I've prided myself on being an extremely ethical person. Too ethical, perhaps. But then it's things like ethics that make relationships work." The smoke Gerd had blown out first hovered about their table before finding its way toward the windows.

Taking gentle hold of Dickie's arm, Gerd reassured him, warmly, "Our friendship matters to me a lot. Some little mistake of yours could never hurt our friendship."

Dickie was quite pleased at their being friends still, and, after they'd fetched cups of coffee, grousing ritually about its foul taste, their general conversation became animated once again. Over the next ten days the two friends went to a movie, a concert, and a mixer, where Gerd continued to apply his knack for meeting girls, whom Dickie felt fortunate to meet too. Subsequently, Gerd had been out with a couple of those women, he told Dick, though duly omitting any further details.

"Listen, Dickie," Gerd said to him as they left English class sometime before Halloween. "Have you been to the Museum yet?"

"Which one?"

"Which one?" Gerd laughed. "The big one, the Philadelphia Museum of Art." He said the name in English. "That's the one."

"I wish I had."

"Well, same for me. You don't have Saturday classes do you? Let's go day-after-tomorrow. I'll ask Kathryn to join us."

Aside from the Calder statue he saw daily, pieces of art were something Dickie knew only through photos found in borrowed books back in San Juan. And though that Friday he settled into Furness till closing time, with his lecture notes and workbooks spread out before him, and no one else at his long table or the next, he found it hard to concentrate and not imagine his first trip to a big art museum. He was reminded of the jokes Shane often told about trying not to think of elephants.

Sometime after daybreak, Dickie heard chill winds outside and even felt them touching his bare cheeks and fingers. (There was no heat as yet.) Shivering, hesitating, he headed for the window to see the slender saplings swaying and crinkled leaves cascading under a low, dark-grayish sky.

Shane had his blanket bunched up across his midsection, his arms and legs sprawled out as he slept, snoring. He did not budge during Dick's first shuffles, morning toilette, and slow change of skin into coat, tie, and raincoat. Neither did Gerd's three knocks or Spanish words have much effect on his stertorous, immobile slumbers.

Out in the hall Gerd said, "Listen, I'd like to surprise Kathryn by picking her up in a taxi."

Dickie stopped in his tracks. "Oh... I haven't got sufficient cash on me."

"I pay. It's too cold to go stand waiting for the bus, anyway. Besides, my fur coat hasn't arrived from Chile yet."

Gerd in fact already had a glistening cab posted at the Spruce Street entrance. Dickie sat up front, where he almost nodded off during the brief wait by Hill House, and when he saw Gerd come onto the walkway leading Kathryn by the arm, her gray skirt billowing in the wind, she indeed seemed pleasantly startled at the sight of the yellow cab.

As he pulled open the back door and ushered her in, Abby chanced to approach and walk right by. Gerd greeted her with a wink and his usual wide, warm smile.

"Hello, Gerd," Abby replied, slightly coldly.

Once inside he remarked softly to Dickie, "She seemed surprised to see me, that other one, *¿no?*"

The taxi rushed past Bennett Hall, where Dickie had twice met Mr. McKay for conference hours. The prof also taught a Shakespeare class, and Dickie planned to take it someday soon. He lost himself in reverie, ignoring the couple's conversation and hardly noticing the drive, imagining himself back on the island, where days this chilly and of this hue were simply not conceivable. At some point he realized he'd forgotten his umbrella.

He had expected yet another red brick structure, like the Academy's or maybe those at Penn, but the Greek pillars now looming into view suggested to him some older buildings in San Juan, though bigger.

Gerd gave the gray-haired black cabbie a large tip with one hand and a pat on the back with his other, saying, "Many thanks."

"Thank *you,* sir, and you all enjoy your stay," said the driver, with exaggerated politeness.

"So tragic, the treatment of the Negroes in this country," Gerd mused philosophically while leading Dick and Kathryn up the big, wide stairs into the Museum portico.

Bigger too, correspondingly bigger, was the crowd of visitors inside; big was the sheer amount of pictures and sculptures, room after room of them; and each familiar item was strangely bigger, and much sharper, than the photographs thereof Dickie had seen in assorted art books.

"This is wonderful," Kathryn said, beaming with delight as they entered the Modern European Painting section. "You and Dick had a great idea, coming here."

"Oh, think nothing of it," Gerd insisted, smiling. "We do it for the sake of culture." (He pronounced it "KOOL-choor.")

"Oh, look," Dickie exclaimed, "they've got Picasso's *Three Musicians* here."

The three friends gasped, ambled across the empty room, and now stood in hushed amazement, for there indeed it was, the trio — the guitarist in his orange-and-yellow diamond suit, the moustachioed piper in a white clown's smock, the hooded monk singing some song of eighth-notes, and in the lower-left shadows a shaggy brown dog. And from outside, in downtown Philadelphia, three pairs of human eyes eagerly fixed on the performance.

"Just imagine," Gerd declared, "at this moment, on this planet, no one except us is looking at this picture."

Dickie and Kathryn first responded with a brief silence, then laughed simultaneously at his joke.

"Do you know what is my dream?" Gerd went on, more earnestly. "I would like to have a genuine Picasso in my home, perhaps even this one." He pointed.

"Well, if you do," Kathryn replied with her big smile, "I hope you'll let us ordinary mortals see it!"

Gerd pursed his lips and nodded firmly. "All of my friends will be invited," he assured them both.

It had been two hours since their arrival, and on occasion they'd dispersed here and about. Now, almost as one, they turned, saw a free bench, and went to sit down together, in a row, sighing audibly while stretching their leg muscles. Picasso was behind them.

"Say, look over there, isn't that Seurat?" said Dickie, pronouncing the name as if it were Spanish. He stumbled to his feet and idled up to a pair of pictures, checking out their names. Sure enough, "Georges Seurat (1859-91). *The Painter at Work,*" read the plaque next to the drawing. The other, in rich, shimmering hues, was identified as *The Models* (third version).

He alternated between them, standing back or coming close so as to take in details.

The hum of Gerd and Kathryn's mutual mumblings, dampened by the soft shuffles of a newly-arrived tour group and its female guide, wafted over to him from the bench. Then came the click of Kathryn's high heels, nearing ever so leisurely and mingled with the sounds of Gerd discoursing on Impressionists.

"Beautiful. So experimental," Gerd reflected.

"Yes," Kathryn concurred.

"Very Dadaistic," Gerd continued.

A sudden and mysterious inner jolt, an about-face spin, and Dick sees Gerd calmly stroking his moustache, unperturbed; and, with a dizzy feeling in his head and a sponge-like lightness in his body Dick blurts out, just a shade louder than is usual, "Dadaistic? What...? What d'you mean, Gerd, 'Dadaistic?'"

Gerd shows a touch of patient, polite scorn, then grimaces, folds his arms, raises his eyebrows, and, pointing with his chin, explains authoritatively, "Those dots. Typical of the Dadaists. Everyone knows that."

Something beyond his control roiled Dickie's insides, hastening his speech. "Gerd, that is *not* what the Dadaists did. This stuff is... oh... it's... damn, I can't remember." He snapped his fingers once, glanced over at the painting. "Some French word."

"Says the expert," Gerd commented drily.

For the first time Dick noticed raindrops streaking a tall window in the neighboring room. He turned to Kathryn. "D'you know the word I mean, Kathryn? What d'*you* think?"

She appeared only slightly upset. "I... I haven't taken any art courses, Dickie, so really, I can't say. Gerd does seem to know what he's talking about, though. Tell you what, why don't we look it up in some book after we're done here?"

Gerd's face was not much altered, but his Spanish featured something of a growl. "Look here, Dickie," he said, "you're spoiling a most lovely day, behaving like an obnoxious little brat." Lips curling inward, he added, "And if you don't know beans about French art, *carajo,* then do me a favor and keep your blesséd mouth shut." Following his passionate "*¡Joder!*" and a deep silence, Gerd voiced a sigh, shook his head with a smile of amiable concern, and gently took hold of Kathryn's elbow while explaining to her in his customarily soft, urbane, reassuring English, "Kathryn, please pardon our excluding you these few instants, but you see, we communicate much better in Espanish, Dickie and I. And I simply had to tell him to grow up and stop being so, so... immature."

Dick felt momentarily paralyzed and mute as he saw both of

them slowly move on to the next painting (by Signac, he'd read previously). He turned around, started first walking, then scurrying at an even brisker pace, traversing once again all of the former galleries yet scarcely conscious of their aesthetic attractions, gazing mostly down toward the floor and managing not to bump into bystanders or pedestrians.

Before reaching the museum's front entrance Dick caught sight of a short, plump, white-haired, grandfatherly-looking guard, sitting in a corner near some Greek or Roman busts, he wasn't sure which. He walked up and, slightly breathless, asked the fellow where he could catch a bus back to Penn campus.

The man showed surprising vigor as he jumped to his feet. "Mr. Cavallieri," said the badge on his lapel. He took Dick firmly by the arm, and, in a grainy voice and a residual foreign accent presumably not Spanish but Italian, twice spelled out to him the full, detailed instructions. "So don't you go getting lost now," he emphasized, wagging a right finger with mock-gruff friendliness. "Plus, make sure you've got your umbrella at the ready, or you'll get soaking wet!"

Oh, he was right, Mr. Cavallieri was, for the rain outside had grown into a steady shower and the directions from him were proving to be letter-perfect too, Dick reflected as he made out the covered bus stop in the distance and took long, hurried steps through the slow downpour, dodging the small puddles that had already formed and feeling thankful that he'd at least worn his new trench coat.

He remembered the free-floating theme for English class, on a cultural event of their choice, and he thought he'd write about his visit to the museum and the French paintings he had seen for the first time. Squinting, he wondered if that was his bus coming into view, and speeded up his pace. Despite his use of a cupped hand as visor, his glasses were quite wet, and he wiped their outside lenses with a still-dry hanky. As he pushed back a dripping forelock it occurred to him that writing, unlike music or sculpture, requires no particular physical or muscular skills, just things in your head like a large vocabulary and a love of well-turned sounds, oh, yes, and better typing abilities than he now had, true enough, and perhaps over the next few years he would fit in more English courses and learn about how writers write, how they use words to tell of what they know. And improve his typing.

The bus was not his, he realized as it slowed down to a stop, brakes hissing. A student-age couple, clothed in black and carrying plastic-covered easels, got off, chattering excitedly to each other; she had unusually long black hair, he, a woolly, unkempt brown beard. Meanwhile a Negro family in their weekend best ran out from the shelter to the door. The shale-dark wife wore a floral print, her lighter-complected husband a dark suit, their twin toddlers, neckties, and each boy was kept dry by a parent's umbrella till he'd climbed fully aboard. The bus's tires splattered Dick's right sleeve and hemline as it took off. He saw the first couple heading for the museum, umbrellas also in hand. There was no other bus on the horizon, but he found welcome relief under the shelter and sank right down onto the grooved bench, assuming a long wait ahead.

Maturity Personal
by Richard Dickerson

I.   I kicked the masturbation habit yesterday. Today, I picked up smoking. I feel a deep and serene satisfaction in having finally become a man.

   Growth is not always a slow, silent process.

II.   It's a lovely Spring evening in New York town, and I'm off yet again to a rip-roaring, mind-blowing, soul-searching party. A chance to mingle with a set of mature, informed and with-it city dwellers such as myself. I mount the brownstone's well-worn steps and eye the graceful brass knocker with a manly decisiveness, spoiling to show blonde, sweet-tongued Marsha just who I am as I stand here with a bold new protrusion from my own space, a king-sized French Gallia held tight between my teeth.

   I'd always wanted to arrive at a party with my equipment in plain sight. Not that there is anything out-of-the-ordinary about my particular endowments (4.7" X 0.9" at zenith). My non-gratuitous act would be purely mnemonic in its intents. It would forcibly bring home to my fellow gringos and other foreign folk a reality too long occluded by social conventions, to wit, that the thinker of these thoughts is incontestably male.

   ¡Pues macho soy, no lo olvidéis!

   Human beings in these United States forget far too easily the essential aspects of this brief existence, such as,

   a) ordinary decency,

   b) good manners,

   c) the Categorical Imperative,

   d) that "Man has no Nature, only History,"

e) that an ounce of prevention is worth a kilo of cure,

f) that the ends-means distinction counts for us too,

g) that our growing brushfire wars are cause for serious concern,

h) ditto for the rise of conglomerates,

i) plus the urban crisis,

j) life's pleasures, fleeting joys undone by death, and

i) a great deal more.

Over-ripe societies cry out in pain for a Socratic avatar who will take on the burdensome task of stinging his coevals into a reassessment of their mental as well as physical baggage.

(He takes a long puff, exhales without removing the cigarette, seizes the knocker and twice bangs out the rhythms of the opening notes of Beethoven's Fifth Symphony. After ten seconds or so clicking foot-steps are heard, and the hostess throws open the door, her long golden hair dangling loosely down to her waist. She wears red high heels and a psychedelic chemise, also with plenty of red.)

SHE: (*Warmly*) Well, Dick Dickerson himself! It's so good to see you again! 't's been a while, hasn't it? Haven't seen you since our last class meeting. (*Tosses her hair back.*) C'm in, c'm in, we're only just starting. (*She leads him down the hall.*)

HE: (*Nods, still puffing. He follows her, in strong silence initially.*) Hi, Marsh, how're you doin'?

Ahaa. Never has she laid it on so thick, this dame. There's but one possible reason for so unprecedented a show of attention and respect.

Armed to the hilt with my new-found weaponry, I enter in full preparedness, ready to brave all aggressors on the battlefield of *virilitas*. Prometheus once again brings fire to the world, or rather to *his* world, for his own undivulged uses. (Why share it? Someone could turn it against him someday!) This is more than just a stick of tobacco I have before me.

III.   My cigarette is the moral and physical equivalent of:

a conductor's baton

Michelangelo's chisel
Hemingway's number 2 pencils
a sorcerer's magic wand
a teacher's pandybat
a judge's gavel
a bishop's crozier
a shepherd's staff
Pope Paul's staff
the country parson's crucifix
a church-scribe's feather-pen
a fencer's fencing-foil
Mickey Mantle's baseball bat
the sceptre of Caesarism
any of the Grand Turk's collection of scimitars
a canecutter's machete
Camus's cigarette
a *guerrillero*'s tommy-gun
a lethal walking-stick
Bogart's cigarette
a pistol.
Flaming weed-stick in hand, I publicize my kinship with the rest of humanity. *O Mensch, jetzt bin ich dein!* The male half, that is.

IV.   Clinging to a cigarette, I grant, does not begin to approximate the old feeling that was wont to seize me when, hand in my pocket, I played with my *cojones*. But then to grow up is, precisely, to make personal choices. And there are consolations to be had. Starting now, my arm enters into action at drinks or dinner, participates in the cocktail chitting and chatting. My hand will henceforth move in a much-widened sphere of influence, more various zones, leaving after each of its manly sweeps a souvenir of smoke.

Cigarettes vest me with authority. Masturbation had partly emasculated my personality, what with one arm or another caged in its corresponding side pocket. I was in fact doubly truncated:

one extremity properly clad, the other needlessly concealed from sight! But I have regained them both, as it were. My arm now joins in the human throng, parading something-like-my-you-know-what in its chief fingers. This baton-cum-chisel, pen-cum-sword, is for brandishing, even as I had once yearned to wave my good John-Thomas at some people (a temptation I most prudently, nay, priggishly resisted).

V.	YESTERDAY		TODAY
	unzipping of zipper	>	tearing open of pack
	extraction	>	extraction
	fondling	>	lighting
	swift, passionate		slow, deliberate
	hand movements	>	hand movements
	huffing and puffing	=	huffing and puffing
	Onan's dripping seed	>	ashes sped by the wind
	relaxation of muscles	>	cigarette at tether's end
	reinsertion	>	disposal

VI.   The new way is less exhausting than the old. The fewer and slower motions of my hand induce in me far lower degrees of fatigue. Seventy-five strokes of my sexuality are the equivalent to about one with my cigarette. Also, more of my bodily apparatus is put directly to work (lips, teeth, tongue, larynx, trachea, bronchi, lungs; thumb, index finger, middle finger, wrist, forearm, elbow). A most efficacious way of preventing localized muscle cramps. And so I felicitously satisfy combined criteria of the functional, the social, the hygienic, the aesthetic, and the morally correct.

VII.   Is cigarette the logical extension of penis? Or merely its socio-psychological surrogate? A Swiss semiologist may well deem it an entirely arbitrary sign that represents the *idea* of penis. Certain Anglo poeticians, to the contrary, would maintain that cigarette is the objective correlative that concretizes the *emotion* of penis. On the other hand we must concede to the

Teutons and grant first of all that cigarette is superstructure originating in the material bases of production, penis mode in this case. Still, material origins notwithstanding, it is arguable, as other Teuton factions claim, that cigarette takes on an impetus and significance all its own, a relative autonomy *vis-à-vis* penis. So that there emerges a kind of "elective affinity" (*Wahlverwandschaft*) between them: travelling in parallel paths they may reflect and partly duplicate one another, though never do the twain meet. Cigarette is only cigarette, with rules and values all its own, while by the same token, penis... Yet it *is* true that, in Toronto, cigarette functions as *medium* whereby we get penis's *message*. So aren't they just about the same thing?

VIII.   Two further benefits:
   A) The aforementioned Promethean fire that glows in my life, and with a warmth that is literal, with real and palpable flames. In contrast to one's being "turned on" by way of metaphor only, my cigarette is a veritable crackling fire, a light that shines in darkness and radiates several hundred degrees of truly ardent heat.
   B) Screen of smoke, giving me a remote and misty aspect. I thus become formidable, mysterious, undecipherable. Moreover it extends my territory, aggrandizes my temporary holdings with a quickie smog that keeps the enemy at a safe distance. Cigarette smoke is offensive gas as well as defensive carapace.

IX.   Writers can write about me! As of now I'm excellent material for good clean family reading targeted for American homes. No author with a sense of delicacy could have penned the following:
   "With the honored guests safely departed, their chariots slowly vanishing on a verdant plain's horizon, young Publius languidly pulled out his prick from his pantshole and joyfully jerked off for an hour and three-quarters."
   As of tonight, more wholesome sentences can claim yours truly as their subject and predicate. A sampling:

A) "Obviously pleased, Maestro Dickerson nodded at the bushy-haired timpanist, waving his cigarette with an authoritative air about him."

B) "A look of inspiration flushed over the sculptor's bearded face. A crimson sun was sinking majestically by the Tour Eiffel. Nervously, he laid down his chisel and lit another cigarette."

C) "Casanova's thoughts of the Marquise coalesced into a devilish plan as, trance-like, he gazed at the midtown skyscrapers' grid of lights through the smoke of his cigarette."

D) "'Are you mad, my dear fellow? You've got to be joking! We cannot allow that sort of foolishness here in your rooms!' Warburton pounded the grey-coloured desk, vigourously shaking off the remaining ashes of his burnt-out cigarette."

X.   (*Finale. Allegro con brie.*)

SHE: Well, Dick, I believe you know just about everybody here. Meanwhile what do you say to a cold drink for starters?

HE: Right on. Kinda hot tonight. Whaddaya got?

SHE: Most everything, really! Cuban rum. Scotch whisky. German beer. Oh, and a special treat, real, genuine Soviet vodka. Столичная, I think it's pronounced.

HE: (*Takes a long puff of his cigarette.*) Hmm...sounds pretty good. How about some *Jerez fino*?

Enter the knight, his lance in his hand. Ahead there looms life and its unending tournament, the proving ground for the just. (Clish-clash clish-clash clish-clash clish-clash. Clish.) I'm ready to face life unquixotically, on its own terms.

The Revenge

"SHHH!" Dick Dickerson hissed, on impulse.

There was a brief silence, followed by the sound of a female voice, giggling. A deeper, male voice mumbled something indiscernible.

"SHH!" someone hissed back at him.

Shrugging his shoulders, Dick tried disregarding the voices and staying focused on his books, which were scattered wide and piled high inside his library carrel.

His Master's exam was just three days off. Since Thanksgiving he'd spent all his free time going at least twice through each item on the official reading list as well as the work of the chief critics, Harvard ones in particular. Worried over his lack of background, he had even holed up in his Conant Hall single room to study day and night this last Christmas and New Year's. And during the final month of the long winter he had been shutting himself off inside his lone cubicle, largely oblivious to the Yard outside, keeping the green window shade down, sometimes skipping class, and often staying doggedly through the very last seconds of closing time, much to the annoyance of the uniformed guards.

Now it was 9:15 on a drizzly April evening. The noise he'd successfully blocked out since his late lunch at Lehman Hall had returned abruptly when, five minutes ago, a little group had taken shape somewhere by the stairway, chatting and joking loudly, and showing no signs of moving on.

And that was why a distracted Dick had let off the fricative consonant that, in English at least, traditionally exhorts silence, in the reasonable expectation that its targeted individuals would whisper, or vanish, or otherwise desist.

What else is 'SHH!' for? he reflected to himself.

Dick heard a swish of fast footsteps approach from behind his corner cubicle.

Turning around, he saw a stubble-faced male in tight chino pants glance at him, purse his lips, go "Sh!" and rush on without a break in his stride.

More giggles burst out from afar. A lower-pitched female voice seemed to have joined in with the first, creating a soprano-contralto accompaniment.

Everything had been a matter of just seconds.

Dick recognized the guy, had often seen him busily sprawled out at the tables of the main reading room or leisurely munching away with other graduate students, English Lit. types, in Lehman or Harkness Commons. Before tonight, Dick had perceived him as just another nameless Harvard face, one out of hundreds he knew by sight, if handsomer than most, with his straight, dark hair, fine-chiseled features, and graceful, long-fingered hands. His constant beard-stubble and use of leather jackets gave him a manly, tough-guy air.

The total stranger, by mocking an ordinary, impersonal, run-of-the-mill request, had assumed an adversarial role vis-à-vis Dick.

Grimacing, Dick wiped his eyeglasses, then returned to reading the dialogue between knight and squire, "when down the road Don Quixote suddenly saw, coming right toward them, a great thick cloud of dust, at which he turned to Sancho and said:..."

Knowing that behind the dust-clouds are herds of sheep, and that the knight thinks them the pitched armies of Emperor Alifanfarón and Pentapolín the Bare-Armed, Dick looked forward to a few smiles as Don Q. attacks the rams and ewes, when suddenly he sensed light, faster footsteps originating in the opposite corridor and heading toward his desk.

From the corner of his eye he briefly glimpsed that it was he, even he, the self-appointed taunter and now his nemesis at Harvard, who hissed a softer, swifter little "Sh!" and sauntered back towards the stairway, to more female giggles.

Dick felt a jolt of fury and a physical swirling deep inside his chest. Not realizing he'd actually moved, he found himself on his feet and scurrying in between the bookstacks, in search of the offending trio.

Sure enough, standing by the metal stairwell, his hands behind his neck, was the very guy, now flanked by two women, one brown-haired, one blonde.

Dick stopped about five yards from the group, arms akimbo, addressed handsome leader as calmly as he could. "Look, man you're not funny/I'm studying for my orals for chrissake/so whyn't you do me a favor and keep it down or just move on for chrissake/jesus god leave me alone" was what he heard though he wasn't exactly sure he'd uttered.

His adversary responded with a thin grin, followed by yet another "Shh!"

Both girls cupped their hands over their mouths. The brunette turned around and walked off a brief distance, her pony-tail flopping this way and that.

Neither of Pretty Boy's two cheerleaders, presumably also English grads, rang a bell with Dick, who, reaching over to a nearby book-cart, grabbed from the pile a stiff, sharp-cornered quarto volume and held it high, ready to fling it as a makeshift missile at pretty boy's oh-so-pretty face.

The taunter dropped his hands down from his neck and recoiled slightly.

Dick laid his would-be weapon back where it had come from, then returned, silently and speedily, to his book-strewn cubicle. Exam panic had prevailed over the violently vengeful fantasies spinning dizzily inside his head.

Dropping into his chair, he surveyed his little stack of loans from Harvard's multi-million-volume holdings. His eyes roamed, landed on a heroic Don asking a perplexed squire:

"You don't hear the whinnying of horses, the blaring of trumpets, the beating of drums?"

"All I hear," answered Sancho, "is the bleating of sheep and rams."

"Your fears keep you from hearing correctly, Sancho. Go off a bit and let me be solitary, for I am sufficient unto myself to bring victory to whichever side I honor with my assistance."

Saying which, he spurred Rocinante and, setting his lance in its brace, rode down the slope like a whirlwind, shouting out loudly, "Ho, knights, ye who fight under the banners of Emperor Pentapolín, follow me! Ye shall see how easily I avenge him on his enemy Alifanfarón of Trapobana!"

Saying which, he rode right into a squadron of ewes, and began spearing them boldly and bravely as if he really were wielding his lance against mortal enemies.

So Dick read, and in his mind's ear there flared up the orchestral brass cacophony that mimics the sounds of sheep in Strauss' *Don Quixote,* a piece he'd happened to hear played at the Boston Symphony just last Thursday and which he'd then written an enthusiastic review of in this week's *Boston after Dark.* A couple of his profs occasionally warned him not to let the music journalism cut into his coursework.

"*Ay, profesor,* it won't happen, I assure you," he always replied. "But I need the money, and it's a nice break from the book-learning."

The critics were calling, the critics were calling. Dick too was a critic yet would've much preferred being a musician, any musician. After imagining himself seated in the brass section of the Boston Symphony, with he and fellow players engaged in merrily imitating the baa-baaing of sheep on muted trumpets, he sighed audibly and turned to one of the half-dozen volumes lying open on his desk.

The Baroque stands between the select linear clarity of the Renaissance and the reiterative linear clarity of the Rococo. The Baroque fills our eyes with great volume. The volume of the dust clouds came towards Don Quixote and Sancho even as Baroque destiny does. Volume, dynamism, conversion — eternal vs. temporal, infinite vs. finite, free will vs. destiny — all comprise the Baroque unity of the battle with the herds of sheep and the slingshot-wielding shepherds. In this scene, Don Quixote's mad, humanistic, Renaissance simplicity confronts ordinary yet ovine Baroque abundance.

Shifting to a more recent, oft-cited tome whose pages had dovetailed with those of the first, Dick read, "The herds of sheep appear as armed hordes to Don Quixote, yet as mere sheep to Sancho Panza. Which of these is appearance? Which one the reality? We have here the free play of perspectivism, relativity *avant la lettre,* the impossibility of achieving true knowledge — in short, a world bereft of epistemological foundations."

The noisy threesome were at least shuffling up the stairs and receding, albeit noisily.

Leafing through the various critics, Dick wondered for the fifth time that day whether becoming a lit. professor was really his heart's burning desire. Following his senior year at Wharton, his dream of a position with a classical record firm — be it an RCA or a small, offbeat label — had failed to materialize. By then he'd found out that classical albums amounted to less than five per cent of all U.S. vinyl sales, and that the minimal office staff involved in producing Bach or Beethoven LP's tended to inhabit the tiniest and most hidden halls within the music companies' glistening glass towers.

So in a spirit of resignation he'd accepted his very first offer, at the international-sales division of the Omni-Telectrono Chemicals and Containers Corporation. Their legendary headquarters were right in midtown Manhattan, and in his first months there Dick put in long hours at his forty-fourth floor office, dictating letters in Spanish to bilingual secretaries, phoning regularly to keep up with Latin American clients and to pressure prospective ones, drafting long memos in which he thoroughly summarized market conditions in sixteen Spanish-speaking republics, keeping track of the bribes to Latin American ministers that constituted a normal part of annual operational costs, and constantly churning out all manner of reports addressed to offices located up, down, and across the Omni-Tel skyscraper as well as to overseas branches large and small.

At that time too he had asked himself, also after seven months, "Is this how I want to spend the rest of my life?"

His immediate boss, a long-faced, broad-shouldered, smooth-shaven redhead called Pat Rhodes, took an inexplicable liking to Dick from the start — presumably because they were both Wharton (Pat from '58, Dick from '65) and had attended overseas high schools (Pat in Jamaica and Cuba, where his dad worked for Alcoa). So sometimes they'd shoot the breeze about life at Penn or about profs they'd each had, switching now and then to Spanish (which Pat pronounced with thick American diphthongs and frequently confused *pero* [but] with *perro* [dog]). Still sporting Sigma Chi pin and tie clasp, he occasionally ribbed his subordinate about having been "one of those god-damned independents." At least once a week he'd insist that they go for lunch at the company cafeteria some thirty-seven floors down; Dick went along out of politeness.

One clear, warm day in October, as they staked out a small table by a window, they noticed a crowd of demonstrators out on the street, marching downtown five abreast and chanting rhythmically, "Hell, no, we won't go! Hell, no, we wont go! and then "One, two, three, four! We don't want your fascist war!"

"Well, hell, yes," said Pat, pouring ketchup onto his fries, "looks like the asshole peaceniks are at it again." He made a dismissive gesture with his free hand. "I'd like to see them speak out like that in Moscow."

"Yeah," said Dick, not knowing exactly how he felt as he sipped from his Pepsi.

"You know," Pat continued with a cool indignation, "it kind of gets me. Here they are, living in the greatest country in the world, and these jerks won't go fight for their American freedoms. 'Cause that's why we're over there, you know, to defend their right to free speech. Look, I did my stint in the army. Total waste of time, but I did what I had t' do. Hey, by the way, how do things stand between you and your friendly draft board?"

"4-F. Nearsighted," Dick replied. He pointed at the left lens in his light-brown tortoise-shell frames.

A hard, grainy male voice could be heard shouting through a bullhorn. "Whaddowewant?"

"Peace!" they all answered, as one.

"When do we wannit?"

"Now!" The sounds echoed off building walls.

Pat's own supervisor, a former college-football star named Biff, now happened by, tray in hand. "Jee-*zuzz,* they're at it again," he said to Pat with an air of quiet complicity, then added, sneering slightly out of the corner of his mouth, "Looks like a Nuremberg rally to me."

"Sho' nuff," Pat replied, a phrase Dick still associated with his freshman roommate at Wharton.

"Peace, hell," Biff continued, gesturing toward the demonstrators with his geometrically configured jaw. "Fastest way to peace is to atomize Hanoi. I mean, *look* at those guys, can't tell 'em apart from the broads. Send 'em all to boot camp for haircuts. You c'n quote me on that." Pat chuckled at his boss's wit. Biff's manner now changed. "Say, before I forget, gotta show you my shiny new Mustang."

"Hey, well, I'm in the market for new wheels, you know. Lemme check out your new limo sometime soon."

"Drive you back to Bay Shore. Smooooothest ride you'll ever have." Hugging the tray with his left hand, Biff made a gliding movement with his right. "Listen, I've also found a place where you can get your car detailed for just over two hundred."

As Biff waved good-bye, saying, "Later," Pat flashed him the A-OK sign with thumb and forefinger.

"'Detailed?' What's that?" a bemused Dick asked. "Some kind

of super tune-up?"

"Young man," said Pat with mock solemnity, wrapping a napkin around his burger bun, "you've got a lot to learn about this U.S. of A. 'Detailing' is a thorough cleaning and waxing job done by professionals. By *hand*. Makes *evv*ery square inch of your car gleam like diamonds." He pronounced "every" as if it had two "v's."

Dick did not yet own a car. "Kind of expensive, no? Two hundred bills?"

"Well... not if it brings some sexy tall blonde into your front seat," Pat answered with a raise of the eyebrows and a suggestive half-smile.

For the most part, Dick noticed, the guys at Omni-Tel chatted about cars and investments, actual and potential both. The secretaries talked mostly clothes and shoes, and shopping centers out on "the Island," and often went on buying sprees down Fifth Avenue during lunch. Both sexes referred to purchases and the dream thereof by brand or model names, as in "my latest London Fog" or "my new Camaro."

Yearning for some chance to talk or merely hear of other topics, Dick entertained the thought that things might be better at other companies around town. Still half-convinced, though, that, as Pat liked asserting proudly, "America is the greatest country in the world, New York the greatest city, and Omni-Tel the greatest firm," the following week Dick tentatively made the rounds and approached a couple of dozen company employees — ages ranging from late-teens to mid-thirties — to see about organizing a book-discussion group.

Meetings would be held once a month, for starters. He offered his own place on Central Park West for a trial run, and devised a voting system whereby members would select titles.

Much to Dick's surprise, the recurring response to his lengthy, elaborate suggestion was a flat, polite, "Oh, I don't read," which more or less brought the conversation to an end.

One particularly stunning secretary — Trisha down the hall who wore her raven-black hair in a spectacular upswept coif —

gave him a puzzled look and inquired, "Book-discussion group? What's that?"

The combined experience of Trisha's dark beauty and innocent reply had in fact jelled into a revelatory moment of truth for our hitherto bewildered Dick Dickerson, and by next day he'd abandoned his cultural quest within Omni-Tel's plush corridors. Stopping at a nearby news stand after work, oblivious to the Christmas décor around him, on sheer impulse he purchased a *Village Voice,* tore out the "Rentals" pages, and, in a lightning decision, went on to spend his weekend checking out available apartments downtown.

It was a snowy, slushy start of the New Year when Dick called a cab and — Samsonite suitcases, stereo set, and book- and record-filled cartons in tow — moved from his majestic old picture-window place overlooking Central Park to the small, ground-level studio that he'd just sub-leased, from an English professor, on lower McDougal Street near Prince.

Thereafter Dick steadfastly refused to work past 5:30, citing as explanation his being enrolled in "two really tough courses" at Columbia and NYU's night school programs. Surveys of Hispanic literature, they were described in Dick's memo to Pat Rhodes as "Latin-American Studies classes" and therefore "of vital relevance" to his daily duties and future career at the Omni-Telectrono Chemicals and Containers Corporation. In reality Dick wasn't sure just what (his distant Puerto Rican upbringing aside) they might be relevant to, though he did know that what he liked about them was precisely their having nothing at all to do with his day-to-day business at Omni-Tel's international-sales division.

Weekends he'd settle into one of the many espresso coffee houses on Bleecker Street, sipping and smoking as he did course reading or simply dipped into the volumes he'd plucked out, on loan, from the English prof's bookshelves. If the weather was good, he might hang around Washington Square Park and take in the occasional political demonstration, where at times he'd encounter fellow students and their friends. One of them, a slight, nap-haired, Jewish girl-prodigy of 21, name of Sue, was handing out anti-war leaflets after delivering a brief oration of her own, in which she denounced "our terrible and criminal bombing campaign against a proud, peasant people who represent no threat to us." Spirited and spontaneous, she invited Dick to a spring housewarming party being given that night by herself and her two housemates up on Riverside and 116th.

"And maybe we can bug you with our bad Spanish," she said with a big, modest smile.

Dick shook his head and assured her she spoke the language beautifully.

There at the party he smoked his first hashish, which for him heightened all surrounding colors into a neon-like glow. In addition he re-encountered Carl, a bearded, almost-folksy philosophy student, one of a loose circle of "Beats" whom Dick had known a little at Penn and had taken to joining at assorted campus hangouts his last year. Thanks to an old friend of Carl's at the *Daily Pennsylvanian,* Dick had managed to produce his first efforts in music criticism, sweating over every word for entire nights, though by his fourth review he'd begun feeling some satisfaction at the printed result.

Now as he finally declined the roach-holder and lit up a Viceroy instead, he heard Carl suggest he try writing for the *East Village Other,* where the very same college friend had just started covering City politics. On the long sofa cross the room, Sue and her two roommates were singing and swaying as one to a slightly scratched-up "Here, There and Everywhere." Carl joined in at the second chorus, Dick at the bridge section, he stumbling a bit over words that, along with its surprise changes in key, oftentimes had him fending off welled-up tears, as was the case tonight.

For Dick it was exciting to be picking up on a past life that he'd previously come upon too late and departed too early, too abruptly, he thought. Graduation and Omni-Tel felt to him almost like an accidental and unreal hiatus, following which his chosen lit. classes and the peace rally — he understood — had led him to Sue, whose little party had led him to Carl, whose helpful tip in turn had led to the scruffy, cubbyhole offices of the *Other,* where by pure chance, Carl's friend (and acting City Editor) told a hopeful and astonished Dick, well, we recently lost our hot-shot music critic to the better-paying *Voice,* and, look Dick, why not cover the Met's *Bohème* and the next John Cage happenings for us? We'll start you off at twenty bucks a throw, yeah, I dig, peanuts compared to your Omni-Tel paycheck, but hey, what the hell, give us your fast, zippy style once again, none of that gray, pseudo-objective, midtown prose, you know what I mean?

And so Dick duly boned up on Puccini's sad plot and on Cage's antic humor before arriving at both events, his press credential proudly in hand. Taking in operas and concerts gratis and getting paid, however meagerly, to cover them, soon proved a great deal more pleasurable than his routine charge of keeping tabs on those South American government officials who were the happiest recipients of high Omni-Tel largesse. Besides, Dick's prose style came out surprisingly fast and zippy after a half-dozen drafts on his Olivetti portable, and an ensuing crop of assignments from the *Other* prompted in him stray thoughts of becoming a critic full-time (though deep inside he wondered, wistfully, if he really could, given his lack of training in music's technical side).

The doubts blossomed into a thorough complex when, at an end-of-finals bash at Sue's place he met a dark-haired Irish cellist named Kathleen, who held a degree from the Royal College of Music, knew theory, played in chamber ensembles about town, and did free-lance reviewing for the *Voice.* While knowing that Kathleen's head start was largely the result of her having had good luck and the right parents, he found himself so intimidated as to be unwilling even to listen to records the remaining weekend, though he did duly attend and write up the Jean-Pierre Rampal recital that same Sunday.

Most everyone whom Dick knew at Omni-Tel lived out on Long Island. Occasionally they bragged about never having set foot in the Village, "where all those weirdos are," as Biff once joshed in the cafeteria queue.

With a guffaw Pat quipped back, "Weirdos *is* the word!"

Dick hence didn't much worry about being seen in his latest haunts, though he assumed that, should they get wind of his new associations, his standing at the firm would not be helped. He hadn't forgotten how, at one of their very first lunches, Pat had described a temporary secretary of his from two summers ago.

"I tell you, Dick, that girl was strange," he said, slowly emphasizing the last four words. "Used to come to work on a *bicycle* with all her stuff in a knapsack. Then, at noon, she'd open up a lunch pail and go sit by herself in some corner and read that *Village Voice,* or maybe some book. Wore her hair all the way down to her waist, too."

Recalling that moment, Dick sometimes thought of publishing his reviews under a pen-name, but finally decided on "R.F. Dickerson" instead.

As far as Puerto Rico was concerned, Dick hadn't been back since senior Christmas break a year and a half ago. The island's warm temperatures and a few old friends certainly were a draw, but the growing political quarrels with his parents — with father especially — had long made any visits to the family fold a less than happy prospect. By letter and by phone the conversations were stormy enough, but right at home the daily front-page news about Negro sit-ins and marches generated endless bickering at mealtime and beyond.

"Just what do these people want?" father might ask with a resentful bluster, waving the latest *San Juan Star* with his left hand.

"Well," Dick replied cautiously, "how about the right to order a bite to eat at a diner whenever they're hungry?" With more conviction, he added, "Or the right to vote?"

"That's fine and dandy," father'd say. "So how d'you go about it?"

"You get Congress to pass a civil rights law," was Dick's slow reply.

Father's pink face turned red, his voice reedy. "Dickie, my boy, that'll only make matters worse. Last thing we need is for the federal government to go meddling in our lives." He wiped both corners of his mouth with his cloth napkin, and, shaking his head, pronounced philosophically, "I've said it before, Dickie, and I'll say it again: the problem is human nature. You cannot legislate morals. Otherwise you pave the way for another Hitler."

As usual, mother sat silently during the disputes, lips pursed, though sometimes she'd join in and inquire earnestly, "Dickie, do you really believe passing a law will end segregation just like that?" Tightening her reading glasses, she'd then reflect, "You have to change people's hearts first. And what about States' Rights? There's two sides to every question, you know."

From maybe hundreds of such exchanges Dick at last inferred that the two weren't actually listening to what he was saying to them. And then, as the troop deployment and body-count reports from Vietnam began their weekly climb, the dinner quarrels became more heated and irreconcilable, and Dick in turn came to feel oddly relieved with each return trip to Philadelphia, even to Wharton. Neither did there linger in his mind any residual longings to re-visit elder kin out in the Midwest — aunts, uncles and grandparents who used to sneer soft-spokenly at "that communist Luther King," and who liked informing Dick sympathetically, with an affectionate pat on his shoulder, that he'd been "completely brainwashed by those folks back East." Dick's grown cousins, for their part, had more or less ignored him, if they happened to be around when he was.

As a result he oftentimes thought of people around the Village as "family," even as he wondered how long he could keep up his thrice-divided (or was it four-times fractured?) life. For a spell he'd considered saving frugally in order to start up his own business — a record store downtown or a maverick record label along the lines of, say, Nonesuch. In just a year, though, he'd heard too many tales about guys at work, his own boss Pat Rhodes included, who'd previously aired like notions of venturing out as entrepreneurs, only to end up staying five, fifteen years, perhaps forever, within Omni-Tel's privileged fold.

Deciding to try out another path, early that fall Dick applied to a few graduate schools in Spanish and Comparative Literature, on all three coasts. Meanwhile the war and riot news eclipsed most civil-rights news, the endearing pet-name "hippie" replaced the more suspect and Russian-tinged "beatnik," and Dick's memo assignments were further widened to take in Spain and Brazil, where the public servants he kept track of were mostly colonels and brigadier generals. As a result of Dick's top-notch performance, in mid-March he was invited by Jeff to sit on a committee charged with putting together an in-house pamphlet, for distribution to the firm's overseas stations, and tentatively entitled *Cultivating Alien Government Officials: A Handbook for Omni-Tel Sales and Marketing Staff.*

The project threw him into a dilemma.

This goes well beyond the limits, he thought.

It's one thing to report on organized kickbacks, another to shape and formulate them, give them advice and consent, he thought.

I can't go through with it, he thought.

Losing sleep, tossing and turning the whole weekend after the first full meeting on the booklet, Dick considered doing an anonymous exposé for the *Other,* only to discard the notion when at the office next Monday morning.

For a myriad of reasons, he also balked at mentioning any of it to Sue or Carl or other such friends.

It was sheer, blind luck that ended Dick's winter of discontent when, to his surprise, he received in April an acceptance letter, his first, from Harvard, with the special proviso that, in order to qualify for the M.A., he "take three additional courses in the pre-modern period."

Dick sent out his RSVP to Harvard that same day. In time they also came through with a small fellowship, and he calculated that, along with his Omni-Tel savings, some continued free-lancing for the Other, and maybe, possibly, *Boston After*

Dark, he might make ends meet. After all, Dick by then had covered performances of every one of Beethoven, Brahms, and Tchaikovsky's symphonic works, live and on LP, and he hoped to discreetly utilize up in Boston some of the same ideas he'd been banging out for the last year and a half from his Greenwich Village studio.

As a Master's degree student, Dick worked far more hours than he ever could have as an Omni-Tel small cog. Besides having to play catch-up within a field that he'd only studied in depth in night courses, he was grinding out reviews just about weekly — some of them full-length, others quickies — of Symphony concerts or like events for *Boston After Dark.* About his only human contacts outside of class were at Lehman (fast lunches with fellow students) or occasionally over at Harkness (dinners with dorm neighbors). A brief affair, in October, with an Anglo-Argentine pianist and mother of two, fizzled out with the return of her estranged, repentant husband. Another fling, in November, with a freckle-faced Indiana redhead, who liked mocking her erstwhile boyfriends, and bragged early one morning about having dumped all 363 love notes from her latest ("He wrote *ev*very day" she said with a little smile), ended abruptly when Dick laid down his coffee mug, quietly put on his shoes and coat, and ignored her inquiries as he rushed out saying, "That turns my stomach. I will not be next." The winter's temperatures averaged twelve degrees colder than Manhattan's.

But, what the hell, purgatory has many, I-can't-say-how-many levels, Dick reflected, and hiding amid the silent, darkening library stacks stood a bit less remote from paradise than hearing constant car talk in Omni-Tel's encompassing white glare. From time to time, nevertheless, the old longing would well up inside of him, his wishing to have been a pianist, or perhaps a sculptor, his yearning for those special realms where little else mattered save for the beauty of sound and shape, where rhythm, contour, and color are the thing, the one and only thing. He couldn't read music, however, and hence couldn't play pieces nor participate in sight-reading sessions for musical ensembles — choirs, chamber groups — though now he could write about those pieces and about other people's performances of them. And he could at least sight-read the Spanish language, and somehow play on that instrument someday.

Dick rolled up the dull-green window shade and noted a young couple lolling about on the lion statue's base, frolicking under the mist-like drizzle. The boy, apparently Asian-American, was pushing her off playfully; she, a blonde, grabbed him by the cheeks and kissed him on the nose; he lay his head on her shoulder. Dick shifted his gaze upward, saw rows of freshmen in white T-shirts, framed by rectangular glass windows, diligently at work or standing about, chatting with their dorm-mates. (He envied them their fresh start here, where there was no business school they could enroll in yet.) Through the Yard a small group of activists in U.S. Army jackets and loosely-dangling hair, presumably home from a rally, filed quietly by, holding aloft a large anti-war banner. (He felt drawn to them, yet equally constrained by his own alienness, his Puerto Rican-ness that set him off from this Yankee life, from its doubters and dissenters included.)

His fatigue finally claiming him, Dick placed most of his loan books onto the cubicle shelf. He turned off the lights, trudged up three flights of stairs to the circulation desk, and dropped off two dull tomes by one of his profs. Heading for the front staircase, he caught sight of his recent nemesis, the hated trio, now expanded by a hand-holding blond couple into a quintet, and engaged in further banter by the "A-B" section of the card catalog.

As Dick walked by, he heard a single "Shh!" Turning around, he stopped, saw no response from any of them, yet could hear Mr. Taunter gleefully retelling his captive newcomers about his and Dick's little shushing war in the stacks.

"Excuse me," Dick inquired, "but, by any chance, do you know if 'Sh' stands for shithead?"

"I beg your pardon?" said the guy, with but a minimal glance at Dick.

Said the brown-haired wench from the original threesome, "C'mon, Larry, let's drop it for now." Larry scarcely paused, however, and went full speed ahead with his nasty narrative. His accent and intonation were clearly British.

Dick swung about and rushed down the marble steps, purposely, passionately indifferent to the Great War wall paintings and rare-book display cases punctuating the front hall. Scattered ice-patches could still be seen dotting the corners and crevasses of the massive outside staircase.

The air being moist and thick, he popped open his umbrella. Not in any mood for more cramming at Lamont, he went instead for a late doughnut and decaf at the Harkness snack bar, where, as it turned out, male grad students of every age and color had claimed all of the tables but one. Filter cigarette and plastic cup in hand, Dick settled in, and proceeded to fix his gaze on the big blue mural as he quietly plotted his revenge.

Eight months at Harvard, and the Puerto Rican provincial in him could still feel astonishment and awe at his sitting, legs crossed, just ten feet from a Miró while he casually puffed and sipped, much as he'd once walked, day by day, past a genuine Calder down at Penn campus. Also as at Penn, he wondered how many of the continental Americans in this room knew what was on the wall and knew who'd done it, knew for that matter who Miró was. Despite four years in business school and another two at Omni-Tel, he continued sensing within himself a wistful desire, if not to paint pictures much like this one, then, perhaps, to make large triangular sculptures that would grace the Peabody Museum lawns or Gropius courtyard.

At a nearby table, a pair of well-built Law School types were discussing the two Lesley College girls they'd recently doubled with, and were carefully planning their next move toward conquest. Otherwise the room was all smoke and murmurs and Miró.

By the time he reached his last puffs and sugary decaf drops, Dick had hatched his retaliatory scheme. Artistically conceived, the revenge on Larry would be a small, private work of the imagination, open-ended and improvisatory, like an ongoing, avant-garde jazz piece, indeterminate in length and with a surprise finale as yet unknown to him, to R. F. Dickerson himself, the working script's sole creator and proprietor.

The Master's exam, while long, held no surprises, and next morning Dick's first emotions were sheer relief followed by a raw excitement at the thought of carrying out his plan. A warm sun mitigated the chill spring breezes blowing across Oxford Street. After duly attending Latin class, he walked the diagonal path toward Widener front entrance, trod triumphally up the broad steps, crossed through the colonnade and climbed the marble staircase. This time he paused to glance at an old Spanish map of the Caribbean on exhibit, and take in the allegorical Great War frescoes, particularly the phrase, "BATTLING IN A RIGHTEOUS CAUSE."

He reached the top of the stairs, bypassed the card catalog's "A-B" section, and sensed within him a rush of uncertainty as to whether the "Shh!" man would be sitting at his customary spot at the far end of the reading room, right next to the literature reference books.

He was.

Dick ambled in that direction. There was by pure chance an empty chair across from his intended quarry. After tossing his Latin book onto the corresponding table space, Dick unzipped his windbreaker and, with a slight whoosh, sent it sailing onto the neighboring seat rest.

Neither party acknowledged the other.

Before sitting down Dick reached up for the two more recent (and therefore heftiest) numbers of the *MLA Annual Bibliography,* carefully pulled out both volumes. From a height of some twelve inches, he dropped one, then the other, side by side within the line of vision of his chosen prey.

With a brusque movement Dick pushed back his own chair and made some minor racket as he settled into his new work station.

Opening his book, Dick cleared his throat, a bit louder than was normal for him.

While leafing through the day's Virgil assignment, he drummed with his left-hand fingers on one of the *MLA Bibliography* volumes.

Turning to the Latin exercises, he hummed Beethoven's *Pastorale* Symphony, first movement, *Allegro ma non troppo.*

Then he combined the drumming and the humming as he continued with the Beethoven, development section.

There was no discernible reaction from the guy, who kept on taking notes on 3" by 5" cards.

Dick lit up a Viceroy, blew some smoke rings toward his opponent's work space, and sent out further puffs throughout the length of this king-size cigarette. He saw no other smokers in the sparsely populated smoking section, though of course it was still early in the day.

He hummed again, now a blues bass. (He envied the bass players, so invisible and unassuming, yet so essential.) And he drummed some more, now on the table top.

Mr. "Shh!" man coughed vigorously. Dick coughed back, mimicking the exact sound.

The guy cleared his throat; Dick echoed the rhythm and pitches.

The little antiphony went through a *da capo* and two variations before the guy, his face expressionless, got up phlegmatically and walked off, pencil in hand. Seeing in the temporary lull a chance to do reconnaissance, Dick casually stood up, and, stretching arms and neck both, took in the florid signature and address occupying the upper right corner of the "Veritas" notebook.

Larry Starr. Child Hall.

"LS" read the initials on the slightly faded, oxblood-colored attaché case.

Dick headed outside, ambled into the foyer.

"¡Hola, Ricardo!" he heard someone say.

At first startled, Dick turned and recognized Alejandro, his neighbor from Conant Hall, studying for his doctorate in Latin American history. The two of them often had dinner and long conversations at Harkness Commons. Their brief, friendly encounter ended with an exchange of Spanish puns and hearty chuckles — at which point Dick glimpsed his game, Larry Starr, now calmly withdrawing a drawer from somewhere in the "Z" side of the card catalog.

Hands behind his back, whistling the *Pastorale*'s Scherzo, Dick sauntered toward that section, whence he whisked out a random drawer and planted himself next to his target, whistling still.

Even as Dick reverted to first movement a minute or so thereafter, Larry departed, leaving drawer unshelved on top of side table. Dickerson did same, closely following him into periodicals room whilst whistling "The Worms Crawl in/The Worms Crawl out" in time to subject's slow shuffle.

For the next two days Dick pursued these routines, about an hour each time, with such variants as were appropriate or necessary, and with as yet neither negative nor positive results. Larry was not there next Monday, however, and Dick thought the guy perhaps had taken refuge inside the stacks. Having fully scoped out the reading room, Dick strode past circulation, flashed his Bursar's Card at the student monitor, and scurried down the metal staircase towards the vast "English Lit" collections on level two. He scouted the entire floor, checking out the names on the I.D. cards of each unoccupied carrel, and was about to give up when, there in the very last corner, surrounded by and absorbed in his library books, was the handsome hisser himself.

The adjacent cubicle Dick settled into had a full profile view of the lion-statue, unlike his own desk another story down, while the people walking between classes or on their way from lunch seemed fittingly smaller. There was no one else in the vicinity, and Dick felt free to do most everything (save smoking) he had been doing inside the reading room and out in the foyer. That is, he hummed and drummed; he whistled; he coughed and cleared his throat repeatedly; and he mimicked his adversary's coughs and throat-clearings.

"Hola, Ricardo."

He made a little jump; it was Alejandro again. Following some spirited, and voluminous Spanish chit-chat, Dick pointed with his finger. "See the guy in the cubicle next door?"

Alejandro glanced over and replied, also in Spanish, "Yeah. Why do you ask?"

Dick recounted briefly the first "Shh!" episode and current revenge play, eliciting broad smiles and, finally, loud laughs from the Nicaraguan. "For your arsenal," he noted.

"Gracias."

"Seems like an arrogant s.o.b. anyway. But, look, man, you're half-crazy. What're you hoping to get out of this?"

Dick reflected for a moment, and answered jokingly. "Maybe something Oedipal, getting back at my dad? Or maybe it's my revenge for those days at Wharton and Omni-Tel. Who knows, though? The guy's a Brit, and it could be I'm taking vengeance on the Empire..."

Shaking his head in disbelief, Alejandro shifted to Yankee English, "Well, good luck with everything. Later, Dick," he said, waving good-bye.

"Hasta luego."

Throughout all of Dick's verbal/musical countermeasures he fully expected Larry to say something, and therefore had his responses at the ready and rehearsed.

If there was just one "Shh!" from Larry's side, Dick would parry with a threefold echo, diminuendo.

If the guy approached him, saying, "Excuse me, will you please stop?" or "Christ almighty" or "Come *on*, man," Dick would flash him the face of a movie-TV moron and, front teeth protruding, serve back to Larry his same words, "Ex-*cyooooz* me" or "Christ al*miiiigh*ty" or "Cum *aaaawwwn,* maaaan" or the like.

The guy never said a word. Still, Dick felt no disappointment and indeed reveled in the knowledge that the enemy and erstwhile hisser knew full well that any visible, let alone audible, reply on his part would constitute a loss to his forces and moreover that Larry knew that Dick knew that such was the case. It was almost as if Dick were Larry's conscience incarnate.

And that was why, at the end of next day's cubicle duty, Dick laughed an operatic "HA-HA-HA!" and pretty much assumed that Larry would infer the reasons for his laughter.

Nevertheless, Dick had not as yet gotten satisfaction. He felt a Faustian longing to extend and explore his new-found project and gave serious thought to such proven tactics as putting in for delivery of three different pizzas to Larry's room around midnight, or for twenty magazine subs under Larry's name, or maybe telephoning him a few times at two A.M. and asking desperately for Cindy or Mindy or Marsh, then finally inquiring in a cheerful, high-pitched voice, "Hi, this is Cindy, any calls for me?" — though in the end he rejected those old chestnuts as too obvious, too time-consuming, and less than legal.

And so, instead, after an enjoyable hour at the library, he crossed the Yard, happened by Larry's ground-floor room at Child Hall, and slipped under the door an envelope bearing Larry's name in full and therein three blank sheets of white bond paper, stapled, or a clipping, any clipping, from the *New York Times*.

Or he purchased a recent *True Confessions,* located a passage saying, "I love you," circled the three little words in a sunburst of red ink, cut out and inserted the folded page into a small pink envelope, and posted the billet-doux from a mailbox by Symphony Hall just before making his way through the hordes to cover a much-awaited concert, all Rachmaninoff, for *Boston After Dark.*

For the following episode he bought some cheap, deep-purple lipstick at Bence Pharmacy, hid inside his Conant Hall suite, bedaubed his lips and left their imprint on the margins of yet another amorous page. Later that evening, writing with his left hand quite slowly so as to suggest the evenness of female script, Dick penned a brief, unsigned, passionate note saying, "Larry, dearest, when will we meet again? I want you, I need you, and I lust for you right *now!*" Next morning, though, Dick looked at both items more than once and placed them inside his desk drawer for further consideration.

Dick's new vanguard methods by no means replaced the established, classical techniques which he'd worked out in the library, and which he in fact elaborated on elsewhere. At Lehman Hall he twice caught sight of Larry sitting with a girl, and Dick made for and claimed the free space providentially available next to them at their long table the first time, and at the nearby square one the next. Whistling the *Pastorale*'s opening bars as he sat down, he tore open his brown bag, picked up on the respective musical passages between bites of this and sips of that, and discreetly lobbed large puffs of smoke toward Brit boy's territory.

Whenever Brit boy laughed or coughed, Dick served back the same sound from out of the corner of his mouth, though louder, so as to be heard above the noontime din.

More than once Dick piped in nasal falsetto the last few words of some of Larry's sentences. The girl, a different one on each occasion, actually looked over at Dick with a frown of bafflement, even as her friend evinced no reaction and said nothing.

Engagement. Fulfillment. Pleasure. Rapture. Happiness. All of this and more Dick had got from his experience thus far. His one major regret was that the waking day as well as the remaining weeks proved much too short to allow for additional growth and polishing of his resources and his craft.

Meanwhile mid-May burst forth astonishingly beautiful and balmy, and the mingled scent and sight of millions of blossoms, ranging from deep pink to lacy white, served further to enhance the mood of high-spiritedness about town. Dick let up temporarily on his campaign in order to get ready for exams, go over the bewildering array of Latin verb forms, and sit quietly on Widener front steps watching the sparrows, squirrels, young pups, and all manner of people zigzagging across the paths and spruced-up lawns. The long-awaited explosion from hissing agent-provocateur Larry Starr had never materialized, somewhat to Dick's chagrin, though the joys he'd felt now lingered potently in memory. He did, moreover, have a revenge of sorts.

It was the start of reading period, and the mix of no more classes with spring warmth made for a festive air, indoors and out. Dick sat lazily at a Lehman Hall square table, peeling a tangerine. At his left sat dark-eyed Milagros, or Mili, a fellow islander and former classmate through most of Dick's twelve years down at Espíritu Santo. Their acquaintance had sprung up anew on a late morning last September, when Dick was scurrying back from drafting his trial Symphony review and checking facts at Widener reference (where he'd also vaguely noticed fateful Larry). Already late for a class, as he mounted Boylston steps he heard from behind him a Spanish-inflected voice.

"Dickie? Dickerson?"

He turned around instinctively.

"Aha, ¡hola! Remember me? Mili Vélez?"

Before then he'd never seen her wearing anything but the school uniforms, yet it took him just seconds to recognize the diminutive little talker in braids who'd always held a front-row seat, and who liked singing funny songs, in English, at their school parties. Off and on his mind had casually recalled certain boys who'd talked mischievously about staring up her dress during chapel, others who'd listed her among the seventh grade's five prettiest. Her dark hair, the braids long gone, was now long and straight.

"I've been here a year now," she explained, "doing French. They'll promote me back home, if I get a U.S. doctorate. Right now I'm more involved with Fair Play for Cuba, though. And you?"

Dickie could scarcely contain the odd excitement that the surprise reencounter with a steadily-receding past had aroused in him. Talking fast and freely, he ran through his own study plans, and his music reviewing, and his experiences back at Wharton and at Omni-Tel.

"Six years total," he said regretfully, now almost out of breath. His eyes fixed on a fat, furry squirrel darting among some scattered peanuts. "Complete waste of time. And all to please my pop." With his chin he pointed at the darting creature; Mili grinned; passersby stopped to take in the small animal's questing skittishness.

"Yes, they *are* cute," said Mili, seconding his observation. "One thing we don't have on our little island." Then she tilted her head and looked at Dick with a strange smile. "Listen, Dickie, those years really seem to have changed you. You're almost another person. You used to be so shy and quiet, you hardly ever talked, except to answer the nuns. I don't think you and I conversed even once."

"Oh, well," said Dick, shrugging his shoulders. "I'm still shy, but I'll make it up by talking with you as much as I can. I sure need it, given my rusty Spanish."

It was Mili who'd first shown him Lehman Hall, where they'd gone for lunch later that day and several times since. And now, near year's end, they once again sat relaxing amid the midday hubbub.

Dick bit into a tangerine slice. At his right sat Nell, Mili's lively, bespectacled next-door neighbor at 6 Ash St. A self-described "strawberry-farm girl" from Vermont, she usually wore black denims and Western boots, and liked reciting passages from Shakespeare and Yeats, stroking their words one minute, then mocking the big theorists she'd recently been having to bone up on in their stead.

"Hey, what's it all worth, these myth critics?" she asked, plucking a cigarette from out of Dick's new pack.

"Myth critics? Who're they?" Dick inquired.

"They get their ideas out of Northrop Frye, the heavy up in Toronto. He's pretty good, actually. But the little Northrops, the small Fryes, they hunt for myths and archetypes everywhere. 'The Fisher-King Myth in *Pride and Prejudice*.' 'Cain and Abel Archetypes in Trollope.' That sort a thing."

Dick felt bewildered. "Weird. I'd had some vague notion that stuff was out there. This sounds kind of demented, though."

Mili added, "Or mechanical. A formula."

"Yeah, well, y' get the impression they really think poets crank out poems according to some recipe book. Shee-it. It's not as if poetry gets written that way." She took a long puff of Viceroy smoke. "Criticism by numbers, like."

"Next thing you know," Dick speculated, "they'll be seeing archetypes in the latest race riot."

Nell nodded, a look of loving malice on her lips. "Well, *indeed,* now that y'mention it, one of Frye's top disciples did just that in a recent lecture here!"

Mili waved and beckoned at someone entering the dining room.

"Y'know," Nell continued, "there's some hot-shot scholar who's been claiming that critics, not poets, are the true artists. Oh, man, gimme a break." She raised an index finger. "*One line* of good second-rate verse counts more than all their little theories put together."

Mili smiled a broad smile as she pointed eagerly at the fourth seat. "Here comes an interesting guy that I met yesterday. Is it okay if he sits here?" she asked Nell and Dick, who both nodded. "He's from London, I believe."

Now chirping a melodic, "Hel-lo there," and warmly beaming back at Mili stood none other than Larry Starr, who dropped his paper bag onto the white tabletop, and whose angular facial features suddenly changed shape the moment that his soulful gray eyes alighted on Dick.

"Larry," Mili gestured, "I would like to present two friends of mine..."

"Oh... how do you do...," Larry blurted out.

"Yes, we *have* met," Dick interrupted with a little smile of his own.

"Yeah," Nell observed flatly, "we had Milton together last fall."

Larry made no further movement.

"Please, Larry, sit down with us," Mili urged him.

"Oh, so sorry," Larry said, "but I must be moving on." And saying no more and without further ado he snatched up his brown bag and rushed off toward the food-line area.

Dick turned his whole upper body in order to stare straight at Nell. "You know him."

"Sort of." She extinguished her cigarette. "He's a first-class shit. Pretty good-looking, as you c'n see, and smart, too. He's also slept with two different friends of mine, gotten 'em all starry-eyed — if you'll pardon the pun — then dropped each of 'em like they were wet kleenexes."

Mili looked somewhat disturbed. "So he's not a nice person."

Nell gave her a longish glance, cut into a piece of pie-crust, and said, "Like I say, he's smart."

Rubbing his hands, Dick now jumped into the fray. "Well, have I some great stories to tell *you*." And he began telling them what has been told here concerning his own strange, less-than-eventful "relationship" to the handsome hisser, Larry Starr, and with each new episode their laughter turned *più forte,* a soprano-alto-tenor counterpoint that filled the crowded dining hall even as they saw sheepish Larry heading sheepishly for the front door, plastic-covered coffee-cup in hand. And for the next half-hour they spoke of Larry exclusively, with Nell's and Dick's alternative recitatives periodically cadenced by three-voice guffaws; and they talked of Larry yet again over lunch at the same table some days later, though now with no added sightings of their subject further to goad their mirthful exultation.

Larry did not enroll at Harvard the next fall. Dick of course nourished half-comical notions about his campaign having drummed the guy out of town.

"Looks like your strategy worked!" Nell first said to him one bright September morning as they happened to cross paths on Widener steps. Tightening her horn-rimmed glasses with her thumb and middle finger, she told him of the English boy's return to merrie old England, far from his taunters. Giving Dick a little tap on the arm, she exclaimed "Congratulations!" and, conspicuous in her black denims, continued descending the wide staircase.

From that day on Dick casually wondered if his curious adventures with a now-departed Larry might be worth a story or perhaps a stage play (realistic? experimental? some mixture of the two? — he simply could not say as yet). Besides, how do you go about telling of a situation in which so little happens, so unilaterally, and in so limited a space? All this Dick asked himself in Widener reading room while drafting the new season's premier Boston Symphony review. (They'd done a brisk *Pastorale* and a fiery Seventh. Good old Beethoven. Never fails the audiences.) He recalled the tragedy by Lorca that both opens and closes with the tyrannical country matriarch bellowing her command, "Silence!" (or *"¡Silencio!"* actually). And he pondered the long-range possibility of someday writing the first short story ever to begin as well as end with the monoconsonantal, hortatory, everyday English utterance, "Shh!"

Problems of Post-industrial Society
by R. F. Dickerson

As a Puerto Rican proverb says, *Un pelo hace sombra.*
Or, to put it in a less laconic English, "Even a hair casts a shadow."

Imagine, then, the rich, luxuriant shadow cast, during my morning walks in the sun, by the countless hairs of my fully-grown moustache.

It's an impressive moustache, long, brown, and bushy, radiating a quiet power as it droops resolutely down my lower cheeks and blows about languidly in the afternoon breeze.

And there's so much there, I must proudly say. There's a new part of me, a new excrescence, or extremity, or whatever it is the taxonomists like calling such phenomena. I look in the mirror after work or after bed, and am surprised. And I say to myself, "Why that is *me* growing out there! More of me *growing!* Yes, more of me, as yet, *still* grows!" And what can matter more than personal growth, after all? So I ponder this addition, and feel quite pleased, for at twenty-five years one's options begin narrowing somewhat. Never will my body surpass its current five foot nine. Nor can it grow save laterally, a mode I rule out resoundingly, insofar as ruling out anything is possible today.

And so, some months ago, finding myself more or less *nel mezzo del camino* as they say in Firenze, I sat down in pensive silence on my gaily-colored sofa, the Andante from Beethoven's Seventh coming in quietly over WQXR.

Or rather it was the orlon cover not the sofa itself that was gaily-colored, just as it was a floppy twin-bed mattress and not a sofa proper, on which I pensively sat.

85

And so, as I sat, oblivious to the Sunday evening traffic swishing by some twelve stories down yonder, I stared at the long, faded wall mirror across the room. And I proceeded to sort out the forms of natural increase then remaining me, to wit: 1) a beard, 2) a moustache, 3) long nails, and 4) long hair.

All but number two I found wanting.

For what prospects accrued to these options? I then asked.

Dreadful few, I fast concluded. No. 3 lacks practical precedents here in El Norte, while no. 4 is just fine for others, who're free to let their aft-locks grow and flow as they wish, but it's not me, really. Beards, no. 1, seemed better, having at least a history, but they're too... too... too — — salient, that's the word, they're too salient for my style. Regretfully, I ruled them out as well.

On the other hand, there, cross-legged in my pensive silence, I at long last espied and closed in on the possibilities of a moustache, which, with its reduced field of action I spotted right off as my legitimate means of expression, like the piano was for Chopin. I wish to give something of myself tho' not my all. I'll take restraint, anytime. There's a lot to say for set boundaries, as one of my lit. profs said to us about Boileau or Pope, I forget which. For one must pick and choose, cull, sift, weed, and winnow out — an act of decision, ZAP! (as they say in NYC) — and then, methodically and magisterially, set off wheat from chaff, sheep from goats, men from boys, and whatever it is the expert separators separate.

Today the total picture differs somewhat because of the arrival, on the scene, of my moustache. I walk amid these big buildings and know that the visual look of the city and my own place in it are ever so subtly altered. This I have been confirming these past few weeks when, on entering the street-bound elevator, I note with astonishment how the security mirror gives off an image markedly different from what it showed last spring. There within that round convex fixture I see a large circumflex of dark bushy brown upon an ovoid surface of light-olive-to-ruddy-white.

Then, three floors down, another groggy male tenant boards the elevator and sees not just one but two brand-new shapes, assuming of course that tenant stands at the appropriate angle.

At ground floor, after remarking these nuances of change, I watch the groggy tenant amble off, deep in his thoughts, where the datum of my moustache lies happily stored, forever. I arrive on the street, where I feel this unmistakable sense of taking up a few more inches on the roistering urban canvas. There is more of me. There are strands of new material brought into being by me. They modify indefinably the former balance between light and shade. They consign last spring's designs to past history.

Cars of all nationalities, three and four abreast, rush down-hill, hitting one, two, three green lights, trying for more. Clean-shaven men scurry by, clinging to their monogrammed oxblood attaché cases. A perfumed and lissome model, sporting sensuous suede, visibly hails a cab. Frizzy-haired Columbia students and Barnard girls in jeans sit on a bench, talking politics. Grayclad schoolchildren clamber onto the downtown bus.

Not unreluctantly, I walk thirty-six short blocks in the direction of the Omni-Telectrono-Chemicals and Containers Corp., their building that is. In my brisk pace I'm conscious of occupying increased parcels of urban air and human memories, more space, physical and mental, than previously occupied. I know that people make way for me, at any rate more than they made last month. They must step aside if they're to avoid bumping into me with my additional terrain.

This very same matrix of events, *mutatis mutandi,* obtains when I retrace my steps uptown late in the afternoons.

Saturdays and Sundays I head for one of the parks and add my body to yet another of those numerous demonstrations, and me and my moustache help swell the crowd a wee bit, thus rendering it all that much more forceful.

All these gains, however slight, are of inestimable importance in view of the crisis of urban agglomerations as I think Professor Daniel Glöckvist puts it. For something must be done to offset this oversize city, this vast thicket of big buildings and *fortissimo-prestissimo* stridencies, with its immoderate light and excess darkness, and the fearful glances, the melancholia.

What else can I do, after all? I'm no public speaker, no tactician or organizer, and then what is it one organizes? Nor can I handle small guns or plan demonstrations, but I'll contribute what I can. Each of us does what he does best, pursuing the struggle in his own way, as some speechmaker said in the park (I forget when). In times of dwindling freedoms we must utilize all remaining freedoms, and one of those yet-remaining freedoms is, precisely, the freedom to grow a moustache.

The struggle, I said. The struggle against what? Against the war, I guess. The men on TV, the guys across the hall, the doorman downstairs, myself, we all hate the war. But there's something I actually hate more. I hate big buildings, all of them, the one where I sleep, the one where I work or buy lunch, the ones where I take night courses or have a beer. These big buildings, they cover the sky so much I just about forget what the sky looks like. And the ocean, with its awesome expanse, is hopelessly blocked from view.

I feel so hemmed in I even bitch about these buildings at the office. The steno nods, smiles, then bitches too.

But big buildings keep popping up while small buildings vanish. Is there a law that makes big swallow up small? Oh, sure, bigger is better, as gringoes like to say. And Prof. Glöckvist asserts early on in *Problems of Post-Industrial Society* that, come the year 2010, all buildings will inevitably be big, and that that will be good, barring of course the exceptions.

But I don't like it, and yet it goes on, despite my dozens of letters to the *Times,* the *News,* and the *Post* (of which two published, their rapier wit intact). I've carried pickets, chanted slogans, reasoned with passersby, fulminated at City Hall. Bigger buildings nonetheless continue to sprout, leading me to conclude that our words are short-lived and travel not far, and that whoever erects these big buildings doesn't understand or heed our voices, or won't heed them.

Besides, however voluminous or eloquent my words, I'm too frequently drowned out by the jets, the F-111s and B-52s periodically swarming by in squadrons of three. The café scuttlebutt I've overheard, both here and downtown, is that the planes are headed back from blasting faraway peasant villages.

Can this really be? What TV news do they watch? I wonder, the noise of the jets is bad enough. What must the blasts be like?

Well, I'm for the villagers, whoever and wherever they may be.

I'm surprised at my saying this... I wouldn't dare say it at work... Surely I'd get roughed up or ridiculed... But those planes, the shadows they cast, too vast, all. Sometimes they hover directly overhead, their shadows enveloping us marchers in a cold, swift darkness, and I automatically think "Eclipse! Solar eclipse!" An enormous black iceberg brushes my skin and batters my face, it seems. The shadow of my moustache will of course never attain such proportions unless my moustache itself somehow becomes considerably larger, its shadow thereby taking on a *force de frappe* to rival that of the airplanes.

Still and all, "*Un pelo hace sombra,*" said the cabdriver to me back in old San Juan, as he pocketed the tip and nodded goodbye.

And three airplanes, or any three big buildings, in turn, cast one hell of a valley of shadow, or deathly shadow.

BUT BEAUTY IS A SUBVERSIVE FORCE. IT IS MORE DANGEROUS THAN A GUN, MORE POWERFUL THAN ANY OF THE BOMBMAKERS. BEAUTY, AND ONLY BEAUTY, WILL PREVAIL!

I read that a few months ago, just as my moustache was beginning to sprout, in *Moustache,* America's monthly magazine for moustache wearers. It sees in us its readers the hope of our troubled nation's future. I hit upon this highly informative publication by sheer happenstance, for it was just about overwhelmed in the downstairs drugstore's magazine rack by other periodicals such as *Beard, Rosé Wines, Snowmobile, Better Bathrooms, Good Biceps,* and *Dope.*

And there amid that array of special-interest magazines I found the one that best suits my needs. Between its brilliantly multi-hued covers *Moustache* runs such items as:

self-help columns on the care of one's moustache;

intellectual articles on the ever-changing styles in moustaches;

socially concerned essays that demonstrate how economic growth and productivity increase in direct proportion to the number of existing moustaches;

short uplift pieces that praise the private joys of a moustache and see it as the key to individual success;

medical features singling out moustaches as an important source of Iron, Calcium, and Vitamins A, B, and D;

thumbnail sketches of famous figures who sport moustaches, whom staff writers occasionally interview;

serial novels about a stout-hearted, trimly mustachioed hero with whom a haughtily sophisticated high-society dark beauty falls hopelessly in love;

whimsical cartoons about us members of the moustache-wearing class;

heated polemics against the beard-wearing class;

reviews of books by mustachioed authors (in which the links between the author's literary, and moustache, styles, are traced);

ads for a range of moustache trimmers, dyes, waxes, tonics, combs, and scissors, not to mention false moustaches for the less-than-fortunate;

oh, yes, and announcements concerning moustache clubs, conventions, and clinics being held throughout the land.

And that's where I read that *Beauty is a subversive force* and *more dangerous than a gun* and so forth.

It was the May issue, I think, a lead editorial entitled, "Moustaches: The Subtle Revolution."

Well, it was a most comforting statement to read, truly and extraordinarily comforting. It buoyed up this psyche which, what with the never-ending war news and the ever-sprouting buildings, certainly did need buoying.

A moustache, according to that editorial, will furnish its

owner and its passing observers with, let's see, here it is, yes, with "a viable alternative to the cigarette butts and ketchup-stained napkins and the overstuffed trash cans blighting our streets. A moustache is the free individual's way of simply saying 'NO!' to the jet planes that befoul the air, of standing up to the mighty skyscrapers that envelop us in their cold purplish lights."

Yes, yes, that's it! I know just what they mean, those editorialists! Good heavens, what the heck, society can't do anything and government only makes things worse, as the editors went on to say, but we as individuals must do something.

And so my moustache will serve as, what is it, yes, a viable model for spiritual transcendence, for assertion of the Self against the onslaught of impersonal forces. I know now, thanks to that editorial, that, wherever I happen to be, my moustache will stand for other and better ways, will haunt and encourage whoever has just seen those overstuffed trash bins and then encountered my moustache, will stay in his mind like a magnet and secretly convey to him how good our short life on this planet can be...

I remember the time when, back in the days during which my moustache was but an incipient stubble, I mounted the elevator and went to ask my boss if it was alright with Omni-Tel if I let my moustache grow. I asked from the doorway of his office, staring expectantly. He seemed part of the big skyline which I could see unfolding from his 88th floor picture window as far as the blue fringes on the horizon. In the meantime I stood there in silence, fidgeting, my hush puppies buried deep — stuck I almost thought — in the lush white carpeting.

"By all means, Dick," he finally said, slowly. "For you are a free agent. Your personal actions are entirely your concern. You are employed, after all, by Omni-Telectrono-Chemicals and Containers, one of the free-est Companies in what is by far the free-est Country in the Free World. I mean — good heavens! — after all, really now, it is not for us to say what Length the Hair, nor, for that matter, Where the Hair may Be. Why indeed I myself am a case in point, for I have just begun to grow Sideburns. Ours being an enormously dynamic and rapidly changing Society, why, one must do his individual best to keep up with the Times. By all means, grow a Moustache, why, grow two of them if you want."

Imagine my amazement, tho', when he began nodding repeatedly, rhythmically, and then mused out loud, "*For Beauty is a subversive force. It is more dangerous than a gun, more powerful than all the bombmakers.*"

My jaw dropped. That's what he said. Somehow I got back my bearings and nervously blurted out words to the effect of, Uh, where... where had he read that?

"Oh, I got it out of *Sideburns,* America's special-interest magazine for sideburns-wearers. An editorial, May issue, I think, about the Sideburns Revolution. Extremely useful publication, by the way. Carries self-help columns on the care of one's sideburns; intellectual-type articles on the ever-fluctuating styles in side-burns; socially concerned essays that demonstrate statistically how economic productivity increases in proportion with the number of existing sideburns; serial novels..."

I tried holding back, in vain tho'. I interrupted, "How did you come across this... this... magazine, sir?"

"Oh, well, you see, my brother-in-law owns the mag and writes the lead editorial. So you see I get a free copy every month. My brother-in-law, he's quite a fellow. Through hard work and effort he's built up his own magazine empire called ASIP, Associated Special Interest Periodicals, Inc., you know, magazines such as *Beard, Hairdo, Rosé Wines, Snowmobile, Sky-Diving, Better Swimming Pools, Better Biceps,* and *Dope.* ASIP's got its own small skyscraper right down the street, you know. Yes, quite a fellow, my brother-in-law. Come to think of it, he owns *Moustache* too, the magazine for America's moustache wearers. Matter of fact, uh, Dick, how would you like a trial subscription?"

I told him I already had one.

"Ah, well. No, Dick," he went on, "remember, planting

bombs in our Country's mighty skyscrapers is simply not the answer. Violence gets us nowhere, you, me, everybody. Only Beauty, individual Beauty, can save us all. I know, Dick, I am convinced, that Beauty will ultimately prevail."

"Maybe so, sir," I said. "I hope so, sir," I said.

Well, I left that office a bit shaken. As the elevator whooshed down I was glad that the old guy'd granted me his permission and was pleased that someone at Omni-Tel actually shared my very own conception of beauty, unlike, say, my father or my... Still, I've never known just what to make of those things he told me. His own brother-in-law... That paragraph... ASIP, Inc... I can't grasp it. Do all sideburns-wearers too go about asserting to themselves that *"Beauty is a subversive force"*?

Well, whatever those rival forces happen to believe, I know my realm, know that there are times when my moustache is the only speck of beauty on the block, the only subversive element in what is a desert of fear and conformism. In fact I don't want to brag but (*glowingly*) some gals at Omni-Tel are of the opinion that mine is the most beautiful moustache they've seen, ever. And certainly, beauty of the highest order must serve some purpose in... that phrase... yes, in our ever-precarious social fabric.

And maybe my moustache not only *is* something but *does* something too. After all, everything in this universe does something. What does my moustache do? Maybe it can help bring down big buildings (my dream, my very dream). Sir Isaac Newton after all made the noteworthy point that every particle in the universe is attracted to every other by a force varying as the products of the masses and inversely as the square of the distance between them. Assume then that the particles of my moustache, for the sake of a round figure, weigh 1 gram, while the big building that houses Omni-Tel weighs 10,000,000,000 kilograms, and the distance between the big building's center of gravitation and my moustache is 100 meters. So, if I sit on a park bench and stare intently at Omni-Tel, and if we go by the formula:

$$F = G M \ X M,$$
Omni-Tel being $N = 10,000,000,000$ Kg
and my moustache $M = 6.670 \ X \ 10$
(that is approximately $1/15,000,000,000$) we then get:
a) $10,000,000,000 \ X \ 1/100 = 10,000,000$
(product of the masses)
b) divided by d, $10,000,000/10,000 = 100$
c) multiplied by G, $100 \ X \ 1/15,000,000 = 1/150,000,000$
d) $1/150,000,000$ newtons, the force by which the Omni-Tel
building and my moustache attract each other when at a distance
of 100 meters.

Not very much, to be sure. It's just a bit more than there had
been before, that's all. And granted it's neutralized by the
somewhat greater gravitation of the Earth itself. Whatever you
say, tho', a little bit more is still more, a little bit better is still
better. The most minuscule contribution is a contribution withal.
Before I raised this moustache, its components-to-be were
scattered about, lacking in concentration. Now they have been
brought together into a focal point where their divers elements
are conjoined. So that they form 1) a locus of beauty, of
aesthetic power fiercely concentrated, the power of art no less,
but 2) are also a new source of physical strength, a gravitational
force ultimately capable of bringing down big buildings. David
brought down Goliath, and my moustache can bring down big
buildings. For beauty is a subversive force. Beautiful moustaches
are a subversive force, and if everyone grew a moustache, big
buildings would crash down. Or at least they would last much
less.

I wonder what effect my moustache can have on the airplanes
tho'. They do fly high. And far, very far. Here they simply
rattle our windowpanes, but overseas, the café rumors have it,
they dump 40,000 tons of TNT every hour and take great
pleasure in destroying everything underneath them, and I've
heard they shower those faraway lands with tiny razor-blades
that cut deep into the skins of the rebel peasants and their
spouses and children and even rip the llamas, the yaks, and the

water buffalo to shreds. Can wearing a moustache really help the peasants? Are moustaches any match against a mad sadist in a jet? I wonder. But perhaps, in my way, I can help. It works like this:

SCENARIO I: I walk into my usual downstairs drugstore and single out a tube of Crest toothpaste. A clerk, amazed or dumfounded or appalled, takes note of my moustache and tells his boss about it. The boss resolves to take note of my moustache next time around. The others are told they can follow suit, and a week later when I drop in for some Tiparillos and the latest issue of *Moustache* the activities of the head pharmacist and his handful of personnel are all slowed down slightly as they furtively take note of my moustache. Consequently their sales transactions are momentarily sluggish in the wake of their mild shock at this minor novelty. And so, with an ironclad logic, the clients get their tissues and bath oils and birth-control pills a minute or two later than they had expected. And lo! I've succeeded in slowing down a small portion of the big machine by minute or two, the upshot of this being that they're late for their coffee dates and love-trysts and maybe even a business deal where some lethal military hardware such as those razor blades is being negotiated.

And, to backtrack a bit, the cashier takes my money slower than she usually does with the aim of course of getting a good look at my moustache. As I move on she keeps staring at me out of the corner of her eye with the result that she is slow in handing over a pack of 4-X condoms to this impatient young customer who's just run out of his monthly supply and is in a hurry to get a move on and use the stuff with his teenage girl-friend who regrettably is at her most fertile today and who, as we shall see, baby-sits in her spare time. He arrives at her place a few minutes later than he had expected because me and my moustache ultimately caused him to botch his routine and hit all the red light signals or to miss his train just as its doors slammed shut. And so he is late in arriving at her place. And though they do screw they also finish late owing to his being

initially exhausted and annoyed in spite of her being filled with
the most ravishing desires in her long wait for him. And so she
in turn is late in departing and again with an ironclad logic
arrives late for her baby-sitting job where a lonely housewife
(whose husband is a bomber-pilot long ago downed and held
POW by a peasant village) is anxiously waiting to get away from
the house and to a motel so as to see her own secret lover who
is on day's furlough from his Air Force base where he works as
a navigator. And because the baby-sitter was late the housewife
also is late and so the lovers ardently prolong their session
somewhat and consequently the navigator is some ten or fifteen
or even twenty minutes late at the air base where his navigating
services are urgently needed and so landing and refueling
operations are at a slump and — who knows? — maybe even
slowed down a good fifteen or twenty or twenty-five minutes
because our
      local *Luftwaffe*'s
      horny navigator's
      prurient lover's
      sex-starved baby-sitter's
      slightly concupiscent boyfriend's condom purchase
took place at a pharmacy where things were moving rather
lethargically for no other reason than that I have a moustache at
which the entire personnel took unofficial time off to peer, the
final outcome of it all being that fewer bombs and razor-blades
fall on peasant villages that day and with luck maybe a life or
two is spared.

    Or, from your friendly neighborhood think-tank here's:

    SCENARIO II: I'm in a supermarket line one Wednesday
afternoon and as my turn comes up the darkly sensual cashier
addresses me directly and comments admiringly on my
moustache saying *how* much she simply *adores* it because it's so,
well, so *darleeng* and "Ooh-là-là eet has so much... euh... as we
say in Bruxelles, so much *charme*, so much *mystère*, such an *air
joyeux*." At the adjoining register there's this crisply Nordic
cashier who rings in enthusiastically with "*Ach, ja*, it iss so, *als*

wir say in Salzburg, so *reizend,* so *bezaubernd,*" and as I thank them heartily and head towards the exit door I hear the darkly sensual cashier declare with conviction, "*Monsieur, est-ce que vous saviez que la beauté c'est une force subversive? qu'elle peut détruire des royaumes entiers?*" I smile nonplussedly and wonder inside of me just what magazine *she* got *that* from, surely not *Sideburns* or *Moustache.* And I hurry out just as that Nordic cashier begins saying, "*Ja, die Schoenheit ist sicherlich eine subversive Kraft.*" But, to backtrack a bit, this entire scene has been witnessed by my next-door neighbor Ned who was standing open-mouthed behind me in the queue, observing my little triumph with this exotically enticing duo... poor guy...

So meanwhile back at the food counter the darkly sensual cashier curtly adds up Ned's groceries and gives him his double Triple-S blue stamps in frosty silence while the Nordic cashier doesn't even look Ned's way, he painfully perceiving the contrast. And so he decides then and there to grow a moustache. And a few hours later at a bar he confides to his beer-drinking buddy Fred what he saw happen at Grand Union earlier that day with the important decision that followed in its wake. Then Fred too considers the possibility of growing a moustache. So when Fred gets home that evening he tells his roommate Ted about me and Ned and the affair of the cashiers, and so Ted also decides to grow a moustache. Later he relays the entire story of me and Ned and the two visions of loveliness and Fred to his rather brutish half-brother Ed who is an emotionally retarded bomber-pilot filled with complexes, terrified of women, and thus rather horny. So he's about to try anything, even grow a moustache. So he grows a moustache, which later gets him in trouble back at the air base with Capt. Head, his martinet of a commanding officer who won't let him fly until he shaves off his moustache. Consequently bomber Ed doesn't get to razor-blade any peasants to death that particular day. Or on the other hand maybe Capt. Head lets him fly but only begrudgingly thus making him feel guilty and depressed. But at the same time Ed is become quite vain about his moustache. And so, with all these psychological complications together with his slightly increased cosmetic duties and physical weight he is become something of a sluggard. And so on one of his bombing missions that day a farmer some 10,000 feet below trains his AK-47 on the airplane and scores a pal-pa-ble hit and brings down brutish Ed, whereas the farmer wouldn't have succeeded had Ed not had a moustache and had I not had a moustache. And so I feel quite good because it's good news whenever bomber Eds are being shot down and, well, to bring us back to the subject at hand, as you will see from this scenario, I, little mustachioed me, Dick in the big city, together with the helpful collaboration

of Ned

and Fred

and Ted

and Head

plus two cashiers

am ultimately responsible, am the prime mover in the row of falling dominoes which leads inexorably to the shooting down of bomber Ed, and saves a peasant family and their mango trees.

My moustache casts a shadow. Hopefully in the long run it can also cast down a bomber pilot or two, or perhaps plunge his mind into downcast moods. At the least it casts the shadow of a doubt about big buildings in the minds of local passersby, casts even a ray of beauty onto this city of late-summer sadness.

I can't define the substance of my moustache, it so evades me, but then I find it so hard nowadays to separate shadow from substance that it's enough if something of mine has substance, casts a shadow at all, and if I can distinguish them, whereas when I traverse those downtown spaces, it is all so unimaginably dark dark dark within the shadow of big buildings that, unless I get close up and carefully examine the angle made by the wall and the sidewalk I can't tell where shadow ends and big building begins. Are there limits? Over and beyond that the planes cast a recurring shadow so large you think it's smog or thunderheads not jets.

Yes, are there limits? Oftentimes in the cocktail lounges, here or near the office, a complete stranger will come up to my table and remark that our whole civilization has gone mad, that it's all decline and fall from here, and someone drinking bourbon at the counter then chimes in and, staring through his bourbon glass, crabbedly remarks that, despite the colossal wealth in our shop-windows and all the Air Force bases from pole to pole, we are now but a shadow of what we once were.

I too sense this somehow, but I can't say why, and when I inquire of them what they mean they just move on to the next barstool and say the same things. Nor do I encounter any printed explanations since the subject just doesn't come up in *Moustache* magazine or in Glöckvist or in the evening news. Come to think of it, *Moustache* magazine never mentions the war, not even in connection with moustaches, nor does Glöckvist. Where is it? How can I find out? As it is, my own reading plus the run of daily routines at Omni-Tel are time-consuming enough.

Oh what was this once like? What gave it its substance of yore, as opposed to the shadows of today? I simply don't know, nor can people answer whenever I ask them over at the Omni-Tel office, they just shrug their shoulders and say they're not interested, they read nothing but *Beard* and *Hairdo* and *Big Biceps* and especially *Dope*.

I often wonder as I head home, what evils lurk in those big buildings, those persistent jets? For we live in their shadow, know them by their shadow mostly, but I know my own moustache, I bask in its luxuriant shadow, I'll think apocalypse, I'll dream of the scenarios that lurk there, deep in its substance.

Here for example is a real hair-raiser:
SCENARIO III: .   .   .   .   .

 .   .   .   .   _____
buildings. ...   .   o r   i s   i t
XXX?..........................SCENARIO CCC or MMM........
............................or ....
beauty

Part Two

Others

A Report on a Concert

This text originally appeared in a scholarly volume entitled *The Fine Arts in Puerto Rico: Papers Read at a Symposium Held at the Fontainebleau Hotel, Miami Beach, July 1967.* The "Contributors" section has a note about the author:

Gumersindo Núñez y Vázquez de Antequera lives in seclusion on his family latifundio, a sugar plantation pre-dating the Theodore Roosevelt era. Though not fond of public appearances, he made an exception in order to read his paper at the conference.

We wish to acknowledge our gratitude to Señor Núñez y Vázquez for permitting us, despite the delicate subject matter, to reprint his highly informative essay. — EDS.

Ladies and Gentlemen,

People get murdered every day, of course, so I hope you will not misconstrue my account or its implications. What happened was indeed unusual, but, given numerous precedents in our past, we hardly were shocked. It all took place in the Teatro Tapia — itself something of a case in point. Now, as a visual artifact, that building, admittedly, is dull; even sympathetic tourists find it an unmemorable bore. Modest, scarcely imposing, it has yet to instill the good San Juan bourgeoisie (by far the most gullish and naive in all the Americas) with subjective wonder or civic pride. A block of sooty greystone built circa 1900, it is utterly bereft of the warm, nostalgic, afterglow of history; wanting in plate-glass windows, it lacks the modernist sheen. It is neither old nor new; not in Grand Style, it also missed the quality of intimacy. You look at the thing once and quickly forget.

How deceptive appearances can be! For few of our own people

think of this prosaic hulk as the setting for numerous strange events, surprise-dramas inconceivable, I daresay, to Carnegie Hall or Covent Garden habitués; nor could I imagine the likes of my report taking place in any one of those concrete culture-structures that the engineers and planners continue to graft so triumphantly onto the great North-American expressway.

Consider these examples from our musical history, facts known silently by the few, and thus undisseminated. While no frequenter of concerts, I in my sporadic visits to the Tapia have seen Rubinstein fumble a C-major scale, dignified Dame Hess bathe herself in self-indulgent tears over some Brahms Intermezzo, and I.J. Paderewski — that wondrous, gracious, old-school gent — leave a notable imprint of his lesser-known side by proffering a number of Polish profanities, elicited when he triumphantly banged out, fortissimo, what was to be the concert's final E-major chord — and hit F-minor instead.

There is an absurd moment in *Blow-up* (yes, we receive those films) when a popular musician, seized with rage, smashes his guitar to bits. But is anyone fooled? We know it is only a fiction, born of a collusion between an Italian yarn-spinner and an Argentine avant-gardist. I myself have seen better, and in real life at that. I am referring to Josef Szigeti, who, at risk of censure and ostracism, before our thousand-odd eyes reduced his famed Guarneri to about as many splinters by bashing it upon the cherubically blond head of his accompanist, seasoning the extraordinary show with tears and curses. The pianist, it turns out, had taken the finale too fast, too bouncy for Mr. Szigeti's comfort.

My head is aswim with such truly bizarre events... such as the South German maniac, who, for an encore, played in its entirety a piano reduction of *Also Sprach Zarathustra*, threw in portions of *Heldenleben*, and also joined in and sang with the climaxes; or the countertenor from Australia who did all songs in his native accent and announced this as his newly devised revolutionary technique. I often wonder: do these people do this elsewhere? Are they using us for their little experiments?

Anyway, our history is thick as any tropical jungle with this sort of thing, these baubles that give lustre to our concert life and yet scarcely receive a passing reference at lunchtime the next day.

So bear this in mind; please understand that the incident of which, thanks to this convention and its stimulus of privacy, you are now about to hear, by no means shocked our admittedly provincial sensibilities. San Juan in its way has seen as much as London or Paris, let alone Los Angeles or Houston. We have probably seen more, since artists making stops in our country regularly succumb to a species of madness apparently unknown — unpermissible, I daresay — in the concert halls of the Metropolis. I do not know why this should be the case. Perhaps the smell of diesel fumes (the worst in the world) drugs these pampered *prime donne* of the suburban north. Or the trouble may stem from the elusive, even amorphous cultural quality of the place, or — who knows? — from the climate. After all, small islands, notably those in these latitudes, have a historic reputation for fostering lunacy of various sorts.

I speak, then, of an "unusual event" — but the event is only a trifle more so than other aberrant occurrences that Providence has time and again visited upon us. The circumstances, on the other hand, were rather routine. No major expectations were sparked late last summer when *El Mundo* announced a recital to be given, in the Teatro Tapia's Sunday evening series, by some hyphenated-Hungarian virtuoso, an up-and-coming parvenu trailing a few clouds of incipient glory. His program was made up of time-honored sequences: Bach-Busoni, Chopin Waltz in E-flat and a couple of mazurkas, the *Apassionata*, and — a bit of contemporary titillation — Ravel, the *Tombeau*.

Still, a concert is a concert, especially on a dreary evening late in August. And I did know his name; one could sense — on the posters here and there, or in the foreign reviews cited with awe by our leading music critics and then bandied about by musicians in local artists' cafés — a growing legend. I must admit that, as I went about my weekly business, I felt occasional flurries of anticipation and entertained hopes of their fulfillment for the future.

And so on Sunday I arrived at the Tapia, where an audience, familiar to me from these concerts, had taken their seats. A small group, it scarcely exists outside the Teatro's confines, held together and informed by broadsides and gossip. Primitive and unstable bonds, these — but bonds no less real than whatever brings our young bankers to the Friday night symphony. Moreover, these bonds, with unexpectedness among their virtues, are richer and livelier, more meaningful to audience members, who are ever aware of the role of chance in human relations.

Lights were dimmed at exactly 8:30. The pianist walked briskly on stage; due applause was accorded him. He was a handsome fellow in his mid-twenties, typically East European in his sleek gracefulness. The only blemish I could detect at that point was his obsequious smile, too well synchronized with his stylized bow. The smile immediately vanished as he turned to the piano stool.

Before I proceed, something must be clarified. The fact is, I'm no music critic, and so I hope you'll allow me some amount of inarticulateness on the subject. I do hope this warning will not be seen as a calculated subterfuge, a sly bit of self-exoneration. But I simply do not know most of the trade words that the music people here have bandied about, and I therefore must resort to subjective responses, vague impressionistic wisps and metaphors, a purely intuitive understanding — couched furthermore in my brand of English, which isn't English at all but an Anglo froth-on-Romance. It is with these scarcely adequate tools that I will try to convey what I believe happened during those intense two hours. Certainly the nonverbality of music is a lovely thing, the inspiration behind many a proverb and poem; but it is also a privation of Nature, one you will have to bear with yet further patience while I use a notoriously confused and complicated language, the sounds and idioms of which my mind, in the twenty-odd years it took some years ago to complete its full growth, never encountered nor suspected could exist.

From the piano now came the five bare notes of the celebrated opening phrase, pinlike emissions preparatory to the imminent volley of sound. They seemed to leap out at me; I shuddered in my awareness that something new and undiscovered was taking on musical shape and arousing us from a spiritual slumber. So new was it that no one could have foretold its nature or its magnitude. The piece was not unfamiliar; but until then we had heard it with a certain sensorial deadness, like the color-blind before a Raffaele or a Giotto. A felicitous convergence of piece, pianist, and place was now rendering Bach more pertinent to our needs than all the family reunions and Sunday masses regularly shaping our lives. Raw psychic powers, concentrated intellect — they had spanned two centuries and united our minds with the scattered stuff we held in common, stripping the veil, giving us a glimpse of our darkest emotional depths.

The Adagio, on the other hand, was the obverse side of the Toccata, delicacy and restraint. Each measure came forth with an unprecedented pianissimo, as if anything much softer would have been sheer silence — an impression then further belied by yet further *diminuendi*. There was an awesome rightness to it all, as if the Magyar, in stretching the limits of an ordinary Steinway, had rendered Bach's conception for the pipe organ temporarily obsolete. There we were, experiencing unheard-of nuances of texture, levels of dynamics as yet unavailable to the most new-fangled electronic instruments. And it was most agreeable to hear the odd twists and turns of the coda (always a joy to my slightly eccentric tastes,)* their outlines often blurred in church performances, now displaying their fresh harmonic progressions within a sharply distinct set of contours.

Such purity, we found out, is not without interruptions. The lapse was brief, ten, fifteen seconds at most. But it was so disturbing, it resembled an elegant, well-bred lady who suddenly

---

*This parenthetical statement was omitted during the public reading of the paper — EDS

shucks off the game of genteel innocence, with all its flowery
phrases, and, mouth distorted, inexplicably emits a few words of
vicious, unrefined cruelty. Likewise, halfway through the fugue,
our Hungarian lost control of both hands and then pressed down
on the loud pedal, turning Bach's crystalline counterpoint into a
vile and messy blur. The musical effect was horrid enough, but
we were even more disconcerted by his body all atremble and his
face nodding in fear from side to side, while he repeatedly cried
"No!" to an unseen force. He then pounded the keyboard with
his fists, as if to exorcise the malicious poltergeist that had
turned his neat succession of sixteenth notes into a swarm of
quavers on the loose.

This was followed by one of those shrieks we hear maybe once
in our lives, a sound claimed by no language, and which
nonetheless we recognize as a cry of desperation. And it brought
him results: the ultimate puppet master seemed immediately
pacified. The Magyar returned to his magical realm as if nothing
had happened, just as scratches on a long-playing record, once
passed, do not intrude upon the grooves that follow.

The applause was tumultuous. And in it there was more than
the admiration of small-time dabblers for an achievement
hopelessly beyond their dreams. I could sense a more genuine
appreciativeness mingling with their symbolic approval, a real
warmth, the love-like feeling of a hostess toward a visitor who,
though rude and irreverent, can fundamentally be trusted.

But disappointment was to strike again: the same run of events
came with the Chopin, and the intruding element became worse.
He first granted us the rapturous ecstasy we had known during
Bach; his rendition suggested the crisp elegance natural to a
nineteenth-century dancer; it evoked the shared spirit of
European aristocrats intent on living out the October of their
lives amid resplendent chandeliers, dazzling neo-baroque
ornaments, long and spacious halls.

The Magyar upset it all with a relapse into chaos. There is a
little moment in this waltz, slower than the rest of the piece,
where an insistent three-quarter time briefly subsides, giving the

dancers a lyrical respite. In an imaginary anti-world, where climax consists of increasing not the volume but the nuances, of lowering not raising one's voice, those sixteen measures of G-flat would be not a pause but a cadenza, a singular flourish of near silence. But our guest artist, who had just created new touchstones and revolutionized taste, now fell prey to a banal sentimentalism quite normal for our San Juan — but just not right for Chopin. He played this G-flat section (marked *meno mosso*) — he played this section *molto più lento, ma stremattissimamente rubato*. And with such distressing results! — graceful two-measure phrases that first sang soothingly but were at once seized by a grotesque convulsion; and *decelerandi* that reached the end of their curious curves, only to swoop and spread their wings like a seagull turned monster. Meanwhile, his heavy breathing, with its inimitable grunts, seemed Nature's most fitting soundtrack to this horrific music drama, our shaking heads its best choreography.

And then, that wondrously simple three-note phrase brought back the joyous sounds that the pianist had previously held up to us. For all I know, he may have purposely snatched them away in order to punish those who would take his playing for granted — after all, as many of us too well know, anything is possible here on this earth. Well, he ended the piece, and we cried "Bravo!" although not too far back in our minds the classic gestures of bewilderment — nervous hands facing up, ruffled brow — clamored for release. Only our polite traditions held them back.

But our bafflement still hadn't reached its peak. Now, there are real dangers in blanket statements, I recognize this. Moreover, one knows how many individuals, out of an undefinable need to verbalize their private assortment of makeshift absolutes, will welcome those occasions when they can pronounce something or other as best or worst of its kind. And even if these categorical outbursts, their emotionalism clothed respectably in sober words of reason — like a lunatic in a three-piece suit — are not as a rule taken seriously, I feel in some way justified in saying that the Mazurkas were the very worst playing I have ever heard, that in them he seemed to have summoned up all the technical inaccuracies and errors of taste that others had committed separately — and we promptly forgiven — in hundreds of concerts throughout the century.

I have no doubt you would agree with me, had you witnessed this disaster. How else could anyone have judged him? There I sat in respectful silence, honestly wishing this young man well, and instead I was bombarded with wrong notes, unintended dissonances, upside-down dynamics (*forte* for *piano* and vice-versa), sheer omission of sections that the audience had scheduled for an appearance, plus a rigid angularity in his interpretation, music rendered geometrically when any fool knows it should be done gracefully, like a delicate weft of interlacing curves. Throughout it all something made him hold tenaciously onto the pedal as if it were his last available foothold in a crumbling structure. Meanwhile he had assumed a fittingly rigid posture: thighs and torso in a ninety-degree angle, only his forearms moving. The one sign of disaffection on his part was the strange grin of troubled folk, which to others often appears as a vindictive grimace.

Only when he ended the Mazurka abruptly with a seventh chord, shrugging his shoulders, did we realize our breaths were held. We had been waiting in suspense for his ancient magic to reappear, a wish now thwarted. And our listless applause came in contrast to the electrifying public love that, moments earlier, had seized and unified an atomized coterie; now you heard discrete cracks, loose sounds reminiscent of the stringy, breathy orchestral gibberish normally preceding the oboe's concert A.

It was intermission time now, but the hall remained dark. We sat still, holding back mixed torrents of stricture and praise. We were saving it for the foyer, where we'd give our frustrations civilized shape. I assumed in all sureness that we would file out silently, as if in a procession, feeling wistful about our losses. This is what will happen, I thought.

But two minutes went by in a dark, frozen stillness, and that cherished moment when flimsy cooperation blooms into active camaraderie simply never came. Or at least not exactly that. The Magyar's head now peeked in at stage left; the rest of him entered and tiptoed silently over to the piano stool, where he collapsed like a bag of stones. He gazed briefly at the ceiling, ran one hand through his hair, punched his hip with the other. He turned to us; a strangely hollow voice — I could have sworn a ventriloquist was doing the talking — spoke up. (The translation, by the way, is mine; I have corrected his atrocious grammar and syntax, with no attempt on my part to mimic his odd accent.)

> *Ladies and Gentlemen,*
> *It is with utmost pain, a pain matched only by my personal anguish felt at these befouled performances, that I bring such lamentable news to the illustrious body of citizens gathered here tonight. Circumstances beyond our control, however, demand that I do away with the intermission. I know too, too well that the intermission is very dear to all your hearts. But I feel that the decision is ultimately in the public interest, for your welfare and for mine both. And so, that we may make the best of our brief and happy spell together and in such a way render the fittingest homage to our glorious heroes' bones, I find it an absolute and imperative necessity that I begin the Beethoven, now, within brief moments [a vile phrase, obviously lifted unthinkingly from Iberian Railroad departure announcements]. Those who have no stomach for my modest alterations will leave the room in respectful silence; however, they stand warned that their hateful act will bring them grave consequences.*

He remained immobile, as if to put the gaze of guilt on whoever was considering escape. But the measure was unnecessary, as he had just taken us across the boundary separating vague uncertainty from plain confusion. We were all paralyzed as a result.

We heaved a sigh of relief when he put his hands on the keyboard — a relief quite short-lived. The minute he began to play, we realized he had completely omitted the first movement and proceeded, without explanation, to the Andante! More, his playing, while not a lamentable disgrace this time, showed little to distinguish it from the flat, tasteless doodling of a pedantic adolescent. The entire slow movement went by in this fashion. Its faster-moving variations were a reminder that Carl Czerny had studied with the Viennese master — save that, in this case, we were witnessing a curious process, the reduction of a teacher's highly developed art to its elementary rhythmic components. The upshot of this inverse metamorphosis is a dull, if clever exercise.

Suddenly, just when I felt myself dozing off, I heard that unforgettable diminished chord — and the Magyar mysteriously resumed his sweeping, pre-Mazurka style of piano playing. The chord, surely the chord, did it. It is simply amazing how a great composer can fashion such an aggregate of sounds, so unlike anything else, so unique and yet so right, that the astonished listeners, reacting as if they had just met an extraordinary person or read an extraordinary book, are shaken from their sleep and become aware of a myriad unexplored possibilities, both in themselves and in the world. The strangely-shaped diminished chord was the pianist's midwife, violently extracting the revolutionary standards carried by him somewhere in the back of his mind. Here were our hopes, being satisfied once again!

He reached the first climax. It was an overwhelming fortissimo, so massive it seemed solid, tangible, as if the incredible density of notes could have been seized and caressed — when The Enemy put in a final appearance. The Hungarian switched his styles; again he floundered hopelessly, scurrying random fashion all over the keyboard. His legs danced about; he looked like a hysterical white rat, trapped in the gigantic maze of a sadistic North American psychologist. As for ourselves, these periodic disruptions of preestablished musical order had led us to a state of mental malfunctioning, the prelude to a total breakdown.

Suddenly the music stopped. The silence, so abrupt and empty, seemed even more terrifying than all of his bad playing.

He arose from the piano stool with a jerky movement. Throughout the sonata his features had appeared fixed and immutable. But his poker face now changed to a look of despair. Tears fell fast; pointing at someone with his left index finger he cried out, "I won't stand for this anymore! Why don't you behave? Why can't you leave me in peace? The Beethoven is ruined, I'm a wreck, and it's all your fault!"

I was quite surprised when I realized this harangue was being addressed to a chap just three rows in front of me, especially since he had sat perfectly still during the concert's worst moments. Everyone knew him without knowing much about him. A small and delicate Rumanian, soft-spoken and shy, he had been pitilessly knocked around by the European wars before settling in San Juan some twenty years ago, where he ran a modest antique shop near González Padín. He attended all the plays and concerts, where he always greeted me faithfully with a reserved smile, suggesting warmth stifled by isolation. His smallish circle of friends and relatives touched upon, but rarely overlapped with, the greater San Juan society. While his antique shop suggested the very best of tastes, his wife — a woman a decade or two his junior, and seldom seen in public — seemed, curiously, something of a brash vulgarian. One sartorial idiosyncrasy of the man tended to cause some discomfort — his predilection for bright green bow ties. Beyond these obvious facts there lay a vast lacuna, unknown to all even in the essentials.

And now to my astonishment I saw this harmless septuagenarian faced with an extraordinary, and seemingly gratuitous, accusation. The piano virtuoso shattered our startled silence: "Yes, you! Don't look surprised! Do you think that idiot look of innocence can fool me?" Still weeping he leaped down from the stage and ran toward the Rumanian, sputtering away in a shrill voice, "Your fault, your fault, it's your fault."

The Rumanian threw up his hands with a gesture of incredulity and attempted to plead his case. "No, no, no, it isn't my fault. Don't suggest such a..."

"You groveling little hypocrite!" the Magyar cut him short. "How dare you deny your crimes, when you have been caught *in flagranti delicto* by the scores of witnesses here? This is perjury!" By now the pianist had hurdled the rows of seats and landed before the accused. He seized him by the hair, slapped him repeatedly. He beat the old man's forehead with his fists, saying, "You horrible, vile creature! What right have you to bring these evils on me? Insolent upstart! Behave!"

To my surprise, I heard voices from the audience furnishing a choral *obbligato*, saying, "Destroy the old man!" "Yes, it's all his fault!" "Kill him, kill him!" and the like. Some rushed over, hoping to carry out these commands. From almost all sides there was encouragement. Many people stamped their feet, others clapped, a few nodded assent. The virtuoso now had him by the throat; the Rumanian, all bloody, dangled loose in his aggressor's hold and repeated mechanically, as if with no ability to rephrase, "I'm not I'm not I'm not" and occasionally "No no don't suggest that!" But the pianist directed more strength onto his victim, gashing his neck. The loudness of his voice, and the variety of his recriminations, seemed limitless.

By now the Rumanian was silent and still, probably dead. But the virtuoso kept kicking him in the ribs, vilifying him more ferociously than when he had been an alleged threat. And then, the dénouement: the attack that had shocked me by its suddenness (like everything else the young man had done) began to disappear, slowly and painfully. As you'll remember, until now the youth had let out torrents of confusion that then stopped in their course, as if by biblical magic. This time it subsided with a slowness almost geological. Rather than an onslaught of silence, there were a number of blank interstices eroding the sound material between them, fusing in the end. It was like watching a city turn dark, one extinguished light at a time.

Anyway, the Hungarian's long seizure gradually lost momentum until its last phase, when two rapid blows were followed by a deathly soundlessness; another blow, a longer silence; five feeble slaps on the old man's face, and Hungarian collapses on Rumanian's corpse, although I was near enough to see an unsteady left elbow propping up his trembling torso.

And what a tableau! Every last one of us was standing perfectly still, as if posing for a science-fiction painter's wildest fantasy, some master dream entitled "Time Has Stopped," while, close by, the stertorous breathing of the pianist served as a reminder that things were a bit less dramatic, more normal than that. And it struck me a few weeks later that this violence had come as a needed rest for our overworked minds, literally a breather for our lungs, paralyzed as they had been by our embarrassment at the pianist's repeated lapses into bad behavior.

Hard upon this dream came the reality of people who move, the unsettling geometry of impermanent forms. Oddly enough, the collective motion was executed with an almost professional smoothness. The virtuoso made his way to the stage and, after wiping his hands on his inside pockets, clambered up like a refugee from battle, even as the spectators returned to their seats with an ease that seemed rehearsed. I have seen such high-quality coordination only at the best operatic productions, where the supporting chorus practices unstintingly to make a complex group movement into something natural, like singing in thirds.

There was a miracle, but it came bit by bit. We waited patiently while the pianist, slouched over like a drunkard, put his hands perfunctorily on the keys. A minute elapsed; there was no motion from his cocoon-like body. He thundered out that chord — he had decided to begin the finale once again. We were as yet unable to judge what we could hear. The little cadenza then issued forth, somewhat unsure of itself as it faced a slightly altered landscape. The speck of sound scarcely stirred up the silence, no more than a sail on the horizon much alters the view of ocean and sky. Finally, the main theme made its reentry; we yielded promptly to its implacable force.

And now, I realize, I must understate everything. So far I've done my best with your troublesome language; I have probably exhausted my most time-tested methods of idiom-to-idiom transmutation. Alas, I have also stolen this moment's thunder. Mere metaphors, empty words — how am I to rely on them now? All I can say is that, until then, none of us had ever felt such overpowering joy, such exultation. The delights the poets sing, and all the happiness we had squeezed from two or three select moments in our lives, dwindled instantly to childish antecedent. The pleasures of time past now appeared but dubious and tentative; the bliss and rapture of the first half of the concert were revealed as a false start, mindless frivolities that we somehow mistook for the summits of sentiment. Within minutes the Magyar had transformed us from raw apprentices into seasoned masters, as quickly as if some modern-day psychosurgeon had insinuated himself into our heads and tampered with them.

The *prestissimo* coda had us all on our feet. Some were straddled on the armrests of their seats, believing that this way they could hear more and better. It is no use trying to describe our quasi-religious ecstasy during the final measures, a state of frenzied excitement that begged for an outlet of cheers and clapping. Beethoven's last chords and our tumultuous applause came simultaneously. Seventeen curtain calls followed. About the Ravel I shall only say that our excitement was still greater — and that there were no interruptions.

Encores consisted of three Chopin études and some awful Liszt. Throughout it all the Rumanian's body remained in a heap where the Hungarian had dumped him, and for all I know it may have contributed in some way to the whole thing. Meanwhile there inexplicably took shape amongst us an unspoken agreement to blame it all on a stroke, with self-inflicted violence to account for the contusions and gore. (Later that evening members of his grief-stricken family together with his gum-chewing wife muttered something about having expected it any day now.) What hidden forces lie behind these tacit agreements are as much a mystery to me as they are to you. Fortunately for myself, an arts convention such as this does not allow for any extended ventures into the psychological.

One last point, something quite baffling to my foreign friends. If hundreds were to go and make this public, in fact if everyone who knows about that concert were to climb the walls and shout it from the housetops, I doubt if there would be a scandal — either on the island or elsewhere. Strange occurrences, as I said before, are normal with us; they proliferate too rapidly for the doltish American reporters to follow them up. Moreover, the memory of these events lingers on merely as a nebulous presence, shared in secrecy by the witnesses, and never questioned. Only on rare occasions does the U.S.-owned *El Imparcial* — more *Daily News* than the *Daily News* — carry so much as a brief résumé, usually in the "Fine Arts" section. (It did this time, and no one seems to have noticed.) Meanwhile, as for myself, except for special occasions such as this one, I don't broadcast it. I am one whom life has taught to accept a great deal, and I have no particular desire to give the world more grist for its thoughtless, pleasure-seeking mill. (APPLAUSE)

The Customer

Saturday again, said the digital clock, and he looked forward
to leafing through all of *The New Yorker*. Its sturdy, sleek pages
were themselves works of art, and its long, tight staples never
came loose, something he, as an engineer, could appreciate.
Recently, at Plaza Books, he'd seen on Christmas special a big
framed wall poster that looked to be an old *New Yorker* cover,
maybe from the fifties or sixties, except it was much bigger, that
was all, really.

To find the magazine down the hall by the threefold row of
mailboxes gave him a strange and tender thrill. There he would
eagerly sort out his flat brown package from among the five
others, still wondering which of those names went with whose
face, and he would've picked up a *Tri-Cities Advertiser* had the
old familiar pile been there, odd that it wasn't today. Saturdays
he seldom received personal mail, and so back in the living room
he'd gently shut the door, loll in his light-green sofa and —
smiling at leisure, chuckling at times, occasionally puzzling at a
mysterious quote or two — he'd go through the cartoons one by
one, first from the front then from the back. Each issue seemed
to start with "Talk of the Town," so he'd read that and then the
shorter stories, usually he'd skip ahead to the movie reviews for
their style and eventually he'd look at the ads, staring at them
for long spells as the day brightened or turned gray.

Beautiful things and places, and unimaginably beautiful men
and women, were always to be found pictured in those ads. One
such woman, he noticed, might appear in several ads per issue.
Never in his four full years up at Troy had he encountered
anyone or anything quite like what *The New Yorker* offered him
every Saturday. Oh, there had been New York City, an easy

116

three-hour ride on Amtrak, but he'd managed to get down there only twice, each time with his tight-lipped, girl-shy, senior-year roommate, no substitute for female company he. Anyway there weren't that many women students at the Institute and he'd never once met a Sage girl, despite those periodic Sage-RPI mixers, and besides he'd had too much studying to do back then, too many problem sets and quizzes, and weekends were often worse save for beers at night with some guys from his corridor. Since taking his lab job in Broome County, however, he'd found he could at least experience New York and its beauties indirectly via *The New Yorker* magazine.

He liked the Cointreau ad in particular. Showed a pair of women's legs dangling out of a steamy, white bathtub, and her arm reaching for the square bottle poised on a white stool, flaunting its funny French name. Week after week he'd noticed the ad in some ten issues, or was it twelve? With each Saturday he might stare at the bathtub scene a bit longer than the last; now he found himself staring, off-and-on, for the remainder of this short, silver-hued mid-December day. He did wonder what her face and hair were like, but his thick-rimmed glasses and beard-stubble kept twitching with desire for her legs. Desire, yes, that was the word he could hear echoing about in his head and on his lips, till night came quietly and early.

He had lunched fairly late on a couple of charred burgers, his favorite food, so he wasn't all that hungry yet. From his ground floor window he could see the snow falling light and steadily, and his bones felt kind of cold. He'd run out of Johnny Walker last night and now needed something to warm up his inside skin. Just for the variety he thought maybe he could try Cointreau this time around. At the lab recently the redhead in red high heels had said Cointreau was her favorite drink after Cold Duck, and the two foreigners she'd been sipping coffee with had nodded and said, "Oh, yes." It had been weeks since he'd gone to the liquor store down at Vestal Plaza malls. He put on his white socks, his running shoes, and his beige parka, then jiggled his front pocket, making sure the car keys were there.

The street lights were a purplish color, seemed even eerier as he drove by them in the snow. He counted the twenty-seven lamp posts, as he sometimes did on the way to work in the mornings, it passed the time. Unlike most of the other guys on the job, married homeowners who commuted from Endicott or Conklin or Johnson City, he lived in an apartment complex a few blocks up from the firm. He slowed down now, noticed how spectrally beautiful the squat, geometric edifice housing Videosonics-Plus Systems Inc. looked amid the first snowfall, with its empty, white-carpeted parking lot serving as foreground and frame. Being with the company made him genuinely proud.

Turning into the Plaza, he glanced over at the Electro-Arcade. The kids were bunching around a single game. Which one? he wondered. A new one, most likely. He warmed up to the idea that someday some teenaged trio could be feeding its quarters into the latest new unit conceived by his subteam at Videosonics, or — why not? — something custom-designed by he himself alone, the upcoming rugged revolutionary in the field, sure thing. He pulled up to midmall in front of Vestal Spirits Stores, then lumbered out with the Dodge still running, saves gas, less dollars for them Arabs, ha ha (he chuckled). It was relatively quiet about the shopping center, unusual for a Saturday. Oh, of course, dinnertime, the families have gone home. He liked the soft violin music, it always echoes through the Plaza, even at midnight when everything else shuts down. Adds class, atmosphere, he thought.

Business seemed slack. The clerk, thirtyish and lanky, sat on a stool, reading the *Evening Press.*

"How y'doin'?"

"Oh, 'evening. Help you?" He put aside the paper, scratched his pencil moustache with his thumb.

"Yeah, I've been seein' these ads for something called *Coin*-true. Got any?"

The clerk stopped scratching, looked at him blankly, then said, "Oh, you mean Quán-trow. Yeah, we got it, comes in three sizes," he said, pointing at them, left. "Which one?"

He glanced at them with a little jump of recognition. "Oh, I'll take the biggest." On his nice new salary he could afford it. Biggest is best.

The clerk turned around and reached for a hefty square bottle, just like the one in today's *New Yorker* ad.

"That'll be twenty-four dollars and sixty cents. Cash or charge, sir?"

He only had gas credit cards. "Oh, I guess cash." He counted out the exact change as the clerk tucked the bottle into a shiny red paper bag. A crisp twenty, four worn singles, and six dimes lay neatly on the counter.

The clerk rang up the sale. "Thank you, sir."

"Thanks. By the way, where're the legs?"

"Legs?"

"You know, the legs that come with the bottle. It's in the ad." He took the slightly crumpled *New Yorker* out of his parka pocket. The magazine opened automatically at the dog-eared page. "Look. See?"

The clerk looked at ad and customer, back and forth. The customer tightened his dark-rimmed spectacles and looked at the clerk. The clerk reflected a moment, then snapped his fingers.

"Oh, yes, the legs, of course, sorry, sir." He opened a little wooden drawer underneath the digital cash register. "Here you are, sir." It was a bright plastic 4" X 6" plaque showing the same ad in bas-relief, the very same woman's arm, the large bottle of Cointreau.

The customer held it in his left hand, gazing intently at the legs, those were them all right. He turned it sideways, viewed it at an angle and searched for her face, wondering again what it was like. Did she sulk or smile? Was she a blonde? Did she wear thick glasses, like his?

"All set, sir? Don't forget your bottle."

"Yeah, thanks." He pocketed the bas-relief, grabbed the red paper bag and walked out the glass door, saying, "Yeah, right."

The snow-covered car was still running.

The Duck Hunter *

Munich, West Germany — For almost 40 years the German people have tried to forget about World War II, and very few contemporary film-makers have dared to depict the horrors of the Hitler era. However, the hottest cinema item of the year, and arguably of the decade, has been *The Tormented Vision of the Teenaged Bavarian Duck Hunter,* directed by Siegfried von Unsinn, a 55-year-old former Wehrmacht captain in the occupation of Paris. With its extended scenes of military violence the film shocked many viewers at the Munich Film Festival, and the French delegation stormed out in protest. On the other hand, numerous Germans have warmly congratulated Capt. von Unsinn for his courage in recalling Germany's sufferings in that now-remote war. Said press magnate Axel Springer, "He tells it like it was."

The film divides neatly in half. The first part evokes Nirgendsdorf, a small Bavarian village. We meet Hugo, Ludwig, and Fritz, three cherubically blond and beardless farm boys. They drink beer at the local pub, hang around street corners in their Lederhosen, go on duck-hunting expeditions in the enveloping forests, and attend Mass in the awesome Protestant cathedral. But it is a torrid day in January, 1940, and draft calls disrupt this idyll. At first enthusiastic, the boys' loyalties are heightened on the eve of their departure, when fellow villagers throw a big Oktoberfest in their honor, complete with schnitzel, knockwurst, and quiche Lorraine. Sipping from his beer goblet, wiping the tears from his face, a much-moved Fritz stutters, "I

---

* This film review originally appeared in *In These Times,* September 19, 1979

120

love this town!"

Suddenly — combat:

We see a hook-nosed Resistance fighter on the Boulevard St. Michel breaking into a ground-floor apartment, where he discovers a day-nursery; ignoring the piteous cries of children and nannies, the cad throws a firebomb in their midst. Fritz, now a Wehrmacht soldier doing guard duty, happens to witness this cruel deed and shoots the terrorist in anger. Three brutish guerrillas then jump Fritz and drag him into their Rolls-Royce.

Now comes the half-hour scene that has caused acrimonious debates and even, in Parisian theaters, riots rivalling those that greeted Stravinsky's *Rite of Spring*. We are inside a houseboat on the River Seine, with the Eiffel Tower and Notre Dame both visible, side-by-side, from the portholes, serving as a vivid local backdrop to the events. Hammer-and-sickle posters, pictures of Marx, Stalin, and Mao, and golden stars of David bedeck the walls. A dozen or so unkempt, scraggly-bearded French Resistance fighters and their Soviet advisors are gambling passionately at Russian roulette, using German POW's (among them Fritz) as subjects. After two of the prisoners have died in the nerve-shattering sequence, Pierre du Pont, the most wholesome-looking of the guerrillas, clutches at his crucifix, straightens his beret, and, as he twiddles his pencil-moustache, earnestly addresses his cell-boss, "We are wasting precious ammunition and moreover the enemy might hear us." Jacob, the boss — a sinister figure with an eye-patch, swarthy skin-color, and a toad-like face — strokes his drooping Cantonese moustache with his two-fingered hand, sucks on his cigar, and screams in a high-pitched voice, "This will stop your nonsense!" then shoots the dissident in the heart. An innocent and incredulous Fritz trembles in his cage at the sight of this terrorist brutality.

Many reviewers shrilly claim that this scene puts the Resistance in a negative light, but subsequent events effectively cancel out this supposition. Night falls over the Seine; the doltish, inefficient guerrillas neglect to lock Fritz's cage, and so he flees the houseboat, ends up on the fashionable

Champs-Elysées boulevard, where he sees the Eiffel Tower shining brightly at the Place Étoile. Pure in soul, Fritz sublimely ignores the aggressive advances of sensuously-clad women of pleasure, who beckon him from street-corners. Outside an elegant café he meets a tall and handsome Count, a worldly playboy with fine-chiselled features, silken shirt and tie, a crisp, courtly moustache, Polaroid glasses, and a shiny-red Italian sports car. In his rich baritone voice Count de la Môle (for that is his name) invites Fritz to a grand ball being given by some aristocrats, collaborators for the Germans.

The two thereupon take off for Vichy, driving North and arriving there in nine minutes flat. Alas, when Fritz crosses the threshold of the 16th century château, he finds out to his horror that the dukes and duchesses are operating a Russian roulette casino, using German deserters and French peasants as paid subjects. Fritz wants out, but a slinky, dark-haired grande dame named Countess Serpentina puts aside her golden cigarette-holder and proceeds to honey-tongue our young swain, cajoling him with promises of warmth and women.

And so war claims another innocent soul: Fritz plies this hazardous trade for a thousand and one nights, performing Russian roulette a total of 44,267 times before the cold-hearted French clique. Meanwhile he accumulates cigar boxes stuffed with Reichsmarks, shipping them home to his quaint, needy Mutti and Pappi, who scarcely suspect its sordid source. And then the crowning blow: even as Anglo-American troops land and march through France, a numbed, prematurely gray-haired Fritz ignores the din of M-16's and B-52's, as do the cigar-smoking counts and jaded countesses, who relentlessly egg their hapless victim on to yet another performance. In his final act, Fritz puts the six-shooter to his head and, following a dull pop!, falls dead to the floor amidst the aristocrats' applause. Another young life succumbs, prey to the dark forces of evil.

French leftists and intellectuals ritually assert a truism: that the Resistance never engaged in Russian roulette. "Sure, Russia was our ally," quipped one critic for the Communist daily

L'Humanité, "but we never went so far as to ape Russian folklore." To these carpers Capt. von Unsinn calmly replied at a press conference, "Fiction is not history, as any schoolboy will tell you. Those roulette scenes are not meant literally. They are a metaphor, a symbol for the random horrors of war." He mused, "War is like Russian roulette; it is a game of chance. A soldier risks being shot at from both sides, neither of which has a monopoly on virtue. My film makes it clear that I hold no special brief against the Resistance. If anything, I show that German boys were exploited and killed not only by hate-filled terrorists but by decadent Vichy collaborators as well." But alas, in the blind passion generated by *The Duck Hunter,* virtually no French critic has taken note of Capt. von Unsinn's cool and exacting objectivity.

The enigmatic full title of the movie refers to the last scene, where — in a grim, Buñuelesque irony — we find out that the entire war sequence never happened, was nothing more than a nightmare in Fritz's head. As it turns out, after drinking too much beer at the Oktoberfest, Fritz and his friends had gone out to shoot a few ducks. But, in the blinding heat of the January sun, a drunken Fritz picked up his rifle and accidentally shot himself in the thigh; meanwhile the rifle report startled the ducks, an angered bevy of which, in a Hitchcockian way, swooped down on Fritz and knocked him cold. Fritz awakes after two delirious days in hospital, and is visited by Hugo and Ludwig, now eager to do their share for German glory. As the three *Kamaraden* lock hands they recite from memory the "Of War and Warriors" section from Nietzsche's *Thus Spake Zarathustra,* after which they intone the final strains from *Die Meistersinger* and *Die Götterdämmerung* as they watch the sun set dazzlingly in the East. French critics cite this scene as evidence of von Unsinn's nationalistic glorification of war, but he insists that the ending is bitterly ironic. "The war is depicted as a terrible German tragedy. How could I glorify a war in which wicked foreigners were shooting German boys for sport?"

Abortive Romances
or the Pianist Who Liked Ayn Rand

I

The successes and the sorrows of young Joe, formally christened José Victoriano González, are the chief subject of this story. Born and raised in Merced, Arizona, an obscure little border town ninety-six auto miles southeast of Tucson, Joe received crucial encouragement and support from two of his high-school teachers, and was the first of his sizeable extended family ever to attend the University.

There he majored in Applied Music (piano, trumpet, and string bass) on generous state scholarships, and found out, much to his delight, that his playing had the potential to charm girls, some of whom, for their part, saw in his playing a resource they might turn to their advantage, without his much realizing they were doing so.

A devout Roman Catholic until age seventeen, he began quietly doubting religion in his final year at Merced High, thoroughly though still quietly abandoning his faith early on as a college freshman, and in time latching onto the then-fashionable thought of Ayn Rand. Thus did young Joe discover the power of ideas, those of rational egoism overcoming the evils of altruism, in particular. But, of that, more later.

At this point let us start out with Joe in his music practice room, seated at the upright piano one mid-April morning in 1961, and dressed in his Army ROTC uniform, which he was required to wear Tuesdays and Thursdays. He had been working on Chopin's "Black-Key" étude, and, having just muffed the final measures, he was poised to attempt the octaves once again, only to be stopped by the sound and breeze of the door swishing

124

wide open, and further startled by the sight of Jennifer strolling in with minuet-like grace and saying, "Excuse me, Joe, I believe I forgot my book."

The scent of her perfume brought back certain vivid memories.

In the room next door a trumpet player was going through Haydn's concerto slowly, note by note.

She walked behind Joe all the way 'round to his right, stretched her smooth, pale arm toward the furthermost top corner of the piano, and retrieved her copy of *Jude the Obscure,* which Joe had indeed noticed though failed to think of as hers, the book being so omnipresent at that time of the year.

"Thanks," she said tersely, heading toward the door.

Whereupon Joe blurted out, "No, wait, I've got to talk with you."

Spinning around on her low heels she looked at him without expression and asked, "Oh, what about?"

And in order to understand just what it was about, we must flash back a full eight months to Joe González's initial weeks on campus and the start of his long correspondence with his elder brother Al.

[September 25-30, 1960]*

Dear Al,

You won't believe how glad I am to be up here. I love all of you as much as ever and miss you guys a lot, really. Have to say, though, studying music full-time and being appreciated as a musician, well, that's something new and different. It also looks as if my fears about college had no basis whatsoever (Freshman English aside — now *that* one's scary).

Say hi to Mrs. Pratt next time you run into her, and give her my thanks once again for helping me to apply to this

---

* Joe was not in the habit of dating his letters. In the interests of clarity, probable dates have occasionally been assigned, in brackets, with a view to furnishing some notion of the time-frame of events.

place. Sad to hear Mr. Gold just up and left. Still, I can't say I blame him for choosing Los Angeles over Merced. He'll play plenty more gigs out there, that's for sure! Could you get me his new address? I'd like to tell him about my new bass lessons and theory class.

Got to tell you, met this girl today, right in my practice room. I'd been trying to get my "Petrouchka" solo up to speed and was getting real nervous, wrists all tensed up as usual.

So I glance up at the window and see this peaches-and -cream face I'd noticed before in the orchestra first-violin section.

She opens the door, floats in, then smiles and says, "Excuse me, I believe I'm assigned at this hour." Shows me her stamped card, and sure enough, it was her turn.

"Oh, boy," I say. "Sorry. Guess I went into over time." And as I slide the score to "Petrouchka" into my old beat-up schoolbag I'm aware of her perfume and how it does something to me.

Same when I see her waving the little red fingernails of her left hand, putting her cloth bag on top of the piano, and saying, "Oh, that's fine. We all tend to get wrapped in what we're doing." And Al, she knew who I was. She says, "You do the piano in the Stravinsky, don't you? It sounds quite good! So does your *Nutcracker* solo. All those instruments you play. Why aren't you at Juilliard?"

I bet yours truly blushed. She's some slick chick! She wore high heels and her legs sure looked nice. Anglo, clearly, but she's got this straight, dark hair, just like Angie and Trini Vargas down the street from us. Doesn't sound a bit like the Spanish girls at Merced High, though, or the Anglo ones either. I wonder if she's from England. Jennifer's her name, Jennifer Jaspers.

She's about the best-looking chick I've met here so far. And believe me, there's lots of them. You know, Al, I never was much good at scoring back home. Wasn't hardly anything rubbing off on me from you and your *cuates*. Really, I'd like to know, how's a guy go about becoming a make-out artist? (If it weren't for those trips down to Nogales last year, my sex I.Q. would still be zero.) 'Course, at school parties I always got stuck with playing dance band and assisting Mr. Gold. And for the zillionth time I ask you, *"¿Has visto a un músico bailar?"*

Well, maybe things'll turn out differently here at the U. of A. And I can always visit Nogales.

Started a job serving meals at Kappa Alpha fraternity this week. "Hashing," it's called. Payment is in meals, so I'll be able to hold on to some of the dough I just got from papá. Don't know how long I'll last, though. The guys in that frat are real animals. Every night before sitting down for dinner, they actually sing a song that goes, "Yes, we love niggers,/ Yes, we love niggers." Can you believe such prejudice? Except for one quiet type who's in engineering and kind of nice, they're all majoring in business.

Love to Mom and Pop and Leticia and Paquita. How's high school treating her? Better than last year? Tell Letty I want to see her as a freshman here before I graduate!

God, I sure hope you turn out to be 4-F. Anything you can do to fake out the medic? I hear if you tell them you're queer, they'll turn you down. Yeah, I know, I know, who wants that on his record?

Cuídate,
José

Dear Al,

Well, so it's gonna be Al the soldier! That's really terrible. I guess it means you're going to have to spend two years of your life in uniform? It's bad enough having to dress for ROTC and go to drill every week here — complete waste of time.

God almighty, I hope they don't ship you to Korea or some God-forsaken spot like that.

I'm really taken with that Jennifer chick. Can't resist staying on in the practice room a few minutes and seeing if she'll show up again. Yesterday she actually did, and she smiled, and I felt butterflies in my stomach at the sight of her straight white teeth. Oh, and I asked if she was English.

"What a funny question!" she says. "Nobody's ever asked me *that* before. I've never been east of the Mississippi." Turns out she's from Palo Alto, California.

Meanwhile I'm packing, she's unlatching her fiddle case, and when I mumble, "Palo Alto, I've heard of it," her face lights up as she says, "Gee, you say it so nicely. No one up there pronounces it like that."

God, I hope she couldn't hear my heart pounding so fast then. Lucky thing she waved me good-bye with her bow, 'cause otherwise I wouldn't of known what to do.

Can't remember if I've told you yet, but one of the things I do here is accompany symphonic choir at noon every day. Just like old times at la High! I miss not seeing tiny Mrs. Pratt up there, though; the conductor here is this big, gruff guy with a walrus moustache called Mr. Mullens. We'll be doing the Messiah this December, when the orchestra takes over and I join up with the double-bass players for the duration.

Abrazos,
José

P.S. Please don't tell mamá, but I've dropped out of Newman House chorus. Haven't been to church all month, in fact. Al, I'm simply not a believer any more. None of it says anything to me, I just don't buy it. True, they throw nice parties at Newman House on Saturdays, and I keep going to them, it's a way to meet girls, but that's about all. I'll have to let Ma know sometime, don't know when.

Dear Al,
Having a great time, wish you were here... Al, there's just

no comparing Merced and the U. of A. Beautiful campus, and so much to do. Not that I don't miss you and Leticia and Paquita and the folks. But I really enjoy being surrounded by all these music people, or sipping coke with them at the Desert Shack behind the Music Building. I go there just about every day now.

And it's incredible, so many people here seem to like me and respect me 'cause I'm a musician. I can't believe it! After all these years being the weirdo, the one who plays classical and jazz and doesn't think much of rock-n-roll. Plenty of Merced girls thought me strange and even crazy because of that. Here it's different, several of the girls I've met so far actually think my being a classical pianist is real cool. One chick, a clarinet player in the orchestra, even said, "Well, I *bow* to you!" when she recognized me as the Stravinsky soloist. Now ain't that somethin'?

'Course, most of those girls are music majors, I realize, so they're biased. But there's also the sorority crowd, and they're something else — so dumb, along with their Freddy Frat-rat friends. (My crude roommate, Jason, was actually suspended from his fraternity 'cause his grade-point was too low!) They're like sheep, sheep in spray-net in the case of those sorority girls. Wouldn't touch 'em with a twenty-foot pole!

Miss you guys. Can't say much about the rest of Merced, though (that *gachupín* priest and his endless lisping sermons!)... Wait, I take that back: there's Mrs. Pratt, she's truly special. She believed in me when almost no other teacher and no girls ever did. Miss her too, and you can tell her so.

Hope the draft hasn't got you too depressed. I'll write you as much as I can when you get sent away.

Love to everybody,
José

Dear Al,

Had an interesting experience this morning. Went down to the Desert Shack after Theory class, and lucky thing there were no music majors there yet, 'cause as I enter thru the back door I hear someone saying "Oh, hi!" And there's Jennifer herself, sitting in the far window booth, beckoning me with her hand. First time I'd seen her outside of orchestra or the practice room.

She had her hair in a pony tail, and on her blouse this brooch in the shape of a dollar sign.

So I slipped into the cream-colored seat, ordered a glazed donut and coffee, and she and I talked about all kinds of things, the U., the orchestra and our conductor, Mr. Smithson, and her favorite music (Rachmaninoff's concertos, Strauss waltzes! Yuk! Of all things! Well, maybe those guys deserve another chance).

"How 'bout Ravel?" I asked her. "Or progressive jazz?"

She looked straight at me with a poker face. "What about them, Joe?"

"Like 'em?"

"Oh, Joe, I can't take them! Ravel's too modern, he makes me nervous. And jazz to me sounds like a bunch of crazy savages screeching themselves hoarse out in some jungle."

"Well," I informed her, "they're my favorites." We paused, but we're grinning silently at one another. Then I broke the momentary ice. "What else do you like, then?"

"Oh... I like my sisters at the house."

"Sisters? You got family here?"

"No, silly boy," she chuckled. "The A Xi Pi house."

"What?" I was shocked. "You're in a *sorority*?"

She pursed her lips and looked embarrassed. "Yeah, I know. It's not your typical Greek association, tho', more of an assortment of individuals, each one unique. What most attracted me about A Xi Pi during Rush Week was that they billed themselves as a house that emphasizes the individual. And the girls there are kind of neat." She put in an order for more coffee. "Besides, Joe, being in a sorority means I won't have to live in a dorm next year."

She's the first sorority girl I've ever talked to outside of class. And who knows? Maybe I'll have to modify my view of those broads. And boy, is she the avid reader. Right on top of her musical scores I notice this thick book, *The Fountainhead*, by some dame called Ann Rand.

"Weird title," I said, gesturing at it with my chin.

Jennifer tapped on the book with her index finger, saying, "Ann Rand is my favorite author, this is my bible, and Dominique is my heroine."

"Mind if I take a peek?"

"Be my guest."

I flipped thru it, saw the 600-something pages of small print, and lay the thing down again. "So what's the message?"

"It's kind of abstract and philosophical," she said with a frown, her voice lowering almost an octave, and her finger describing circles on the book's cover. "But the basic idea is that no one owes anybody anything, and that we are all free to succeed and achieve greatness. Egoism is the highest good, and altruism, conversely, is the supreme evil."

(So I learned a new word today, "altruism!" Looked it up in my new Mr. Webster's just before writing to you. Means "unselfish concern for the welfare of others.")

She continued. "It follows, then, that to be 'selfless' (in quotes) or to sacrifice oneself for others is to live second-hand and actually do harm. Self-sacrifice is usually phony, anyway." Then her voice became normal again. "That's it, then, in a nutshell."

It sounded kind of familiar, don't know where I'd heard it before. Never realized it came from this Ann Rand person. I wasn't convinced, tho', and when Jennifer was finished, I asked, "What about luck?"

"Luck." I detected some sarcasm in her voice. "There is no such thing," she stated almost scornfully. "Superior people choose success. If someone fails, it's nobody's fault but his own. Luck is simply a handy excuse."

"Well, but, look," I said, kind of nervously. "I'm on scholarship. Wouldn't you say that's just plain luck?"

She shook her head real vigorously, and her pony-tail made a little breeze. "No, not at all, Joe. You are here because of your superior talents. And because you haven't succumbed to all the second-hand mediocrity out there."

I was about to bring up Mrs. Pratt when suddenly she says. "Have to go. See you at rehearsal." Next think I know she's up and going and waving at me from the cash register, and then off thru the back door to her violin lesson. What she'd said had me thinking as I slowly finished off my coffee. Maybe I should start recognizing that my musical talents and hard work did get me here.

Five weeks at the U. of A., and I love it. Beautiful green lawns and palm trees, air-conditioned rooms, good music for a change, and sharp dames like Jennifer. (God, she's built! You should see her from behind.) I can scarcely believe any of it, Al, you really should of applied last year, probably you'd of gotten your 2-S. Well, couple of years from now maybe you can put in your application, 'cept by then I'll be the senior and you the freshman. That'd be some switch, no?

Love to all,
Joe

Dear Al,

Today my English prof said to us, "Probably the best thing about a college education is that it teaches us how little we actually know." Well, college must be doing yours truly lots of good, 'cause I'm finding out I don't know much about nuttin'. (I still wonder how I managed to land OK grades at la High.) Science, for instance, don't know beans about the stuff, and I'm real scared about Astronomy here.

Managed to build up my courage at Orchestra and ask Jennifer out for a coke at Mac's. Couldn't believe it when she said, "Oh, I'd love to." Not only that, but as we sipped our cherry cokes I asked her for a date to the Stokowski concert this next Tuesday, and she said yes!

Turns out she's half Italian, that's where she gets her dark hair from. "You should see my father's hair, tho,' it's so blond it's almost white. He's German."

On our way back to her dorm I quoted what my prof said to us in class. She had a very different view. "Oh, I strongly disagree." Her voice was almost cold. "Being aware of how little you know can only hurt your self-confidence. And there's nothing more important than self-confidence."

Oh, yes, I'd also been feeling troubled by what she said about luck that last time, so as we turned the corner for Kaibab (that's her dorm), I mentioned Mrs. Pratt to her, saying how lucky I was to have had a teacher who used to let me practice on her piano and who gave me lots of help with my music and my application here...

And she interrupted and got emphatic, Jennifer did. "No, no, Joe, that's not right."

"How so, not right?"

"Nobody helped you, nor was it anyone's duty to help you. Actually *you* helped *yourself*." She was almost vehement on that one. "Which is as it should be, people depending on themselves, making it thru their own efforts alone."

I just didn't know what to say, it's all so confusing. English prof says one thing, Jennifer another, and yours truly doesn't know what all to think. And then there's government. You know me, I can't tell one party from the other. Couldn't get so much as a 4 minus if I took a course in politics. (Let's face it, I'm just this dumb musician type.) But Jennifer is really following the elections, and she's for Nixon, says to me as we climb the front stairs to Kaibab, "He's a stronger man, and we need strong men. And besides he's better for individual freedoms. I don't like Kennedy's civil rights platform, it'll curtail individual liberties."

So what do you make of *that,* Al? Wouldn't ending segregation be *good* for the individual? Shouldn't a Negro have a right to eat wherever he wants? Jennifer's so smart, though, and I suppose she's got information I don't have, so I didn't answer and said good-night instead.

It'll be great seeing you guys next weekend. Six weeks is a long time without los papás. And I've been wondering what that surprise is you say you've got in store for me.

Hasta entonces,
José

Dear Al,

Boy, does it feel good to have wheels! I mean, look, I'm sorry about you and boot camp, but, geez, I do appreciate your lending me the Plymouth for the duration.

So this'll give me the chance to impress some of the women up here, including Jennifer. (Man, you should see the pair of legs she's got on her, real sharp, almost like Hollywood. True, she's got a pimple or two, but...)

Hey, don't get me wrong. I really respect her. I'm not out to feel her up or anything, but no objections if it somehow happens. Now maybe we can drive over to Sabino Canyon and line up with all those parked cars I read about so much in the *Wildcat* (that's our school paper).

The limousine made it fine up here yesterday. And you can count on me to keep it in top shape. Gave it a wash this afternoon.

Love,
Joe

[October 31? 1960]

Dear Al,

Guess what? Jennifer's asked me to be her accompanist. Who knows, though, maybe it's only on account of your car!

'Course it means more work. Have to go to her weekly lessons. Then there's the extra practice, getting the piano part and our ensemble into shape so that we'll do a decent job at her violin jury (sort of like a final exam) next January. Gives me the chance to be with her, tho'.

Found out something incredible: We just had our first-run practice session this evening and got to talking afterwards about extracurricular activities, Jennifer and me, and over coffee at Mac's the fact slipped out that she'd been a *cheerleader* in high school! Jennifer, the great individualist, no less!

"I'll admit," she said, stirring her tea apologetically, "I did it because it seemed like the thing to do at the time. Joe, I was only in ninth grade when I started! But I finally stopped last March. And who do you think saved me from becoming a pom-pom girl here?" She took a long sip, then laid down her cup silently, staring at me straight in the face.

"Well, who?" I asked.

"Ayn Rand." (I finally found out that's how it's spelled, not "Ann.") "She opened my eyes and made me see cheerleading for the brand of tribal, emotional collectivism it is."

Again a new word, "collectivism." Jennifer's great for my word power. *You* look it up this time!

"So I pulled out last April," she concluded.

Have to admire her for that. She's a really nice girl, Jennifer is. Hope you guys can meet her someday. With the car now it wouldn't take long for her and me to hop in and do the drive to Merced. Maybe some weekend when you're on furlough. You'll all like her, I think.

Love,
Joe

Dear brother of mine,

Learned a different kind of new word last night: "grassing." Picked it up from Jennifer, naturally. Nothing like widening your horizons... Wasn't listed in the dictionary, tho'.

Gotta admit, the idea was hers. There we are, walking

back to Kaibab after some pretty intense practice on her Beethoven, and she says, "Let's go sit over there for a while." It's a nice secluded spot near the library where you often see couples making out. So we're stretched out on the hill, the only ones there, and before I know it she's put her head on my shoulder, and next thing you know she and I are, well, grassing. Couldn't have done this in Merced — not that many grassy spots there, when you think of it! She tells me she likes being with me, which is nice to hear. First time any girl's ever said that to me.

Next week is orchestra concert. Hope I don't get too nervous during my Petrouchka solo (the one you guys don't like). The celesta in the Tchaikovsky I can handle fine, but that Stravinsky's something else, and it's got this here Joe trembling just a wee bit.

Love,
Joe

P.S. Jennifer's been talking about taking me to a meeting of the campus Objectivists one of these days. (Apparently that's the name of Ayn Rand's philosophic school, and I guess she's really active in the group.) She says I might have to wear or carry something — a pen, a bracelet — in the shape of a dollar sign, since that's their symbol! Don't know if I want to spend money on something I'd only use once, though.*

Dear Al,

Well, you guys should be proud of this Joselito. His orchestra solos went great! Dr. Smithson even signalled me to take a special bow at the end of each piece, and the applause actually got louder. Jennifer rushed over with congrats and a kiss on the cheek as we were all shuffling off stage, and then we went off to celebrate with a pizza.

She talks about majoring in psychology. I tease her and

---

* There is no evidence that Jennifer ever followed up on this idea, nor that Joe ever did attend an Objectivist meeting. — EDS.

wonder out loud if she's got plans to analyze me. I joked about it over our sausage pizza last night, and she replied, real serious, "Well, I do have lots of insight into human nature. I've known quite a few individuals, and when the time comes, I test them."

"Well, then," I chuckled, "I hope you don't go testing me."

She shrugged her shoulders. "If a guy is weak enough to let me walk all over him, I'll walk all over him." I suppose she was just kidding, I hope so.

We've been to a couple of her violin lessons. It's fun working on a piece together and then playing it for the teacher, who's none other than Dr. Smithson. (He raved about my Petrouchka solo as we entered his studio for a make-up lesson this morning.) Just between you and me, tho', I'm kind of surprised to find out that, as a violin player, Jennifer ain't exactly hot. There's a lot of musical stuff she doesn't know, and when it comes to faster runs she can really mess up. Also, Dr. Smithson keeps telling her to play with more feeling. "Jennifer, how about putting some soul into your Beethoven? This is a joyful sonata about springtime, not some four-finger exercise!"

That's what he said to her. Well, maybe I can help her out with music, and she'll teach me about psychology and Ayn Rand. A two-way street.

I tell you, Al, there's nothing beats grassing, tho' it gets embarrassing at times. After fifteen minutes or so I might have this big wet spot on the front of my pants, and when we get up to head for Kaibab I've got to cover the thing up with my books.

Next year Jennifer is supposed to be living at the A Xi Pi house. Don't know how much I'd like walking up frat row to pick her up, but that's a long ways off anyhow.

Love,
José

Dear Al,

It's going to be great being with you and *los papás y las chavas* next week. And yeah, I can see how you might look forward to getting the hell out of uniform for a few days.

Got to admit, I'll miss Jennifer. She's off to San Francisco this next Tuesday. Funny thing, her ride in the plane's just an hour or so longer than my drive down in the Plymouth the next day. (The way things are going, it won't be long now before people will be taking their Thanksgiving vacations on the moon.) She'll be at a San Francisco Symphony concert on Friday, and guess what they're playing? All of "Petrouchka." Boy, do I envy her.

See you soon.

Joe

[late November-early December 1960]

Dear Al,

Called Jennifer when I got back — no answer. Same thing next morning. Don't want to overdo it so I leave it at that, but then she doesn't show up at practice room either, and I've overshot twenty minutes into her time slot. I was real worried that she'd up and forgotten about me, so it was nice when I found a note on my locker that afternoon saying, "Practice session tonight, same time, same place? J."

We did, plus went grassing. It's a routine I've gotten used to: Tuesday evening practice, Splendor in the Grass (isn't that how the movie's called?) comes next (hey! pun not intended), violin lessons the following AM, orchestra Thursday nite. Sometimes we go for a coke then or a date on the weekend. Real intense.

Tell me, Al, how casual should I be? I don't always ask her out 'cause I don't want to wallow all over her, but I also get jealous when I see her smiling at other guys.

We've especially had fun a couple of afternoons just sitting on our hill next to the library, watching people go by. Don't know what to make of some of Jennifer's reactions, though.

Today we saw this couple I'd been noticing since my first week here. She's got real long hair, and they both wear sandals and are kind of skinny. Much older, too, 26 or 27, probably graduate students or something like that. So we see them walking holding hands, and right in front of us they stop, the girl takes off her rimless glasses, they both giggle, then kiss and hug and move on after she's thoroughly wiped the spectacles on the hem of her flowery dress. (Kind of reminded me of my wiping my glasses on my shirt, and mamá always giving me a hard time about it.)

"Weird people," Jennifer remarks, almost snide.

"Think so? They seem sort of interesting."

She smiled. "Well, let's say they're sort of *different.* Beatniks, I suppose."

I kept quiet, but, face it, Jennifer's got some typical sorority-girl attitudes. What's wrong with beatniks, actually? She's still a pretty cool chick, tho'.

Those are real horror stories you tell me about basic training. Sure hope *I* never get drafted.

Love,
Joe

[January 1961]

Dear Al,

Yeah, I know, I've hardly written you in weeks. But like I said to you at Thanksgiving, the work really does pile up after Xmas. Besides researching two term papers, studying for four finals, and practicing for two music juries (mine and Jennifer's), I've also been teaching myself lots of pop tunes — picked up five Gershwin songs this week! An older guy in my theory class (Wayne Belli, an Air Force vet) says I can make good money playing dance jobs around here — frats, dorms, churches, lodges, etc. Pay is around $25 a night, and it sure would beat hashing meals for the Greeks. (Serving and picking up after those animals at Kappa Alpha hasn't exactly been my idea of a good time. I'll be glad to get away.) It seems Wayne's own piano man and bass player are both leaving school to go into the Navy, so maybe the guy's got me in mind, given that I could substitute for either of them. Who knows? I might be playing for extra cash sometime soon. That way I could afford a bicycle to get around campus faster.

(Next Sunday) We've been doing some hard practicing, Jennifer and me, and it's not always fun. She can get really bossy when she wants her way. We spent about 2 1/2 hours on a single piece tonite (seemed like the whole evening actually), and each time she felt we didn't have it right yet. Still, I've got to admit we've got our tempo and dynamics going like clockwork, which is how a team should be. Haven't done any grassing since vacation, tho', says she's feeling too nervous and overworked, and wants to impress them in her violin jury, and I guess I can't blame her.

Don't want to leave this letter sitting around much longer, so I'll stop now and send it off tomorrow.

Love,
Joe

Dear Al,

Well, we did it. Jennifer and I were a big hit at her jury this morning. Boy, did we wail! A couple of people, including Dr. Epstein, my piano prof, even clapped at the end, something that almost never happens, or so I've been told.

Later that day I ran into Dr. Epstein outside the recital hall, and I can still see his eyes beaming and hear his guttural German voice saying, "Joe, you played *vonderfully,* especially those Beethoven sixteenth-notes."

"Oh, thank you," I stammered out, not knowing what else to say.

"Vill you be vorking with Miss Yaspers next semester?" he added.

"Miss who?" I asked in return.

"You know, your violinist, Miss Yaspers."

It took me a split second to realize who he meant. "Oh, sure, of course," I blurted out. "By the way, how *did* Jennifer do? Was she fine?"

Dr. Epstein suddenly frowned, and said only, "Oh, she vas all right." After another moment's silence, he said, "Vell, good luck on your piano jury tomorrow," and suddenly took off. It was a funny incident, wonder what to make of it.

(Next day) We celebrated the end of Jennifer's semester with a large pepperoni pizza last nite. She's off to California tomorrow for intersession (yours truly still has finals), but she also suggested we both read *Jude the Obscure* over break, so we can get ahead on the reading for our English 3 classes, and then discuss it when she's back. Seems like a good idea.

We got in an hour's worth of pretty intense grassing before we kissed good-bye at her dorm's front steps. Have to say, I'll miss her while she's away.

(Some days later) Started reading *Jude the Obscure,* and I feel so sorry for the hero. He's this stonecutter who wants to go to the university and study old books, but the snobs there won't let him in — and just because he's poor. And his wife, she is mean, tricks him into marriage and treats him real bad, too. Guess I should count my blessings. It's a modern world now, and we live in a democracy.

Al, I'm so glad they're not shipping you overseas. OK, so you won't get to see the world, but this way you can come to Merced more often. And our letters will reach each other faster too.

Love,
Pepe

P.S. I'm playing my first gig with Wayne Belli this coming weekend. Guess where? Newman House! I feel so excited. I'll be seeing some of the same people I met this last September, except they'll be dancing to my sounds!

[February ?, 1961]

Dear Al,

Classes started today, and by pure chance I ran into Jennifer as I was coming out of the music building. She looked sexy in her blue jeans, but, boy, was she in a foul mood. I gave her my friendliest, "Hi, Jennifer!" and all she came back with was this frigid, "Oh, hello."

"What's wrong?" I asked.

She spoke almost thru her teeth. "What's wrong? I'll tell you." Her lips puckered up. "Smithson gave me a 3 in violin, that's what's wrong." Al, she was really pissed.

"Have you seen him about it?"

"First thing I did when I returned," she more or less barked, crossing her arms. "He said," — and here Jennifer's voice changed to a sarcastic "nya-nya-nya" sound — "'Your playing lacks technical facility, and tends to be expressionless and mechanical.'" She uncrossed her arms and clenched both fists. "Ohh!"

I felt bad for her and suggested a coke at the Desert Shack, hoping she'd calm down. On the way she said, still angrily, "I thought we'd played quite well, both of us. I think I deserved a B plus, even an A, or a 1, as you call it here."

The front picture-window booth where we'd first talked last October was unoccupied, and we settled in. After she'd snapped her order at our waitress, Katie, Jennifer continued, livid with rage, "It's pretty damned unfair, if you'll pardon the French." Eventually she spilled some of her 7-Up and shed some tears, and when I tried wiping her cheeks with my hanky, she pushed my hand abruptly away. Didn't make me feel too good.

"Well, Jennifer," I said, "they did clap for us."

"Clapped for *you,* maybe," she growled, using a few paper napkins to clean up the wet spot on her side of the table.

"Jennifer, have I done anything wrong?"

Now biting into her straw, she nodded silently, then said,

"Well, inasmuch as you *have* raised the issue, I will say that you took the Beethoven a tad too fast."

It made me feel so guilty, I just had to apologize. "I'm really sorry. I'll be more careful next time."

With a cutting voice, she said, "That's water under the bridge. A lot of good it'll do me today, when I'm feeling like an absolute jerk."

Things felt real tense, so I asked her about California. She did cool down a bit as she got into her weekend skiing trip up in the Sierras with her parents and two brothers, and the many hours they'd put in simply relaxing or watching TV. Seems to me they do so many interesting things together.

"Oh," I asked, "get to read the book?"

She made a face. "Yeah."

"Sad, no? Poor Jude."

Looking out the window, she said in a deeper voice, "He's nothing but a milquetoast."

"A what?"

Using her straw, she fished out an ice cube and popped it into her mouth. "A weakling. He lets everybody run all over him, his two women especially. Never asserts himself once."

I was more or less flabbergasted. "Jennifer, how can you say that? The guy's dirt poor. He's got practically no family. All he wants is to be at the university, and he can't get in."

The sounds of the ice cube crushing between her teeth were loud and clear. "Poverty? Joe, that's a lame excuse. He deserves everything he gets." Then she swallowed. "He's weak, that's all. If he wants to be a student, why doesn't he show some individual initiative? By the way, Ayn Rand's heroes don't have families. Or their families are horrible altruists. And yet it doesn't stop them. They succeed."

We sat there in silence a few minutes, she chewing on a couple more ice cubes, me scouring for the last few drops of coffee with my spoon.

Then I see Wayne Belli coming in the back way and ordering a large coffee to go, and when he catches sight of me he says, real fast, "Hey, Joe, how's it goin'? Listen, some new dance jobs comin' up, gotta run now, tho'," and we wave at each other as he hurries out.

Jennifer perked up and looked curious, so I told her about my first paid gig the other nite, how I'd initially felt sort of nervous yet really took off on several of my piano solos, how I managed to put in a few minutes of trumpet and bass during two slow songs, how the dancers clapped for us after every set but the first. And how I'd gone and bought a bike, used but like-new, the next day.

"Joe, that's wonderful!" she said with her nice big smile (finally). "Calls for a celebration."

"Well, how 'bout a movie this Saturday?"

"Sure, Joe!" She's got such a nice melody in her voice whenever she says "sure."

Al, how's this all sound to you? She did come 'round at last, but I feel as if I'm getting mixed signals from her. Should I let it ride and see what happens? Or should I pull out? You're the expert, and I'm in need of your advice.

Love,
Pepe

II

Now, in the practice room in April, Jennifer was staring down at him, saying nothing. He in turn avoided her eyes and observed his left hand randomly improvising parallel-ninth chords, in whole tones, up the keyboard. The trumpet player next door was attempting the Haydn at full speed. On the other side, another pianist was playing the opening chords of the Rachmaninoff Second Concerto.

He wiped his glasses on his ROTC necktie.

"Well?" she asked.

"Well, this," he ventured nervously. "I've been meaning to talk t'you these last few months." Immobile, she still stared. He spoke faster. "I just can't figure it out, Jennifer, I mean, what happened? how come you stopped wanting t'be with me? after

all, you started this whole thing, but then you got so strange."
His full stop was abrupt.

She gave an impatient sigh, stamped one of her heels softly,
and bit on her lower lip, always keeping a firm hold on her
violin case and book. Her grin was a small one; her green eyes
looked his way, unmoving; her voice was proper and well-
modulated, even business-like. "Joe, I wonder what ideas you've
gotten into your head. Did you somehow think I was supposed
to live for you? I'll spell it out for your benefit: I live only for
myself. After that there's my family, and then maybe a few truly
superior friends at A Xi Pi house."

As she ran her right hand through her hair, Joe for the first
time saw the slender, delicate gold bracelet, made up of tiny
dollar signs, sliding and tinkling upon her wrist.

"You're real selfish," said Joe, on impulse.

She smiled. "That's right."

Hands on his knees, his heart beating faster, Joe went on, "So
if I never really mattered to you, why didn't you just tell me
earlier? I feel like a first-class dope."

Her smile widened, but her voice remained unaltered. "Well,
Joe, what was I supposed to tell you? 'Watch out, you're going
to get the short end of the deal?' Honestly, if you think I've been
mean, well, believe me, I can be a lot meaner..."

"Then why did you let it drag on like you did?" he interrupted. "That was real thoughtless and inconsiderate of you."

She shrugged her shoulders, thinned her lips. "Joe, I'm not a
considerate person. You're talking the language of compassion
there. Well, compassion is something one feels when looking at
a squashed caterpillar. I don't feel sorry for anyone. I don't
believe in self-sacrifice. And I will not do penance for my
virtues."

Joe was unable to negotiate her statements. As he loosened his
necktie all he could respond with was, "Y'know, I really
suffered because of you, couldn't sleep for nights on end,
couldn't study, couldn't even eat, hardly."

The smile on her face became a smirk. "If I may say so, Joe, suffering is a disease. You were thinking of me all that time? Well, perhaps you should have been thinking of yourself. I certainly think of *my*self first and foremost."

He looked away from her, toward his piano score, the G-flat key signature. "I can't believe the self-centered way you see things."

She rolled her wide-open eyes as her voice took on a gravelly tinge. "'Self-centered'? Yes, and that is healthy. You'll get no altruism from me. Altruism is a weapon of the weak. I am selfish and proud of it."

Joe's hand did a legato chromatic descent, flubbed the middle octave, then stopped. "You've got a real knack for running a guy down," he finally reflected.

She looked up toward the ceiling, softly stamped her left heel again, chuckled once and made a sweeping gesture with her free hand, palm facing outward. "I won't say anything."

"Aw, c'mon, Jennifer, what is it?"

Her green eyes were somewhere distant as she took a barely audible breath. Save for her smiling lips she did not move while speaking to him. "You see, Joe, I'm much stronger than you are. And I need a man, a real man who will take control, who'll push me around and put me in my place. Otherwise I'll push *him* as far as I can. Someone so weak should expect no better."

Hands poised again on his knees, his gaze fixed blankly on the keyboard, Joe attempted to speak but could not.

"And remember, I warned you: I usually get around to testing people in my life. So you cannot claim lack of mutual consent. And Joe, you simply failed the test."

Joe could only move his head, which turned, almost by its own accord, toward her. "Was the test that night out in the desert?"

Her grin was ever so slight, her voice just above a whisper when she replied, "Yes."

[Saturday, February ?, 1961]

Dear Al,

Don't know where to begin, it's so damn crazy. Jennifer

and I've had the weirdest time together, and I can't make no sense out of the whole thing.

Remember how she and I were going to celebrate my first gig by going to a movie? Well, I see her rushing out of a practice room early this afternoon and ask if she'd like to go see *All about Eve,* with Bette Davis, not at a theater but at some new coffee-house type place called Vesuvio's. And she doesn't smile even, just puts on this pouty look and says, "It's up to you, Joe," and simply walks off. And that evening when I come for her in the Plymouth she barely nods "Hello" to me up at Kaibab lobby and sweeps by me in her cape (it's chilly tonite), then runs toward the car, gets in and slams the door shut herself and won't say a word all the way to the café. Lucky thing the flick was just starting, 'cause I wouldn't of known what to do if we'd had to sit around waiting in pure silence.

The film wasn't in color, but it sure did grab me. Eve seems like this sweet, nice, pretty girl, an orphan and a war widow who wants to be a famous actress. So she works out a scheme to make friends with Bette Davis and her crowd, and slowly takes advantage of them, causes them all kinds of grief, and leapfrogs over them all to make it to the top. The Bette Davis people finally see thru her game and realize what she was up to but can't do a thing about it, it's too late. Turns out her story was phony and her nice sweet orphan-girl bit just an act — she's a class-A bitch and incredibly nasty!

I was on the edge of my seat for most of the two hours and felt nearly speechless at the end. I turned to Jennifer.

"God, what a movie! 'Little Miss Evil' (that's what Bette Davis calls her) really says it all! So creepy."

And then she smirks and gives me this funny stare. "What do you mean, 'creepy'?"

"She's such a horrible person," I replied.

Jennifer raised her eyebrows, sort of a superior look. "Why? Because she's strong and independent? Apparently you don't like seeing a woman being successful."

"Jennifer, she's not independent, she exploits people. And what you just said about me is real unfair." It was so frustrating, Al.

She made some kind of animal noise and breathed out loud thru her pursed-up lips. "I can't stand that word, 'exploit.' If Eve gets what she wants, it's thru her own talents and efforts. And if *you* can't see that, Joe, then it's your Latin values coming out."

Al, how do you answer that one? All I could come up with was, "That's simply not true, and anyways it's not the point. The girl is an evil little bitch."

"From your old-fashioned religious standpoint, maybe. Why so defensive, by the way? It looks as if you can't take criticism."

We were getting nowhere fast, so I clammed up and let my eyes roam about the place. It was actually kind of neat, with maybe a dozen marble-top tables and a nice aroma of coffee. They put on some jazz when the movie was over, Thelonious in fact. People there were really different, never saw so many beards in my life. And on the wall next to us I saw this long, skinny poster showing a poem and a guitar, and you wouldn't believe it but the poem was in Spanish, by this guy called Lorca we read in class last year.

Our short, slim waitress had the curliest dark hair I've ever seen, and she moved incredibly fast in her huaraches. And you know, Al, that gringa *smiled* at me when she came for our order, something Jennifer hadn't done all day.

Most everything on the menu was new to both of us, never had a capuccino before. So, to play it safe, we each ordered hot cider. As we waited I asked Jennifer what she thought of the place. She said nothing, smirked again, and looked away. I noticed she had her dollar-sign broach pinned to her cape.

We sip our drinks in silence, and I finally ask, "Want to go for a drive?"

She shrugs her shoulders and says, "If you do."

Night was cool and crisp, the drive north silent still. "Kinda nice, these mountains," I say, just to say something.

"Mountains? It's desert."

"Well, sorta both, isn't...?"

"It's desert."

Feeling crappy, I slow down, bear right, and ask, "Jennifer, you want to go home?"

She lets out this whoosh of air and answers only, "Joe, it's up to you, whatever you want." By then I can see just a few houses lit up out there. A moment later she adds, "Oh, God, it's so ridiculous."

"What is?"

Now I hear this impatient sigh, followed by a long flood of talk from her, tho' not much of an improvement over her silence. "Here I thought I was a good violin player, and all I get is a lousy C, a 3, I mean. And after so much practice. And then I get a 2 in Psych. Just great for my self-confidence. I feel like chucking violin lessons and going back to the cheerleading squad."

I took my foot off the gas pedal. The car coasted. I held her hand tight, and said, "Jennifer, don't talk that way. You're great, you're smart, you know so much. Why should you want to be some pom-pom girl?"

And then she nearly shouts, "And what, pray tell, is wrong with that?" I let go of her hand. She continues. "Who are *you* to say what's good or bad for me? Don't be such a self-righteous snob."

"Okay, okay, I'm sorry." By now I'd parked on the narrow shoulder so we could talk better, but she sat stony-faced again, breathing heavily like some baby dragon.

Finally she says, "Joe? Would you mind if I stepped out for a minute? I need the fresh air."

I hesitate, but answer, "Alright, go ahead."

She's out in a flash, leaving the door wide open. I shut it, turn on the headlights, and can see her cape flopping and tossing about, her milky white legs pushing up and outwards and gaining speed. To my surprise she keeps running inland, receding amid the sand and sagebrush, and then vanishes from sight. I sit there, real nervous, watching the occasional car zipping by me on my left, the bright full moon and wispy clouds floating directly over some coal-blue ridges up ahead, and I start wondering where Jennifer's at and what she's up to. I've left the lights on so she'll find her way back easier, but the minutes keep ticking by, and seeing as how I'm getting worried about my date and your car battery, I blow the horn a couple of times, climb out and yell "Jennifer!" loud as I can, then honk again and shout her name once more, with longer sounds.

Finally from among a clump of tall, slim cactuses the pyramidal outline of her cape looms into view, and it's sheer relief to see her legs advancing at a gradual, rhythmic gait, and her chalk-cold forehead facing steadily toward the ground, with her invisible arms probably locked in a firm grip across her chest. Halfway thru her slow return, a small cloud slithers past the moon, and her figure darkens into a streaked silhouette. She looks like she's stepped out of an old black-and-white ghost movie, like a *Twilight Zone* show that's sprung to life.

As I rev up the engine she throws open the door, tumbles in, and lashes out, "I am so furious. I've never been so embarrassed in my life."

"How come?" Got to admit my insides were all shaken up as I executed the U-turn.

"Howcum?" she mocks, and I can't begin to imagine the grotesque look she must of had on her eyes and cheeks and lips. "Can't you see the houses? Don't you realize there might be people hearing us out there?"

"Jennifer, it's dangerous in the bush, there's rattlesnakes in this country..."

"Leave me alone," she snapped, "I don't need your help."

I slow down, pull over onto the shoulder, take her left

hand in both of mine, and say to her, softly, "Listen, Jennifer, I like you a lot, it makes me sad..."

"Oh, cut it out. You sound just like my mother. It's my bad manners that's the problem, Joe. Let's go back to the dorm."

Al, that durned radio of yours is no damn good! Jiggled it and banged it, but it won't work just when I most need the thing. So the silent drive back to the U. is pretty intense, and feels even worse at the tail end when I pull up in front of Kaibab. She exits and trots right up ahead of me onto the concrete steps.

"Hey, Jen, how's it goin'?" this loud Anglo voice booms out. It's some crewcut blond guy in a Sigma Chi sweater and sockless Keds, sprawled out on the stairs, and she gives him this wide open grin, her only smile all evening, the biggest smile of her life, I bet.

I felt so damn dumb facing her by the glass doors. Then some double-date foursome shuffles out, the girls chuckling at the guys' Spanish-accent imitations, and suddenly I wished I'd had a shotgun then and there to mow 'em down and laugh, saying, "Ha! Hey, you're so funny!"

But all I can do is stand there looking at Jennifer with, "Don't know what to say."

She shrugs again, something that has always gotten to me. "There's nothing to say." Feels interminable as we stand there till she turns around, says "Bye," and pulls at the door.

"Good night, Jennifer," I say, hoping she'll come out again and be nice.

So as you might guess, we did no grassing or parking tonite. And I'm back in Navaho now, where I've been slouching on my bed for half an hour, and am so glad that wise-ass roommate of mine isn't in. And I hate boring you with a blow-by-blow account of my miserable day, I know you've got enough problems of your own with Sergeant Croft and latrine duty and all that, but I'm so shaken up, I don't even know what I'm supposed to think. Tell me, Al, what's with this mess, what've I done wrong? I feel so crappy.

Joe

Dear Al,

Another terrible day. It was unusually warm, so I biked down to the music building, where I did the five-finger exercises I used to drive you all nuts with, didn't require much thinking. Then I started actually having fun, whizzing thru those fast Bach and Chopin runs; their fantasies are a real gas (I practiced them last Xmas, you'll remember). I shut the piano lid with some feeling that I'm good at *something*.

And as I come out of the room I see her sitting absolutely still at the piano across the hall from me. She's got her right hand on the keys, left on her lap, and is wearing Levi's. She's got a funny little grin and doesn't look up when I turn the doorknob.

"Hi, Jennifer, didn't know you played."

She kept gazing at the keys, "Oh, I just goof around a bit." She did some chords, said nothing for a minute or two, then, "Our T.A. in Psych told us about all sorts of music therapy experiments with" — and I really thought she said — "artistic children."

"Hmm. Artistic children? What's supposed to be wrong with them?"

"No," she shook her head impatiently. "*Au*tistic. A-U-T."

"What's that?"

She took a deep breath and explained. "An autistic child is one who lives in his own private world."

"Aha," I said, just to fill the gap. Meanwhile she keeps making triads till I ask, "Hey, like to go for a ride on my bike?" She shaped a minor chord, pressed slowly on the keys; I could feel my heart pounding.

Now she grinned a little bit more, did her shoulder-shrugging routine, but said, "Okay."

Outside it was as still as any Sunday morning can be, perfect for a bike ride. I did my gentle best to help her onto the crossbar, and pedalled off as slow as possible. Just riding together with her had me excited. She giggled once or twice, and it made me feel happy to cruise by one of our favorite grassing spots, with its arched citrus trees and dangling fruit. As I approached a nearby slope, I asked if she'd like to sit up there for a while, and she said simply, "Okay."

Despite the time of year, it wasn't chilly. Strange, I can't recall what all we talked about as I lay there, hands behind my head, feeling the little breeze blow all over me. I expected we'd be talking soon about the weird stuff out in the desert.

Meanwhile she was seated bolt upright, and I don't know when it was she mentioned, real casual, "It's a relief, not having to work up pieces for violin jury this semester."

"And why's that?"

"Oh, I'm dropping violin. I was only taking it as extra credit anyway. I'm staying in orchestra, tho'."

I say nothing, feeling awful confused, and then something real funny happens. Not ha-ha funny, just odd. She stops talking all of a sudden, and a few seconds later she's up and bouncing down the hill. "Well, I need to be at House brunch, 'bye, now," she says super-casually as she marches off toward sorority row.

"Oh, well, OK, I'll see you," I said, but I doubt if she could hear me. I sat up, and watched her purple sweater and dark blue jeans vanishing beyond the benches and palm trees and gray stone fence.

And I felt so goddamn hollow, Al, so empty inside. Couldn't get back to practicing, and I now wonder how much studying I'm going to get done this semester. Sorry to cry on your shoulder, but there's nobody else would listen to me. (I can just hear mamá and papá gloating, "That's what you get for dating gringa girls, Joselito.") About the only other person I've mentioned Jennifer to is my gross roommate Jason, and when I told him a few weeks ago that I was in love with her, he thought it was pretty damn funny. Today I bet he'd *really* laugh, the bastard.

Al, should I simply have run after Jennifer and grabbed her by the arm and said, "No, girl, you ain't goin' nowhere, you're stayin' here"? I've seen it happen in movies and on dorm steps; is that what a guy's supposed to do? I feel almost desperate, please write and let me know soon.

Joe

III

During the two-and-a-half month interim that followed the above letter, Jennifer and Joe had not had occasion to converse with one another. For many a morning after the incidents out on the little hill and in the desert he took to overstaying his time-slot and practicing five, ten minutes extra that she might come to see him or at least claim the room as she had done last fall. But she did not. And the bell that ended Theory class had come to mean more treks down to the Desert Shack, where he might wait alone, or sit with classmates, ordering seconds on doughnuts and coffee, but had yet to espy her in their cream-colored window booth, she, Jennifer, who somehow also arrived just seconds late for Thursday orchestra rehearsals and then suddenly absented herself, fiddle and all, just at the very moment when Mr. Smithson shut his scores and said, "Okay."

[Early or mid-March, 1961]

Dear Al,

Thanks for your Special Delivery letter. Really helped. Still feel hopeless, tho'. Played a gig w/ Wayne Belli at Jennifer's dorm, and thought for sure she'd be there for me to dedicate a tune to her. Didn't happen.

10 PM rolls along, dance floor's livened up, and my "Misty" solo flows out from me real fine, with some of the coolest sounds I've ever made. (Sometimes I like to imagine me and Jennifer dancing real close to Johnny Mathis singing

"Misty.")

But it's our second break, and still no Jennifer. God, was I tense, even took a cigarette offered me by Jake, our chain-smoking drummer, and you know I usually don't smoke. Finally I can't hold back no more, and head for the pay phone in the corner.

"Hello." I recognize her voice.

"Hi, this is Joe."

"Oh, hello," the voice replies. And silence. Phone booth's shut tight but I can hear some Kaibab girls and some guys cracking corny jokes and asking where're you from? and what's your major? and the usual stuff. Jukebox starts playing "Heartbreak Hotel," seems just like the tune for me right now.

Anyhow I explain why I'm downstairs. She answers nothing. Feeling nervous, I blurt out, "How 'bout coming down and dancing some? I'm on break, and there's the jukebox playing now."

"I'm studying," is all she says.

And whatever I say it's what she comes back with. Between my saying, "OK, see you" and my hanging up the phone I hear nothing from her, *nada*.

I sure did appreciate the five clean fives Wayne peeled off for me at midnite, but I could hardly sleep afterwards. Only good thing was that crude old Jason wasn't there to rib me about riding a bike. ("Tell us about your *bicycle,* Joe," he said to me once in front of his frat-rat friends, this asshole smile on the edge of his snide face.) Wake up at 6; lay in bed till 8; now it's 8:30. Al, I thought I'd blow up from trying to make sense of it all, Jennifer like she was our first semester, Jennifer like she's acting now. What's wrong? Is it women? Is it me? You say you think she's crazy, Al, and maybe you're right, but then why was she so nice before? No girl's ever treated me so nice. Can't figure none of this out, makes me wonder why I'm in college or even alive.

Joe

It was a balmy, breezy March morning as Joe biked down to the Student Union Post Office the next day and dropped off last night's letter to Al. No mail in the multiple rows of SUPO boxes, too early as yet. He pedalled on toward the Desert Shack, locked his bike in the rear parking lot, and slipped into a booth next to the counter. The street outside, normally so busy, seemed as still as a framed photo.

Katie, the plump, bubbly waitress with short, gray hair, emerged from the kitchen, greeting him with, "Well, hi there, Joe. Glazed doughnut and white coffee?"

He chuckled fast and nervously, once. "Yeah, right, Katie, how'd you guess?"

"Well, we know everything there's to know about you here, don't we?" She poured the cream, handed the cup to him from over the counter, then the doughnut. "They're both fresh and hot."

The only other customers, a colorful, talkative blond couple whom he recognized as Drama School types, got up and exited through the front door. Their deep, well-cadenced voices floated faintly from the sidewalk curb. They had been seated in the same booth where Jennifer and he had first sat last fall. Katie cleared and wiped their table, now empty.

After slowly consuming half his doughnut and skimming off some of his coffee, he arose to pay.

"Say, why the long face?" Katie exclaimed slowly, ringing the cash register. "It's Saturday, there's no classes, so enjoy!"

Nonplussed, Joe chuckled again as he pocketed the change.

Pointing her angular chin at his abandoned leftovers, she said mock-properly, "You must eat more, young man." And, shaking a friendly finger, "Food is good for piano practice!"

He waved good-bye from the front door.

And then, just as he'd been attempting through last night, he actually encountered Jennifer now, in the Music basement hall. At first it seemed deserted as he ambled on to his locker, hands in his pockets and whistling his Chopin. Then, from the end of the hall she appeared, silent and expressionless, wearing jeans, tennis shoes, and an Alpha Xi Pi sweatshirt, her rhythmical steps silent and her tennis racket hanging firmly in the grip of her delicate left hand.

He stopped whistling in mid-phrase. Right arm slightly atremble, his fingers spun through the trio of numbers until the combination padlock fell open.

"Hello," her high soprano said, a downward major third.

"Hi," he replied without glancing her way, a soft diminished fifth, up. Soon seated at the familiar dark-wood piano he played for a half-hour straight. Nevertheless he could hear her doing orchestral parts somewhere as he closed and laid aside an uncooperative Chopin. He started out his more or less performable Bach fugue, one hand at a time, knowing that she'd be gone by the time he was finished.

In the following weeks, Joe's imagination did far more than the rest of him could do. As he lay in bed those mornings and nights, the most vivid thoughts he had were of his happening upon Jennifer on the Library lawn, she sitting on a bench, her hands folded, and bathed in white moonlight, and then she sees him, leaps up, and runs toward him saying "Joe, oh, Joe," then flings her arms around him in a tearful yet mysterious passion, all in a split second, he knew it happens, had seen and heard about it happening, it really happens, he was sure. And he toyed once, and twice, and yet again with placing a classified ad saying "Jennifer! please come back. All is forgiven!" just like the one he'd seen in *The Wildcat* this last week. Oftentimes he wondered if the romance with Jennifer had actually existed, or if it had dwelled only inside his head, she seemed like some impalpable phantasma, remote and incorporeal, save for her tardy entrances and quick exits at orchestra rehearsal Thursdays.

IV

And now, for the first time in months, in the same practice room where they'd first met and our story had begun, Jennifer and Joe were together again.

"But, Jennifer, what did I do wrong?"

The pianist next door had skipped on to the second theme of the Rachmaninoff.

"Joe. Oh, Joe, you just don't understand. It's what you didn't do."

"Didn't do? But I thought I was being tender and considerate." (In his mind he heard his mother's words, in border Spanish, "Try to be more considerate.") He rolled his khaki sleeves down and buttoned them up.

"No, Joe." The bell-like voice had never been more beautiful than when Jennifer, her face almost roseate from inspiration, said, "All that tenderness was about the last thing either of us needed. You never should have let me get away with acting as I did that night. You should've asserted yourself," she stopped briefly, "and maybe threatened me with a slap or a put-down, anything but sit there and take it from me."

Joe's blood was coursing faster even as Rachmaninoff's arpeggios rose in volume.

"And you never should have let me out of the car. But once you did, I'd actually have felt much more respect for you if you'd simply driven off and let me fend for myself out in the desert and then maybe phoned me at the dorm next day. Or even done to me what Roark first does to Dominique."

"What? Who're they?"

"Oooh, yes." She cut the second word short. "I forget, you've never read *The Fountainhead*." He could see her laugh, but somehow she made no sound. "Anyway, Dominique's this beautiful, brilliant architectural writer, and powerful men worship her. One day she's out in the country, getting distant glimpses of Roark, a genius architect who's been reduced to cutting rocks at the local quarry. She struts about in her high heels, oozing scorn for him as he sweats down below. His own disdain for her is much stronger, though, and she can't resist him. That night the guy shows up at her mansion, flings her silently onto the bed, and teaches her a lesson she'll never forget. Being degraded like some piece of property was just what she wanted. She loves it."

Joe remained steadily mute and immobile.

"There's too few strong-willed men in our world, and too many people content with being second-raters. And Joe," she shook her head, "the fact is, you're not strong enough for me; it became painfully obvious that night."

Joe's grimace was involuntary. "I guess I'm not that lucky, to be so strong."

Again Jennifer shook her head, much faster. "Lucky? No, Joe. I don't believe in luck, I've told you more than once. Really, life is what the individual makes of it. And a superior man controls his life. He does not depend on others." For at least a minute she said nothing and gazed toward the keyboard. Then she hummed briefly to the Rachmaninoff, and turned toward the door. "I must go."

"Wait, Jennifer." The question seemed to come to him from nowhere. "Lemme ask you: Did you start this whole thing just so I'd accompany you on the piano?"

Flushing red, the pretty face took on a deeply offended aspect. Her lips pursed up, looking fearsome as her indignant retort thundered out, "How *could* you say such a thing to me? For your information, Joe, I can manage perfectly well by myself, thank you. Did it ever occur to you that I sincerely admired your superior gifts? And still do? I am shocked at your unfair accusation."

"Sorry, Jennifer, dunno, I was just wondering, OK?" He felt ashamed of having asked, and held out his right hand. "Friends, OK?"

She raised her eyebrows, rolled her green eyes, and, taking a deep breath, spoke more softly. "Oh, all right," was her reluctant response. "I'm not so sure, though, after hearing you suggest something so vile. I don't use people, Joe."

He had already withdrawn his hand. "OK, OK, I apologize, honestly. Friends?" For a long time thereafter, Joe would feel a confused anguish and guilt about his accusation, but now he simply raised his hand once again.

Still radiating her noble fury, Jennifer extended her stiff palm

and brusquely shook his, then hastened out. She left the door
slightly ajar, and the lingering click of her high heels out in the
hall mingled with the sounds of Rachmaninoff's and Haydn's
difficult passage-work.

Joe stared at the keyboard, then positioned both his hands.
Stretching all four outer fingers he surged through the black-key
run as if it were a single and indivisible fluid entity. Flawless,
his very best. He tightened his necktie, straightened his
eyeglasses, and stared again.

Suddenly he reached for his scores, stacked them in no
particular order, noticed his hands were trembling slightly, and
just sat there, his music on his lap. Out in the corridor, the voice
of a redheaded baritone, familiar to him from Theory class, was
cracking some joke about parallel fifths. Another guy guffawed,
a girl giggled. The trumpeter and pianist on either side were
silent.

He donned his ROTC cap, leaped up, gave the door a little
push, rushed out and veered left to his locker, gaze fixed
downward and never once taking note of the still-bantering
threesome, the baritone in a plaid shirt now laughing, in turn, at
the Texas couple's one-line jokes. Joe grabbed his battered
schoolbag, threw in his scores, slammed the door shut, and
caught sight of Wayne Belli, seated far off in the bandspeople's
cubbyhole with drummer Jake, who was also duly clad in Army
ROTC uniform.

As he scurried toward the stairs, always looking downward, he
could hear his regulation plain black shoes squeaking
rhythmically, then Wayne joshing in his ever-jovial voice, "Hey,
there's our house Mex, goofin' off again." Joe bounded up the
stairs two at a time, wondering why Wayne pronounced his last
name *Bel-eye* instead of *Belly,* didn't seem exactly right. Eleven
forty-four, the wall clock said.

"Oh, damn, English class, I'd almost clean forgot," he
muttered.

The bike ride across campus felt almost exhilarating. There
was almost no one on the paths as he coasted alongside the

Library and on to Liberal Arts, where English 3, advanced
section, took place in a basement room. Arriving more than ten
minutes late, he took off his cap and sat alone in the back row,
unable to shake from his mind what Jennifer had told him.
Fumbling in his bag, he realized he'd left *Jude the Obscure* in
his dorm room or his locker. It hardly mattered, though,
inasmuch as there was little Joe could glean from class
discussion while he sat in a back corner, staring at his open
notebook. He did wonder if it were more than just coincidence
when a pretty blonde coed in the front row firmly asserted that
"Jude's problem is he's weak," and he duly wrote down and
pondered her insistent comments on this score. He also caught
a few stray sentences from Mr. Green's short lecture about
Hardy's "fatalism," and considered looking up the word later
that day, yet never did. The entirety of his notes added up to
about twelve lines. Writing to his brother Al later that day, he
related the morning's episode, and finished saying, "Feel
worthless. Wish I was dead sometimes."

V

During the weeks that followed, Joe's lack of appetite led to
a seven-and-a-half pound weight loss. Even his letters to Al
became shorter and less frequent. Still, the Chopin études he
performed in a mid-May recital went well enough, if a trifle fast.
Meanwhile he began being hired to play piano regularly, and
trumpet occasionally, for Wayne Belli's group — "Wayne's
Five" — and its series of end-of-year gigs. The relationship with
the band was thereby cemented, and would last throughout Joe's
remaining three years up at the University. The group actually
played another engagement at Kaibab Hall, and there as most
everywhere else Jennifer Jaspers was in Joe's thoughts. Save for
a brief passing "hello," however, the two never spoke again,
scarcely saw one another in fact.

Because Jennifer was the first girl Joe had ever dated much or
(excepting prostitutes) tasted physical contact with, he remained
strongly attached to the memory of her, dwelling on it in his

mind persistently if not obsessively. Yet he also felt that the romance had remained an incomplete and abortive matter, given Jennifer's grasp of topics of which he, alas, knew nothing. And so, still overwhelmed by the experience, and hoping to understand it and learn from it, before departing for Merced for the summer he spent a portion of his most recent gig payment on crisp new paperback copies of *Anthem, The Fountainhead, Atlas Shrugged,* and a collection of essays, all by Ayn Rand. Reading her books was to be among Joe's summer projects, along with some weekend dance jobs and other forms of employment.

Back in Merced, when not otherwise busy, Joe sat for hours on end in the bedroom he had once shared with Al, or on the front porch of the modest adobe-style house, immersing himself in one of Rand's volumes — much to the annoyance of his parents, who occasionally would come looking for him and urge him to join in a family activity or meals. Being a slow reader, he needed time and exerted no small effort in getting through the two heftier tomes, but eventually he understood and gradually assimilated Rand's thinking, and indeed was strongly persuaded by her logic and art as to the depth and power of Objectivist philosophy. Often he daydreamed of him and Jennifer, reclining side by side on their favorite lawn, holding hands, and reading long passages from *The Fountainhead* to one another. Sometimes he faintly wished he had been blessed with the steely blue eyes and jutting jaws of Ayn Rand's strong, noble heroes.

Joe attended Mass exactly twice that June, if only to please his mother. On the afternoon of July 4th, however, he informed her that he no longer accepted "mysticism" and would not be going to church again, a development she accepted silently. At any rate, whenever he had a Saturday job with "Wayne's Five" he'd usually been staying up in Tucson, so that he wasn't back in Merced till Sunday afternoon. At his mom's suggestion he did drop in one evening on Mrs. Pratt, who was warmly gratified at his rapid musical progress, while her husband, also a teacher, humorously asked Joe how he'd been treating "that old upright heap" they'd sold him at a nominal price some years ago. Joe smiled and said that he still practiced on it every day.

At the time of this visit Joe was temporarily employed part time in a work crew at the nearby stone quarry, and the boss's leggy teen-aged daughter — a tall, aloof, strawberry blonde — actually used to come strolling in her tight capris and red pumps, making him wonder whether he or anybody else could be Howard Roark to her Dominique Francon someday.

Toward summer's end he had thoroughly imbibed Ayn Rand's system, so much so that both Joe's parents (and brother Al, on furlough) expressed to him a certain curiosity about these books, this writer who seemingly had cast a spell over their Joe. In response, he tried summarizing Rand's complex plotlines, as a means of conveying to them her philosophy, though time and again they'd either yawn and doze off without much comment, or give him a bewildered look and reflect, for example, thus:

MOTHER: *¿Qué cosa es ésa?*

FATHER: *Qué ideas más extrañas...*

or AL: *¡Esa mujer está loca!*

Paquita, his kid sister, attempted to read *Anthem* but soon gave up, laying it aside on the turquoise-colored sofa and saying, "This stuff's simply *weird*," which made Joe assume that at her age — twelve-and-a-half — she was just too young to understand. During the last weekend in August, when their parents were off seeing friends in Las Cruces, Joe went for a solitary walk by the quarry and, standing at the rocky ledge while contemplating the rich sunset, he raised his hand and, slowly, made the sign of the dollar.

On his return to University the next month, Joe was hoping to impress Jennifer with his new knowledge. To his disappointment, however, he soon discovered that the girl hadn't come back, and no one really knew why. His casual inquiries yielded conflicting accounts: she had eloped with a football-player sweetheart from high school, she had transferred to USC, she had done both or neither. Joe never found out for sure; nobody seemed to have her Palo Alto address, nor had he and she traded such information while they'd been dating. And it did not occur to him simply to inquire at the Registrar's office.

Meanwhile Joe only dimly sensed the specifically personal, academic, and political reasons that had motivated Jennifer's past interest in him. Rather he dwelled on the disturbing set of concepts that she'd introduced him to in the practice room during their final meeting, and he now accepted the painful lessons of those few months as his necessary initiation into the opaque, strange ways of male-female romance.

Joe was coming of age at a time when notions such as those voiced by Jennifer were far from uncommon fare. Certainly he'd always known that men sought and needed women who'd submit to male control. What was newly revealing for him was to think back on women who had made stray statements eerily suggestive of his ex-girl friend's own. Sitting around Merced High cafeteria, the Desert Shack, or the University's buildings he had actually overheard on different occasions a girl remark to another, "I want to be dominated," "I need someone who'll push me around," or "If a man's weak enough, I'll walk all over him." In the light of his learning experience with Jennifer, he began to grasp that those catch-phrases of late-adolescent and young-adult love-talk were indeed casual instances of the laws of life and love.

For the moral to be drawn from this whole episode, Joe grimly came to realize, was that, yes, Jennifer was right; alas: he had indeed not demonstrated manly strength out in the desert. He now recalled comparable past moments during which he had responded with sickly altruism and despicable weakness when a strong, healthy, superior egoism was what was called for. To his current regret, back in high school he had once allowed flute-player Cristy to send him fetching coffee, instead of his remaining seated and simply telling her, "Fetch it yourself." He had let classmate and neighbor Angie be consistently grumpy with him at junior prom, had let newcomer Lucinda sass him for mispronouncing English words like "covet" or "won" at a party after their movie date, and so on... And yet, though they'd initiated verbal force with him, he'd then seen them home and even asked for a good-night kiss, rather than counter-mock them or maybe leave them stranded somewhere, as they deserved. Brooding on these matters over his sophomore year at college, Joe felt an odd gratitude toward Jennifer and wished he could drop her a note of thanks. But he also knew that any such token of gratitude would be taken by her as continuing weakness on his part.

And so Joe now readied himself to apply the lessons learned from Jennifer. The initial opportunity arose in February, just a few days after the anniversary of their key experience out in the desert. It was on a cool Thursday night; he had biked to a Juilliard String Quartet recital at the Music building and there casually encountered a pixyish little freshman from back East named Sue. He walked his bicycle as they headed for coffee at Mac's (their third time out) and later sat on the grassy mound next to the Library, where they continued to chat about the concert and the new semester.

Then, at some point, as Joe was recounting the first-rate piano riff he had come up with at a gig last Tuesday, Sue got up and started dancing the Twist, a new rock-and-roll style that he did not much appreciate.

He stopped midway through his sentence and asked, somewhat irritably, "Why don't you sit down?"

"'Cause I wanna dance, that's why," was her slightly defiant answer.

Joe bolted up, said curtly, "OK, you dance," hopped onto his bike. As he pedalled off he scarcely heard her shouting, "Joe, wait, no, come back." Thereafter he was approached by her a couple of times in the Music front hall and library, but he just ambled on, saying, "Have to go, see y'," feeling that on each occasion the experiment had proved satisfactory.

An episode the following month provided him another measure of pride. He was at the A & W Drive-in up on Speedway with a cute sophomore from Kingman, Liz Willis, a psychology major and marching-band clarinetist, who for a good portion of their date had been discoursing on her many admirers and boy friends, both past and present.

"Strange breed, men are," she said.

It being a weekday night, cars were few, and service was fast. Joe finished his root beer, signalled to have the tray picked up, and switched on the ignition as she talked, now about Ed, the engineering grad student who had a mad crush on her.

Suddenly he leaned over, unlocked her door and gave it a sharp push, followed by a soft tap on her bare shoulder. "Well, Liz, I guess you should be dating Ed and all those other guys instead. So why don't you get out of my car." He stared calmly through the windshield.

She gazed at him, speechless, and after some seconds had ticked by, shook her small blond head. "I don't understand. I mean... is this a joke?"

"No, baby, it's not."

"Well," she hesitated, "aren't you supposed to escort me back home?"

Whipping his face around, he saw her huge, pained, sky-blue eyes, and stated coldly, "I have no obligation to you whatsoever." Then, pointing with his right index finger, he added, simply, "Out."

Biting a slightly curled lower lip, she plucked up her pink cardigan from the middle of the seat, placed it over her shoulders, slowly stepped out, gently shut the door, and presumably returned to Maricopa Hall by taxi, or perhaps by bus, he never knew, since he never troubled to speak to her again.

Meanwhile Joe was slowly evolving into the "make-out artist" he had once yearned to be. A major step took place next summer, in Tucson, where he'd stayed on to play a series of dance jobs that Wayne Belli had lined up at several hotels and rest homes, some as far away as Flagstaff. Needing to work on some new tunes, Joe headed for his habitual practice room one afternoon, absent-mindedly pulled open the door, and nearly collided head-on with a petite, slim coed with flaming red hair, sea-green eyes, and a UCLA T-shirt. The two of them burst into laughter, struck up a conversation. She was actually from Scottsdale, near Phoenix, a music education major and Spanish minor, who couldn't take the L.A. smog and so'd come to U. of A. summer school to get her science out of the way and also keep up with oboe; Lynn was her name.

On their first full evening out days later they sat at one of the scarce free spots available around the "grassing" area next to the Library. She tried practicing her Spanish with him, he answered only in English. When a lull eventually ensued, the girl slithered up slowly onto her legs, yawning mezzo-piano as, fingers interlocked, she let her bare, freckled, moonlit arms stretch forward.

"And what if I were to step down right this minute?" she now inquired, raising a shapely, besandalled foot just inches above Joe's flat belly.

Thinking fast, Joe grabbed her by the ankle, flipping her down onto the soft grass. She giggled in astonishment, her bright eyes big and wide. Then they hugged and kissed with a tremulous passion, necking as long as her dorm hours would permit, tonguing, petting, and pressing their denim-clad flesh to the allowable erotic limits of the time.

More than once over the next few weeks, as Joe lay on top of Lynn, taking his limited pleasures with her amid the aroma of freshly-cut grass, always by the same fruit tree, he'd wink at her and whisper, "Come on, Lynn, let's go all the way. I know a nice secluded spot up in Sabino Canyon."

She in turn would look up at him with her roguish smile, shake her head in a wide arc from side to side, and reply, "Naughty boy. Uh-uh, that's for my wedding night." The banter, with variations, became almost routine with them. Conversely, as they'd go strolling or be simply relaxing somewhere about the University grounds, Lynn would ask, "Hey, Joe, like to accompany me at oboe lesson tomorrow?"

And Joe too would shake his head, he in a fast quiver, then flash her a small grin and raise his jaw. "Nope. I'm not a boy scout, or some dumb altruist either."

"God, you are really selfish," Lynn observed once.

"That's right," he retorted quickly yet modestly.

As the couple sat at Memorial Fountain one cloudy night toward session's end, at the height of the dog days, Lynn elbowed him and coaxed him yet again with, "C'mon, Joe, I need an accompanist for oboe jury this week."

"OK, Lynn, I'm game," he at long last conceded. "What'll you pay me?" he asked.

Her green eyes now almost glowed bright with incredulity. "Pay? Are you serious? That's so mercenary." She emitted a nervous chuckle. "Greedy."

"Greedy, right," Joe echoed her. "Anything wrong with that? There's no free lunch, you know." He pushed on. "OK, I've got a better idea. We find some quiet place tonight and go all the way; then I'll accompany you on your jury."

After turning utterly silent, she remarked. "That's really disgusting, Joe. You're sick."

"Not at all," Joe struck a dignified, noble pose as he consciously drew from John Galt's speech in *Atlas Shrugged.* "I'm a *trader,* and all I want is fair exchange and equal value. You give me sex, I'll give you top-quality musical service."

The girl merely said, "You're weird."

He blew out a gush of air, stood up to face down at her, gestured with his left index finger as he enounced carefully, "So go accompany yourself." Hands in his pocket, he rushed off, and managed never to cross paths with her for the remainder of summer school.

What kept surprising Joe over the next few years, as he'd often reflect to his brother Al, was the number of Anglo girls who seemed to appreciate his attitudes and actions. Repeatedly he'd pass their tests, prove to them he was strong, and their romantic interest in him actually increased.

On the other hand, the following summer an olive-skinned sophomore from New York called Ruthie, whose exotic features Joe at first construed as gypsy-like, responded differently to his newly-found philosophy of strength. A combined Art and History major at some progressive college back home, she also played decent alto sax, and the two had blown impromptu duets, just for fun, in her practice room.

As they drove up to A-Mountain one starry Friday night, Joe discoursed on his system of selfishness, and in time placed his hand on Ruthie's bare knee.

Calmly, she plucked off the hand as if it were a starched clean napkin, restored it to the steering wheel, and said melodically, with good Spanish phonemes, *"Macho, macho, macho. "* Shifting back to her New York voice she then remarked, "Trying to pull some Latin-lover shtick on me? Looks like Spanish mentality dies hard."

"False," Joe countered quickly. "I picked up my ideas from Ayn Rand, who's Anglo." He raised his chin triumphally. "And," he added with a heightened sense of victory, "a woman, by the way."

"So? I don't care what she is." As Ruthie got more impassioned her New York accent turned thicker. "Besides, since when are Russians 'Anglos' as you say? And for your information," she remarked, "Ayn Rand is full of shit."

"What?" Joe was completely taken aback. A "nice" girl who'd swear like that was something new to him.

"You heard me," Ruthie continued, now more softly, with a smile, "Ayn Rand's full of it and a fascist creep, too. Maybe you're this hot-shot musical prodigy, Joe González, but you don't know zilch about much else." She gave him a charming, friendly smile that contradicted the harsh judgments and made him feel better.

Her two words, "shtick" and "zilch," were also new to Joe, and he asked for definitions on their next night out, since his dictionary had failed to list either of them. "Fascism" and "fascist" did have entries, though he couldn't see how they squared with Rand's opposition to tyrants and staunch belief in freedom, an inconsistency that he later mentioned to Ruthie yet elicited from her only a chuckle, a shrug of her shoulders, and then silence.

She was among the few girls at the time who weren't intimidated by Joe's Randian arrogance. On their numerous encounters during that summer, she spurned most of his attempts at kisses, preferring instead to talk music, which she knew a lot about; she actually liked both Ravel and jazz, much to Joe's amazement and delight. He felt genuinely sad when Ruthie left for good in early August, reflected on how much more interesting she was than Jennifer, though he wondered how much he'd really understood her or she him.

And yet he still looked back with gratitude on his prime mentor Jennifer, she who had first opened his eyes to how male-female relationships work and also led him to the liberatory universe of Ayn Rand. Through Rand he'd learned to think in terms solely of himself and his own selfish worth as an individual, and, correspondingly, to reject all false moralities of guilt and sacrifice. He liked to fancy himself the incarnation of the Argentine aristocrat Francisco D'Anconia in *Atlas Shrugged,* sharing in a secret, lifelong passion with Jennifer in the role of Dagny Taggart.

Joe nonetheless drew a limit on raping a woman. Though well aware of Dominique's ecstatic bliss following Roark's forcible seizure of her (and aware, too, of how much she deserved it), he could not bring himself to contemplate so extreme a measure in his own dealings with women. For reasons that he could not articulate, there were actions Joe simply would not take, despite Jennifer's and Ayn Rand's hearty approval thereof.

Meanwhile, in smoke-filled campus spots and hangouts about town, Joe would join up in casual conversations with men students and fellow musicians, and, to the varieties of folk wisdom being bandied about concerning proper dealings with the opposite sex, would add his new-found insights. The traditional speculations of young males would customarily crop up, old standards such as, "Can't let some dumb broad boss you around," and, "Treat a lady like a whore and a whore like a lady." Or a more ruthless and cynical sort might ritually invoke "the four Fs: find'em, finger 'em, fuck 'em, and forget 'em," and some sympathetic soul would chuckle approval. Joe's own contributions harked back either to Jennifer — "Be nice to a dame, and she'll walk all over you. Rough 'em up, push 'em around, and she'll love it" — or to Ayn Rand — "Gotta be selfish, that's the number-one rule." And, continuing, "Every chick respects a guy who's selfish and puts 'er in 'er place," even as, for emphasis, Joe did the bug-squishing gesture with his right thumb.

"Hear, hear," someone with a thick Texas accent seconded him enthusiastically. Another time, however, a more religiously-inclined fellow, just back from missionary work in Asia, thought Joe's position too extreme and lacking in charity. On both occasions Joe felt called upon further to elaborate his views and hence summed up for each of them certain aspects of Ayn Rand's work, with special attention to the key episodes of Howard Roark and Dominique around the quarry and of John Galt and Dagny inside the train tunnel. In the absence of additional comment from anyone in the group, Joe took the discussion to a more abstract level by reminding them, "Face it, man, it's selfishness that's made this country great. I mean, look at the skyscrapers in New York." He'd point eastward with an outstretched left hand. And then he'd ask, "Who made those buildings, when you think of it? Why're those things there?" He paused. "Because of the efforts of selfish and superior men, that's why."

To a certain extent Joe identified with those superior men. In his junior year, he began synthesizing a unique piano style that brought together elements as diverse as the chordal structures of Bill Evans, the left-hand virtuosity of Art Tatum, and the harmonic palettes of Scriabin, Stravinsky, and Berg. It was something new, especially in Tucson; and, within their music-filled basement halls, friends and acquaintances at the Music building often acknowledged the originality of what they could hear Joe fashioning day after day in the seclusion of his practice room. Wayne Belli was particularly impressed, and, with genuine admiration, standing on the very same spot from whence Jennifer had enounced her ideas on romance, Wayne said to him, slowly, "Those are some *really cool* sounds there. You'll go far, Joe."

In his senior year Joe landed a weekly job playing the cocktail lounge Thursday nights at the old Falkland Inn, downtown. He shuddered and then marvelled at the near-coincidence of names, wondered, privately, whether the place had any connection to the Hotel Wayne-Faulkland, in New York, where so many Ayn Rand heroes and heroines have their most fateful encounters. On the morning of his first engagement Joe dipped into his well-thumbed copy of *Atlas Shrugged* and re-read that passage where genius composer Richard Halley plays his soaring, triumphant Fifth Concerto amid the lofty Atlantis guild of great men.

VI

Following graduation in 1964, Joe sold his piano in Merced, packed the rest of his belongings, said good-bye to family, friends, and Mrs. Pratt, and moved on to southern California, hoping to find his way there as a musician. He had his ultimate sights on making New York by 1970. ("If Howard Roark could, why can't I?" he wrote once in a letter to Al, from whom he'd bought the aging Plymouth a year earlier.) During his first few weeks there Joe stayed out in Claremont with his aunt, uncle, and two male cousins, who were all uniformly awed by his technique and talents, if somewhat baffled by instrumental jazz and more so by his piano style (he played them a sampler in the basement of their church); and they found his Ayn Rand ideas positively "kooky," as the older cousin liked putting it. They helped him navigate the city and locate an apartment in a complex conveniently located nearer to Los Angeles. With a $300 graduation gift from his parents and some savings, Joe bought himself a used upright Yamaha piano.

In his wallet Joe carried letters of introduction from Wayne Belli and from his piano teacher, Dr. Epstein. Shortly after arrival he dropped in on a local buddy of Wayne's, a lanky, long-armed Negro tenor man named Skip, who furnished him a few more names, and whose quiet, delicate wife cooked them dinner. "Wayne's been saying great things about you," the guy said to him casually over that evening's beer and spare ribs, and Joe naturally was pleased.

At first, however, the gigs came slow and less than steadily. Joe soon found out, for one, that his genuinely unique piano synthesis was far less striking in the urban bazaar of L.A. than it had been in provincial Tucson. To his surprise, top musicians abounded (among them none other than Stravinsky, whose house he walked by once), and the main difficulties he faced came not from the power of incompetents and immoral altruists, as Ayn Rand had led him to expect, but from the too few jobs for too many players, of which even the mediocrities were highly qualified and skilled. Most of the existing bands, moreover, were stably constituted and in no need of his abilities as yet. Hence, in mid-August, with a view to making ends meet, Joe auditioned for a half-time post as exercise pianist at Madame Olga's Westwood School of Ballet, where, after a week's delay and a second audition, he was hired. In addition, on bulletin boards at laundromats, supermarkets, and campuses, he thumb-tacked red-inked ads offering music lessons. At first he advertised only for advanced students, but, when no one called, he took on the few interested parties who phoned, regardless of their age and level. He believed his rent and food costs were now more or less covered.

Joe also called on Mr. Gold, his former bandmaster at Merced High, who had moved to L.A. four years ago. However, from Mrs. Gold's tense, pinched voice, partly drowned out by telephone static and the sounds of a sobbing child, he learned of their recent separation and of Mr. Gold's finally having landed — in her words — "some hot-shot contract with one of those big, gaudy hotels out in Vegas." A nonplussed Joe offered his regrets and hung up.

A tip in late summer from tenor man Skip, who had chanced

to see a classified ad for a pianist in a local paper, did lead to a job playing solo piano during band intermissions at an extravagant Hollywood Hills wedding reception. Though none of the combo members said more than "Hello" to Joe, the vision of radiantly beautiful young newlyweds, surrounded by loving friends and relatives, aroused in him vague desires of someday moving within that world. The dream came slightly closer when a ruddy, voluble, executive type in a pink sports coat, hovered, whiskey in hand, over the piano and sang along with Joe's duly clear renditions. At the end of the set he suggested that Joe drop by Kaplan-Quigley Motion Picture Studios, an obscure, poor-man's-Roger-Corman sort of outfit. In all innocence Joe showed up at K-Q early next Monday, expecting to find a job; as it turned out, their lead musician had dislocated his left arm in a weekend surfing accident. So Joe filled in for him on the spot, reading piano and electric-organ charts for the soundtrack of two low-budget, cops-and-corpses items (*Snipers* and *Pushers Die!*)

As he cashed the sizeable paycheck he remembered that Ayn Rand too had first begun in Hollywood, though he was later disappointed when his brief studio stint generated no such further work for him. Every gig seemed self-contained, and each one usually required constant phoning, driving, auditioning, and just plain waiting.

For his first few months, Joe's sole regular income came from pounding oom-pahs and oom-pah-pahs at Madame Olga's, and — less so — from his ever-shifting roster of pupils. Business did pick up in November, when he was invited to blow piano with Skip's quintet at a garish, grandiose "Pre-Holiday Luau" thrown by the biggest U.S.C. fraternity of them all. At the urging of the House president, members of the band wore multiple leis and identical Hawaiian shirts; and Joe's expert riffs and affably boyish manner won over the co-players, who provided him several leads for possible work that Christmas season. One name led to the next, and, when he finally awoke to the late-morning hush of New Year's Day, he felt pleasantly exhausted from the sheer number of gigs he'd played. Thereafter he enjoyed the good fortune of doing dance jobs at least one night per weekend, sometimes with Skip's group, sometimes with new contacts. As part of his formal attire, Joe took to wearing a tie-clasp shaped like a dollar sign, though no one took note of it.

Occasionally he entertained thoughts of launching his own trio. A dream-job starting in mid-1965, however, temporarily altered Joe's life-course: the gracious, 1910's-style Hotel Wellington in downtown L.A. hired him on a three-months' trial basis to play solo two nights a week in their legendary South Seas Lounge, home to many once-struggling jazz pianists and singers.

"COME HEAR JOE GONZALEZ
CARESSING THE IVORY 88!
COME DRINK & RELAX
TO HIS FRESH, NEW, MELLO TONES!"

said the silvery-blue block-letters circling, in round-robin fashion, his tilted, chiaroscuro photo at dead center of the hotel's front-lobby posters. Although nervous at first, Joe more than lived up to expectations. His distinctive technique, range of sonorities, and large and varied repertory pleased many patrons, impressed fellow musicians in the audience, and earned him a brief write-up in the *L.A. Times,* all of which led to a three-month extension of his contract.

With these successes came increased attentions from women, and a series of lively affairs. Joe's phase as a mere "make-out artist" was well behind him, yet his romantic dealings were still firmly guided by the rules of engagement he'd learned from Jennifer Jaspers and Ayn Rand. No girl in fact had caused him much pain in the years since Jennifer, thanks precisely to the far-reaching insights she'd passed on to him that distant April morning in his practice room. Meanwhile Joe seldom visited his next of kin in Claremont, and had not been home to Merced since the week after college graduation, though occasionally he sent short notes relaying to them his triumphs, and also continued to write to Al. He had bought a brand new VW square-back, and had come to regard past memories as a pointless indulgence.

VII

Then, in 1966, things started going wrong for Joe. Rock-and-roll, for one, was fast imposing itself as the in beat, the normal sound, the music of choice for American dancing. Most Greek-house parties, for instance, now hired rock groups, as did the discotheques and the newer clubs and hotels along the coast. The availability of jazz and cocktail gigs rapidly dwindled to about a third of what it had once been, and anybody dependent on those styles for income found it necessary to adapt in order to survive. Some pianists and guitarists pared their chordal ranges down to three, maybe four basic triads, gladly or indifferently in some cases, cynically and distastefully in others. Horn players had it the worst, their role in rock music being negligible. A few side men whom Joe had previously worked with — including Skip — now found the job scene much too tight, and decided to take their chances in Paris and Copenhagen, where jazz, a *Downbeat* columnist had claimed, was still alive and well. Joe was among the four guys who assisted Skip and his wife with last-minute packing business and saw the couple off wistfully onto their New York-bound bus at the Continental Trailways station. In a postcard from Vienna some months later, Skip informed his former drummer, "These German-speaking folks seem to dig our sounds! We're doing okay," and the drummer passed the card around to Skip's friends, Joe included.

As for Joe, his own gigs schedule shrank considerably, and began approaching the blank look of his first calendar from three summers ago. The South Seas Lounge at least happened to be among the area's final holdouts for cocktail, and his ever-improving pianism continued to attract fair to middling audiences. In a sudden, surprise move, however, the venerable hotel was bought up by New York's Omni-Telectrono Chemicals and Containers Corporation, leading to a swift relocation of the older managers, and the arrival of a younger team, business-school graduates strongly sensitized to modern trends. The time was ripe for change, rumor ran, and Joe was soon under polite pressures to simplify and update his act. Less cool-jazz, more loud rock sounds; less Brazilian, more American; less soaring and ripple, more boom-boom.

As he concluded with a Cole Porter medley one summer evening, Joe noticed Tom Ellsworth, a Stanford graduate who now managed the lounge area, sitting casually in his cream-colored suit on the arm of one of the Victorian club chairs nearby. A tall, attractive man, square-faced and blue-eyed, with thin eyebrows and a lock of light-brown hair dangling down the right side of his forehead, he smiled at Joe and, after the applause and tips were done, signalled him to sit down on the adjoining chair for a nightcap.

Some small talk and half a drink later, Tom Ellsworth suggested, still smiling, that Joe concentrate on rock and roll, perhaps also singing along as he played.

"But I can't sing," a baffled Joe replied.

"Well, Joe, you can learn, can't you?" Ellsworth countered, giving him a friendly pat on the arm. "And you certainly could play more folk and rock."

"I do, though," Joe came back vigorously. "About two tunes per set."

"Maybe, Joe, but they sure don't *sound* like folk or rock."

"Mr. Ellsworth, I..."

"Tom, please."

"How's that?"

"Tom. Call me Tom."

"Tom, I can't be forced to play something that's not me. Rock and roll simply isn't my style."

The boss now turned sterner. "Joe, we're not 'forcing' you to do anything. All we're asking from you is more flexibility. Why be so selfless?"

Joe smiled and shook his head as he realized he was living a scene from Ayn Rand. "I'm not being selfless. On the contrary. This is the most selfish thing you'll every see a guy do."

Tom Ellsworth's face took on a colder aspect as his thin brows narrowed. "Suit yourself, then. I only wanted you to be a team player. It's a free country, though, and you're completely free to do whatever you want." He got up and turned on his heels, leaving Joe to finish his drink and pack his sheet music. The only patrons remaining under the soft lights were a thirtyish couple in the back row, boy's reddish hair short, girl's golden strands long. Their lips were still pressed together in what seemed a permanent kiss even as Joe departed.

Joe's contract was not renewed in the fall. Shortly thereafter, the South Seas Lounge was terminated, its space gutted and eventually remade into a cavernous disco place called "Rascals."

Meanwhile Joe panicked. He took on extra pupils, combed every paper's want ads, stayed overtime doing one-and-two-and-three routines at Madame Olga's, and, finally — due precisely to his nerves and fear — botched up a double-bass audition with the Anaheim City Symphony the day before Halloween. Driving home that afternoon in the rush-hour traffic, he wondered if he might've been deluding himself all along as to his talents, and grimly looked forward to a beer and a long nap. As he inched the year-old VW square-back into his parking lot, he caught sight of two strong-looking, square-jawed, broad-shouldered males poised at parade-rest on either side of his front stairway. Their movie-star-handsome faces radiated a look of firm, calm self-confidence that was proudly aloof and inscrutable. They each of them held their thick athletic arms crossed in an exact rectangle framing their taut barrel-chests. Their long, fair, muscular legs, covered with peach-fuzz and delimited by Bermuda shorts and sockless loafers, showed the fine precision of classical sculpture. And their air of high disdain was further enhanced by the cigarettes tensed tightly between their lips.

Emerging from the car, Joe saw the white Greek lettering on their blue polo shirts. Their close-cropped hair also appeared faintly Greek and seemed to shine still brighter amid the light and shadows of the vestigial dusk. They looked strangely alike, and indeed, Joe realized on coming closer that they were, in fact, twins.

In an almost identical gesture, they plucked out and cast aside their cigarettes.

"You Joe Gonzalez?" said the guy on his right, his jutjaw barely moving.

"Yeah," Joe answered. "What's up?"

"Nancy's our sister," said the guy on the left in the very same nondescript voice, though his lips opened slightly wider, baring his top row of perfect teeth.

The first one picked up the ball. "We also hear you've been saying real nasty things about fraternities."

Joe said nothing at first. The three stood frozen in silence for a moment.

Joe had first met Nancy Rearden at a private gig in Hancock Park a month ago. The lively, middle-aged host and hostess who'd hired him had just moved into their recently finished Spanish-style mansion, and Joe was doing background divertimentos to their house-warming party, along with occasional accompaniments to the impromptu serenades by bolder and more festive guests. From the piano he'd seen Nancy drifting around and about the vast, crowded living-room, her dark gown and single-jewelled brooch contrasting sharply with her bright-red lips and auburn mane.

Halfway through the evening, after having seemingly talked to everyone present, she floated by, leaned onto the curvature of the baby-grand, and, in a rich contralto, sang along to both of his choruses to "Summertime." As usual for such occasions he wore his dollar-sign tie-clasp. With the tips of her fingers she lightly applauded his closing cascade of arpeggios, flashing her scarlet nails, and then, pointing discreetly at his necktie, she asked, "I take it you're an Ayn Rand fan?"

Joe nodded and said "Yup" while starting on his intro to "Tonight." Curiously, no one had ever noticed his ornament, or at least inquired about it.

The girl's elegant little smile showed elegant little teeth. "I've read all of her stuff again and again."

The two of them hit it right off, especially since they were almost the only people present under thirty. Though not a blood-relative, Nancy was the favorite niece of Mrs. Rearden, who occasionally ambled by, tossing a terse, "Good work, young man," at Joe, and moving on. Throughout the rest of the gig Nancy kept returning to share Joe's bench, humming or singing when she could, while during his break they evoked their preferred passages from their great mentor, the fateful go-between in this boy-meets-girl episode.

And so, after the guests had trickled out at 1 a.m. and Joe had gotten his $80 check from a gruff, tight-lipped Mr. Rearden, the two went out for a drive on the L.A. Freeway, ignoring a lustrous imitation Taj-Mahal here and a multi-hued waterfall there, discussing Ayn Rand's books and essays all the while. As the hour approached for Joe to take Nancy back to the Mustang she had parked at her aunt's and uncle's house, she admitted to having joined a sorority long ago, but then quit six months later because it was too "collectivist-oriented," and besides she couldn't stomach the charitable works. "People should learn to fend for themselves," she said.

They were both exhausted now. Conversation waned, and Joe turned on the radio. A newscaster calmly reported stepped-up B-52 raids over North Vietnam, prompting Joe to reflect, "Don't know what I'll do if I get drafted. My brother was in the Army, and he hated it."

"Well," she replied in a wry tone, "whatever you do, don't go fleeing to the People's State of England. They've got socialists in government there."

"I know what you mean," Joe responded after a short pause, yielding his left lane to a speeding white Cadillac convertible. "We've got the draft here, though."

"A necessary evil," she came back immediately. "After all, the Soviets are preaching world conquest. They've already taken over one-third of the globe's population, including China."

"Hmm. Can't say I know much about foreign policy," he granted. "But, I mean, should we be bombing peasant villages? Just doesn't seem right to me."

"'Peasant villages' my foot," she echoed with a profound

disdain. "Ayn herself says those villages are enemy strongholds. *That's* immorality for you."

As with Jennifer seven years before, Nancy had gotten Joe to thinking once again. Moreover he sensed an opportunity fully to rectify some major errors from his naive and inexperienced youth, those college-freshman blunders that to this day made him cringe with embarrassment. At the ramp and stoplight that led to the Rearden's neighborhood he heard Nancy's eloquent reminder, "This country's special, Joe. Whatever defects we may have, we're the greatest nation in the history of mankind," and Joe felt a strange uplift within him. "And it's worth fighting for," she summed up.

He even considered making a pass at her as they said their good-nights, but decided to hold off until they'd gone out a couple more times. And so he jumped at her last-minute suggestion that he join her next week at the Philharmonic, featuring Van Cliburn doing Rachmaninoff's Second. (Her musical tastes were uncannily similar to Jennifer's.) Because she frequented Objectivist chapter meetings at U.S.C., she knew all of Ayn Rand's latest pronouncements, and at intermission and over post-concert beer and pizza she updated him on Ayn's recent views on the war, and on the evils and idiocy of the new Civil-Rights laws, which had caused the riots in Watts.

Believing in fair exchange, she accepted Joe's invitation to go see Thelonious Monk in rare public performance at the Venice Jazz Oasis the following Thursday. Unfortunately, from early on that evening the relationship turned sour, for Nancy took to yawning uncontrollably through much of the first set, and giggling under her breath whenever Monk did his lonely dance up on the stage during solos by his sidemen.

An occasional hostile glance darted their way from neighboring tables. With his finger on his lips, with pleading words, now gently, now angrily, Joe repeatedly signalled Nancy to desist. He even grabbed the girl by the forearm toward the end of "Light Blue," threatening her through his gritted teeth, but she merely shook her head in a broad semi-circle, and, writhing in her seat, giggled even more energetically.

Finally, during the lengthy applause and round of hurrahs Joe shot up, tossed a ten-dollar bill onto the wire-spool tabletop, zigzagged his way to the glass door, and made for his automobile. As he fumbled for the ignition switch there came the sound of high heels clicking hurriedly across the pavement.

The engine turned as Nancy's front knuckles rapped authoritatively on the right-hand windowpane. "Joe, open up, c'mon, stop being ridiculous," he heard her voice exhorting him. He smiled as he watched the silver-clad figure scurrying about and over to his side. "Joe," her curled, now less elegant mouth admonished, "you can't leave me here like this. Just what is your problem?"

Joe rolled down his window. "What's my problem?" he replied, raising his voice, then pointed and waved his left finger in her face. "I don't like you laughing at Thelonious Monk, *that's* my goddamn problem. Besides, you've been embarrassing the hell outta me."

Nancy's eyeballs rolled, her lips grimaced. "Oh, come *on,* Joe. That savage music, sounds like jungle noises, I just couldn't believe it." Slowly, mocking, she folded her arms, swayed her body from side to side. "Not to mention what's-his-face lumbering around like some street drunk or crazy animal. And those beatniks in there, it was ludicrous, really."

Joe revved up the engine. "Well, babe, if that's what you sincerely think," he replied more softly, "then you c'n go back to your frat-rat friends and fuck off."

"Oh, you little..." She seized the outside latch and managed to half-open his door, pulling him out a slight fraction. He regained the car door and banged it shut; she tumbled against an adjacent white Mercedes. He drove around, tires screeching, and briefly glimpsed her in the rear-view mirror, looking his way, hands in her well-coiffed hair, and apparently stunned. A small crowd had gathered by the door of the Oasis, watching. Joe's anger over the incident came out in a letter he wrote to Al later that evening.

He had vaguely recalled Nancy's alluding to her twin brothers some time after the gig where he and she had first met.

"Yeah, so what's up," Joe now asked them, briskly and flatly.

"What's up is you don't go treatin' our sister that way," said twin number one.

"What way."

"You swore at our sister. You don't go swearin' at a lady," said number two, raising his jaw. "And don'tcha go puttin' down fraternities either."

"Hey, c'mon, man, she was askin' for it..."

Two's volume grew higher, "You pushed 'er out of y'r car..."

"That's a lie..."

"...and she had t'phone us t'get back home. She was in tears and real shaken up."

"Look, man, she was actin' real bitchy, makin' a fool of me in public, and she got what she deserved."

Their strong, manly, decisive hands grabbed Joe, number one's by the lapel, number two's by the neck. "I don't care what she was doin,' y'damn Mex," said a voice, Joe no longer could tell whose, "you don't go treatin' our sister like that."

Joe felt himself propelled toward the metal bannister, and his left shoulder hit a sharp edge. His glasses flipped off as he tumbled onto the lawn.

"Try any of that with her again and there'll be none of you left," he heard one say.

"C'mon, Hank," said the other, "they're expectin' us at the House."

The car they took off in sounded like a low-flung sports model. Joe lay still for a few minutes, then pawed about for his glasses and hurried dizzily inside, forgetting to check his mailbox. He collapsed onto his double bed, oblivious to the loud, hard beat of "Satisfaction" coming from the stereo next door.

Twelve hours had gone by when he awoke the next morning, still fully clothed, his necktie only slightly loose, his glasses still poised over his forehead.

Several loud knocks on the door made him start and sit up until he remembered with relief that it was a beginning student, showing up for his third piano lesson. A 17-year-old kid who liked hinting that his cash came from dealing in Acapulco "tea," all he wanted to learn was simple chords and basic riffs, with a view to putting together a rock-and-roll band someday.

"Just a sec," Joe shouted, then took off his necktie, put on his loafers, and reeled in a daze toward the door. The thin, scraggly-bearded boy stood there and sheepishly admitted to not having practiced for today's lesson but, producing some bills, offered to pay the nine dollars anyway. Joe took the money and told him to return next week.

Then, remembering about the mail, he reopened the front door and ambled down the hall, still groggy. The sole back item in his blue metal box was a notice, forwarded from Merced, instructing him to report for a physical examination at the local Selective Service center.

Joe's health was excellent. Despite his nearsightedness he passed his physical, and soon received his induction papers. He read them several times and, as he idled aimlessly at the Yamaha, a minor triad there, and augmented arpeggio there, he recalled a couple of guys back in Merced who, when faced with the draft, had simply gone across the border and moved in with relatives. But he saw little future for himself as a piano man in Nogales or Chihuahua or anywhere in what Ayn Rand referred to as the People's State of Mexico, and he tended to assume that, Skip's good-news postcard notwithstanding, things in Europe were much worse for the freedom of the individual. Eventually he set his sights on being an Army musician, only to find out that there were no available slots for pianists or bass players (seldom employed by military ensembles anyway), and that his trumpet-playing abilities weren't good enough for him to make band. He looked into the language program, but the military bureaucracy proved impenetrable and his Spanish too rusty, and he finally ended up in a regular Army outfit. His chief concern by now was that lack of access to a piano would result in his getting out of practice and his technique deteriorating.

In 1967 Joe's outfit was assigned to overseas duty. During the toughest weeks of Basic Training his Ayn Rand books, along with his new round of letters from Al and his parents and his sisters, had served as much-needed consolation. Many times before departure he'd heard officers speak forcefully on the horrors and the threat of world communism, and on the need to stop the Russians over there before they reached us over here, something he had already learned from reading Ayn Rand. Once in Southeast Asia, he found the hot and humid climate well beyond anything he'd imagined, whereas the native people reminded him of people he had known and seen in Mexico, and he wondered on occasion where the Russians were. And when, after a month in the Central Highlands, his unit came under guerrilla artillery fire, an Allied fleet of Phantoms and F-111s misgauged and accidentally hit the far edge of Joe's bunker, where his two comrades — each of them Texas Hispanics — as well as Joe himself were all killed instantly. In his wallet was a much-handled photocopy of a key page from John Galt's climactic speech in *Atlas Shrugged*.

Joe had requested that, in case of termination, his remains be interred at the old Spanish cemetery in Merced. The body having been duly processed and shipped back home, a night-long wake drew family members ranging from a great-grandfather and all four grandparents to both of his sisters, together with a good many aunts, uncles, and cousins, as well as numerous friends, (including those from Claremont and Las Cruces). Shortly after sunrise the relatives and their guests moved on quietly to the small adobe church of La Guadalupe, its white wooden steeple, turquoise trim, and replastered walls emerging in clear outline against the reddish-brown hill and dark-blue morning sky. Also present in the congregation was Mrs. Pratt, seated alone on a rear pew in her white hat and gloves. Chief pallbearer was Joe's brother Al, who now led the silent throng on through the camposanto's rusted gate. His eyes surveying the cactuses, the tumbleweeds tossing about in fence corners, the makeshift wooden crosses bearing colorful religious ornaments, and the dozens of immobile faces gathered before him, he delivered a brief yet eloquent graveside oration, partly in Spanish for the oldtimers' benefit.

The tomb next to Joe's ditch was for Preciliano and Dionisia Gurulé, whose weathered metal crucifix featured a sacred heart, and whose children Mrs. González had often played house with in the past. At Joe's behest, there was no priest present at the burial. A trembling, tense-lipped Al cast the initial, ritual spadeful of Arizona-yellow earth. The two gravediggers, one Anglo and one not, managed the rest.

Hitler Reconsidered *

Hitler Reconsidered: An American Conservative Takes a Second Look at the Third Reich, and Finds More Than a Few Things to Recommend, by Will E. McPazzo. Washington, D.C: Adroit Ventures Institute, 1986. 200 pp. $19.50

Countless sacred cows have been gored by the Reagan Revolution, and many liberal dogmas have been consigned to history's scrap heap. But then, wasn't it about time sensible Americans asked if environmental regulations might be *harmful* to the environment, or labor unions bad for labor? or Affirmative Action actually hazardous to blacks and Civil Rights laws a pox on all concerned? In sum, after five decades of profligate New Deal, Fair Deal, and Great Society spending, the American people are finally seeing the light and realizing that government meddling in the economy only makes things worse, period.

Such at least has long been the contention of Dr. Will E. McPazzo, scion of a renowned conservative clan and Director of the Adroit Ventures Institute, a respected conservative think tank in Washington D.C. On more than one occasion Dr. McPazzo has been known to quip, "I was against the New Deal then; I still am now."

One large liberal totem, though, still remains: the so-called "Grande Alliance" that FDR made with the Soviets against Hitler. Here especially McPazzo brings fresh thinking with his highly polemical book (and runaway best-seller), *Hitler*

---

* This mock book review originally appeared in *The Gharial,* Williamstown, MA. All of the historical data cited in this satire are true, and all of the attributed quotations are accurate.

Reconsidered: An American Conservative Takes a Second Look at the Third Reich, and Finds More than a Few Things to Recommend. As one might expect, McPazzo's balanced and open-minded approach has elicited harsh debate among the pundits. A lead editorial in *Commentary* speculated that "there can be such a thing as excessive anti-communism, and McPazzo's bizarre book suggests as much." The curmudgeonly *American Nationalist,* by contrast, gave McPazzo warm if cautious praise, while *U.S. Report* broke with tradition and ran its first book review ever, noting that "McPazzo has raised some hard-nosed if troubling questions for our time." On the other hand the London *Economist* haughtily dismissed *Hitler Reconsidered* as "a perfectly silly book" and judged "*signor*" McPazzo "a disgrace to Anglo-Saxon conservativism."

With his crackling, whip-like prose that rivals Bill Buckley's or William Safire's or Pat Buchanan's, Dr. McPazzo forcefully argues that siding with the Soviets against Germany in 1942 was "an incalculable mistake, the start of a fifty-year disaster" whose consequences we are still paying today. While solidly deploring the "stupid anti-Semitism of Adolf Hitler and his cronies," McPazzo finds this "heart-rending minus" largely balanced out by a substantial if oft-ignored plus, namely, Hitler's staunch anti-communism.

McPazzo marshals ample data on this score, reminding us, for example, that just two months after taking office in 1933, the Nazi government wiped out the German Communist Party and "carted off its leaders to Dachau," thereby smashing the biggest Marxist party in Europe. "Only a bleeding-heart Liberal would see much wrong with *that!*" McPazzo wryly reflects, noting that, throughout Europe and America, the business communities and conservative press gallantly praised Hitler for his "war to the death on Marxism."

McPazzo's "second look" next zeroes in on crucial Nazi support in helping General Francisco Franco ("a great man" warmly admired by Patrick Buchanan's father as well as by the entire McPazzo family) overthrow Spain's "Red Republic" in

1936-39; and he is so bold, moreover, as to dismiss the "so-called French Resistance" as "Moscow-directed" and "communist-tainted," and hence fair game for Hitler's objectives. What McPazzo finds most laudable in Hitler, however, was his "anti-Bolshevik crusade to the East" and the death-blow it dealt to 20 million Soviets. "Can anybody who killed 20 million Soviets be all that bad?" McPazzo ventures to speculate. In this regard, he quotes — music and all — a song sung by the Young Americans for Freedom in the wake of President Reagan's 1980 electoral triumph: "Deck the halls with commie corpses/ Fa la la la lah, la lah la lah/'Tis the time to be remorseless/Now we wield our sharp stiletti/Carve the pinks into confetti/Fa la la la lah, la lah la lah."

Alas, we know the outcome: the Soviets in 1944 proceeded to embark on their war of westward expansion, invading Germany "without provocation" even as the liberal West stood idly by and appeased Moscow instead. The naked Soviet conquest of East Europe and Eastern Germany in the 1940's provides clear proof that, if anything, "we in the West strongly needed Hitler's anti-Bolshevist bulwark," McPazzo concludes.

German capitalism and its great strides in the 1930's and early '40's also earn high marks in McPazzo's book. By 1940 the German economy was Europe's most developed and prosperous, a classic "miracle." Growth in the corporate sector from 1933 to 1941, particularly in steel and chemicals, surpassed growth in all previous fifty years combined. Moreover, McPazzo points out, in contrast with Communist states, Hitler never confiscated U.S. business investments in Germany, which in 1940 stood at half a billion dollars.*

Indeed, Dr. McPazzo asserts, GM, Ford, and IT&T made large amounts of money in their German truck, tank, and fighter

---

* On this basis, Dr. McPazzo applies Professor Jeanne Kirkpatrick's renowned model and places the Nazi system in the "authoritarian" rather than "totalitarian" category. He concludes, moreover, that "the only truly 'totalitarian regimes' have been Communist ones."

aircraft divisions during the Nazi period. In a supreme irony, it was American aerial bombardment that reduced those firms' German plants to rubble, a violation of property rights for which a contrite U.S. government later paid millions of dollars in damages to its corporate victims.

Nevertheless McPazzo forcefully rejects the anti-Semitism of the Nazi leaders, which he finds "quite abhorrent." Dr. McPazzo, it should be said, has become highly sensitive to allegations that his "second look" at Nazism somehow stems from ethnic prejudice on his part. And in order to quell such rumors he recently published in the Adroit Ventures monthly magazine, *Objectives,* a hard-hitting essay entitled "The Case against Nazi anti-Semitism." Invoking libertarian philosopher Ayn Rand, he strenuously repudiates as "emotional, not rational" the "primitive, quasi-African collectivism" that led Germany to treat Jews not as individuals but as members of a group. (As Dr. McPazzo emphatically asserted on *Firing Line,* long before Margaret Thatcher later did on British television, "Groups don't exist, societies don't exist, I would even say that Jews do not exist. Only individuals do, and their families.") And McPazzo has consistently opposed all state collectivisms, whether they take the form of Nuremberg Laws or Affirmative Action programs.*

And yet even in Hitler's camps McPazzo finds silver linings. He observes with almost childlike glee that "professional Communists" from all over Europe, including 3 million Red Army soldiers, died in the camps too ("And I'll drink to that, by jingo!") In addition there were the half-million Gypsies, "notorious for their criminal element" — in McPazzo's own words — and hence Hitler's way of "getting tough on crime." And he is overt in his praise of Hitler's decisive action against the growing problem of homosexuality. He forcefully

---

* In this connection, McPazzo has gone on record as being against the category of "Crimes against Humanity" that was applied at the Nuremberg Trials. For future use he proposes in its stead "Crimes against the Individual." "I don't give a hoot about humanity," he states frankly in that article; "I care only about the individual."

cites Norman Podhoretz, who in *Harper's* in 1977 singled out
the gay subculture as the chief cause of malignant "pacifism," of
"hostility to one's country," of an "appeasement" mentality that
has long been weakening the West in its battle against Soviet
expansionism.* "You just can't say that *everybody* in the camps
was absolutely innocent," McPazzo soberly reflects. "Would that
life were that simple."

Not that everything Nazi, however, looks rosy to Will
McPazzo — far from it. His concluding chapter makes a point
of confronting Nazism's ugliest flaws, for example the restraints
on freedom of expression. ("Few things are as sacred," McPazzo
remarks, "as the right to speak our minds, to talk back and say
whatever it is we think" — a right that, he observes, is currently
"under siege from campus leftists, multiculturalists and
feminists.") And the absence of elections under Nazi rule
inspires some almost dizzyingly eloquent words of condemnation
from McPazzo's able pen.

His very harshest terms, however, are reserved for the
Reich's byzantine fiscal policies, particularly its governmental
price controls ("arguably among the most repellent features of
fascism," McPazzo angrily notes). Above all he singles out "the
heavy hand of government regulation" that strait-jacketed
countless German businessmen, each one of which, McPazzo
insists, "probably suffered more than all of the world's alleged
underdogs put together." This brings us to what have become the
most controversial portions of *Hitler Reconsidered,* namely, his
paradoxical argument that, though German capitalism prospered
under the Reich, Germany's businessmen actually deserve to be
memorialized along with the other victims of Nazism. He has,
as we know, recently launched a tireless campaign to have
monuments and statues erected in Germany, Poland, and
Washington D.C, in remembrance of what he calls "the
Unknown German Businessman, 1933-1945."

Still, in the balance, Dr. McPazzo believes Nazi Germany to

---

* Norman Podhoretz, "The Culture of Appeasement," *Harper's,*
October 1977, pp. 25-32

have been a safer bet for America than was Communist Russia. In this regard he notes, "Hitler built the camps, yet he never erected a Berlin Wall." Or in the words he quotes from literary critic Diana Trilling, "More people died under Stalin than under Hitler," and the conclusion to be drawn is obvious. Had America encouraged a healthily capitalist and anti-communist Nazi Germany, we would not have spent the following four decades fighting off Russian proxy troops in Korea, Cuba, Indochina, Grenada, Chile, Libya, Angola, Grenada, Nicaragua, and a host of other Soviet colonies.

McPazzo's closing reflections in his "Epilogue" remind us that, throughout the 1930's, Western conservatives "found *much* to recommend" in European fascism. And the time may have come, he quietly argues, for U.S. conservatives to reclaim that long-forgotten legacy. He brings up the little known fact that fewer Americans died fighting Hitler's Reich (50 thousand) than were to perish in holding off Soviet expansionism in Korea and Indochina (100 thousand). "Who, then, was America's real enemy?" Dr. McPazzo darkly asks.

McPazzo's book ends with the words, "I was against Roosevelt's war on Germany then. I still am now. And if it ever comes down once again to choosing between Nazism and Liberal-Communism, I'll take Nazism." *Hitler Reconsidered* is surely fated to become a key document of our time.

The Collection

I

Zoltan Jones was known around town for two things in particular. The first was his vast collection of LP recordings, along with his prodigious, not to say monstrous knowledge of the classics, something we often got a glimpse of in his music reviews for the *Daily Californian*. Second was the guy's name, which, believe it or not, was no contrivance. As the story goes, his Hungarian-Jewish mother had managed to persuade her adoring husband, an expatriate Brit, to name their first-born son after her late beloved dad.

I remember meeting him late one morning in the mid-sixties, at the Caffé Mediterraneum. My new roommate Mitch and I were sprawled out at a square table by the picture window, he busily correcting student papers for his Philosophy section, me leafing indifferently through the Sunday *Chronicle-Examiner,* when this slender yet rugged-looking sort in an untucked striped shirt and very faded blue jeans ambled casually our way, capuccino in hand.

"What's up, old man?" said the stranger to Mitch. He had dark frizzy hair, high cheekbones, and a sallow complexion partly covered with beard stubble.

"Hey, Zolly Jones, how goes it? have a seat." That's how I learned his nickname, from Mitch, who now introduced us.

"Oh," I couldn't help remarking as I stretched out my hand, "you're the music reviewer."

"Yeah." That was his entire response to me for the initial five minutes, during which the two of them started talking New York, from whence they both came. (New Yorkers, I'd long ago noticed, have this code they switch to whenever they connect together, and if you're with them too but can't speak the dialect, well, tough shingles.) Feeling hungry, I got up to fetch some stuffed cabbage and a cup of Viennese.

They were sitting in momentary silence when, armed with my lunch tray, I came back and reclaimed my window seat.

I had always liked the Bach-Beethoven-Brahms Old-Masters crowd, and had oohed and been awed at how much Jones seemed to know about them. "So where'd you learn so much about music?" I asked.

He shrugged his shoulders. "Got to do *something* with your life, I guess, right?"

Mitch was gathering and straightening up his students' papers. "C'mon, Zolly," he said, pointing at me with his thumb. "Tell the guy about your collection."

Jones slowly lit up a Salem, then took in and exhaled a first puff. "I have four thousand record albums," he stated matter-of-factly, and added, with his index finger slightly raised, "operas and oratorios counting as one each."

"Good God, man. How d'you keep them straight?"

He tapped off some burnt ashes, then spread out his hands. "I just do. They're like an extended family. Kind of like Bach and his twenty kids." He mentioned his four different versions of Mozart's *Jupiter,* five renditions of Brahms's Second, three of Mahler's fourth, and so on.

"And I suppose you know the quirks of every single album," I further ventured. The cabbage, I had noted to my chagrin, was only so-so that day.

"Sure," he shot back. "Which guy's Haydn goes too fast, whose the slowest. There's a Beethoven might be romantic and fiery, another that's geometric and four-square. The possibilities are infinite." I could hear the music critic talking.

Mitch, who made no secret of preferring Elvis, Fats, and Jerry Lee to any of those dead Germans, now observed, "Packing's got to be a pretty heavy experience, I s'pose."

"Sheez." Jones had that rare ability to raise one eyebrow, which he now did. "Getting my belongings out here was a major logistical operation. Record boxes beyond counting. Today I guess there's half again as many."

Mitch whistled in amazement.

Zolly, it turns out, was a graduate student in the arcane field of musicology. "It's what they call it," he remarked somewhat jadedly.

"Aha, so that's why you know so much," I speculated.

"Yeah, Jones, that why? Come on, 'fess up," Mitch said, giving him a friendly punch on the arm.

Zolly extinguished what was left of his cigarette. "Look, man, I've listened to the stuff all my life. My mom's a pianist and worked as a music librarian over in Brooklyn. Used to tote the latest records home for me to listen to. I s'pose that's where this addiction started. Anyway, I'm in musicology because of what I've learned from those records, not vice-versa."

"Well, it doesn't necessarily follow," I interjected. "My parents both collected records and even played piano duet, but I didn't come out musical, let alone musicological. Wish I had, though."

Now Mitch stroked his moustache, turned half-serious. "Y'know, Zolly, there's a mystery that's been on my mind."

Jones again raised a left eyebrow as he looked Mitch straight in the eye. "Yeah, well?"

Mitch managed an almost somber aspect as he slowly shut his student rollbook. "Well... uh... what does a musicologist *do*?"

"Good question," he replied in that grainy, dimly sarcastic voice I'd sometimes noted in New York speech. "Depends on your angle, really. Some go looking for motet manuscripts or masses in obscure European archives. Some edit and write about works that everybody's forgotten, like Haydn's operas. Some, like me, want to understand the modern avant-garde better and explain those guys to the public. And others, also like me, get into it 'cause I'm not such a hot-shot string player and I don't compose either."

That was the first though not the last time I talked with Zoltan Jones. Meanwhile we sat around lazily, reminiscing about last year's Free Speech Movement strike, getting passionately pissed over LBJ's escalation policies, and feeling excited about *Jules and Jim,* which we'd each seen recently over at Northside. At some point I fetched a capuccino, Mitch a regular American. Zoltan stayed and had nothing.

Following a lull in conversation and another Salem, Jones glanced at his Timex wristwatch, then asked, "You guys like to come over and see the collection?"

I spooned up the last of my cinnamon-tinted cream and said to Mitch, "How 'bout it?"

Mitch ran a finger through his straight hair and, with a half-smile, said, "Yeah why not? 'Bout the only classical guy I like is Kurt Weill, and that's mostly 'cause of Brecht's lyrics. I'm sort of taken just by the *idea* of Zolly's four thousand, though." He put his student papers inside his black attaché case as we all got up. I left the *Chronicle-Examiner* carefully arranged for the next customer.

There's something about late Sunday mornings in Berkeley, near the start of summer, when the air is crisp and warm, and any rain, one can bet on it, is about as likely as a stray toucan landing somewhere in the tundra. We enjoyed the uphill hike to Zolly's place on Etna Street, a diminutive two-block stretch where brown shingle houses stand half-hidden behind assorted shades of green foliage. And, in a second-story, three-room flat near the corner of Parker, right by a gray and white house resembling a ship, lived Zolly. Zolly and his records.

The place was immaculate and fairly austere. There was a small oval-shaped white dining table, framed by two straight-backed wooden chairs, with some specialized music books opened and neatly dovetailed on one curved end and — the single sign of disorderliness — an unwashed coffee mug and spoon on the other. At our right as we entered was a large, predictably spotless gray couch, and, next to the oval table, a small spinet piano. And lining three of the four walls, in a triple row of shelves that started with the Spaniard Albéniz near the front doorway and ended with Hugo Wolf and one Zemlinsky in the cell-like bedroom, was the Zoltan Jones collection, through which the proprietor now led us for a couple of minutes, like a museum guide on a routine tour.

Each and every one of the record jackets was uniformly sheathed in its own loose plastic envelope. I remarked on the fact.

"Yeah. Same goes for the vinyl inside. A lot of these disks could pass for new."

There was something monkish about it all, with Zolly Jones as abbey. I wondered what kind of sex life he had.

"So there it is," he summed up as we re-entered the living-room area. "A thousand years of man's musical history, stored in these two rooms."

"It's impressive, no doubt," I said slowly as I tried taking in the whole structure.

"Yeah, sure is," Mitch added, placing his attaché case on the arm of the sofa. "Must be lots of dough invested here."

"Well, gotta admit, lots of them I get free from the record companies." He rubbed his hands gleefully. "One of those perks of being a music critic. Hey, have a seat, guys."

I plopped down onto one side of the couch; Mitch slid into the other.

"And what would the gentlemen care to hear, pray tell?"

Mitch raised both his hands. "Hey, Jones, I'm not the one to ask."

Zolly looked over at me. "How about you?"

"Oh, let's see. Brahms's Fourth."

"Sure. Whose? Toscanini's? Furtwängler's? Dorati's?" He pronounced it DOR-ati.

"The first," I said.

His about-face and outstretched right hand were almost a single movement. It was as if he sensed where each individual LP was and could reach for it blind, like a seasoned pianist who instinctively knows the exact placement, one by one, of each of those eighty-eight keys.

Zoltan Jones carefully extracted the disk, and positioned the outer sleeve vertically on a wooden music stand located, presumably for that very purpose, to the left of the stereo set. He lifted the turntable top and, like an antique dealer handling a priceless old engraving, gently pressed down the record in a soft bull's eye. The whole thing resembled a performance.

And there they were, those lush, rich strains, coming to us via Toscanini's NBC players and RCA's engineers to fill and enrich Zolly's spare and minimal flat in Berkeley. Never knew why, but much of Brahms has that wistful feel of early November to it, conjures up images of mid-autumn within me, though obviously not so much of California as of my hometown of Highlands, in northern New Mexico, where I grew up. Soon I was moving my head in rhythm to the first movement's second theme, a tune I've always been taken with, and I wondered what makes it sound so Spanish or flamenco. It's when I listen to such aural beauties that I wish I'd heeded my parents' suggestions and learned to play violin or viola, even triangle or tuba, anything so as to be involved with Brahms's symphonies from the inside. Oh, sure, they're over-played, and can be counted on just one hand; and yet, from the time I'd first heard them on my father's hi-fi set, I've never tired of the Brahms four, and bringing them to life anywhere on earth strikes me as nothing less than a miracle that I envy.

As we entered the slow movement's horn solo I heard Zolly say, "This is what's called Phrygian mode." Then I looked to my right, saw Mozart number 40 in multiple versions, randomly reached for von Karajan's, glanced at the Canaletto print on the front liner, and placed the album on the sofa as I got up for a quick pee break.

"Please put it back," said Zolly with a poker face.

"Oh, right, sorry," I replied, turned around, and did as instructed. Mitch and I cast each other a faint smile.

We sat quietly through the third movement; I remarked to Zolly how, even when he's fast, Brahms sounds languid and melancholy, and the musicologist nodded in assent, "Yeah." By now Mitch had stopped fidgeting in his seat, was even tapping his foot on occasion.

The finale was described by the jacket notes as "tragic," I remember, and while it isn't exactly music to be happy by, it gets fairly exciting, especially under Toscanini. Between movements Zolly had explained its chaconne-like structure, with its recurring bass, and I can sort of follow the first few variations on the opening theme, but to this day I eventually lose track of them, and luckily I had Zolly there that time to point out some of the highlights.

The succession of loud last chords found us all waving our fingers or fists in rhythm, and even Mitch in the end commented, "Hey, this is pretty cool stuff."

"Yeah, Brahms is a good composer," Zolly said with a straight face as he got up and headed for the turntable. "So you've heard one building block out of this edifice. Anything else?"

After our sitting around utterly enveloped by the sounds of a 90-piece symphony, the twittering of a finch outside the window came as a surprise.

"Not right now," I decided after a few moments' temptation. "Got an Incomplete to take care of and I'm way behind. I'll take a rain check on it, though."

"Yeah, and I've got more papers to grade," said Mitch as he picked up his attaché case, then adding, a bit pensively, "You know, this music ain't all that bad. Maybe you've made a convert, Zolly." He may have meant it; he hummed the scherzo much of the way as we trod downhill home. For my part I couldn't resist sharing with him a low-level, obscene joke regarding Brahms's Fourth relayed to me previously by my first true love and only serious girl-friend thus far, a relationship of five years' standing that, almost exactly twelve months ago, had ended in a tearful if amicable parting of the ways. (She had since transferred across the Bay, to Stanford, where, she informed me periodically, her studies and other campus activities were going quite well, thank you...)

But back to Brahms. "Remember how that Fourth Symphony starts out?" I asked Mitch. I whistled the opening. "Well, there's modern lyrics been added to it."

He eyed me half-suspiciously. "Yeah?"

"It goes, 'Fuck yooo, and yooo, and yooo, and yooo...'"

Mitch guffawed like he seldom does. "Hey, I like that." Then he picked up on it, words and all. He'd often break into the song during the next couple of years. Brahms, updated and Americanized, seemed to have further won him over in the wake of Zoltan's lesson.

That initial encounter redoubled my awareness of Zolly's columns in the *Daily Cal.* As I read them amid the constant hum of people on the Terrace or the Bear's Lair the next few months, I could hear his raspy, slightly cocky voice and also sense his priestly awe toward the past masters. At the same time Jones championed those avant-garde moderns whom almost no one liked — Schoenberg, Webern, Boulez, et al. — touting them as this century's Beethovens and Bachs.

In more ways than one, I recall, it was a different sort of summer. For the first time in three years I'd chosen not to spend my vacation months working as a bilingual guide and clerk for the Park Service back home, near Highlands. Instead I'd stayed in the Bay Area and extended my hour-a-day shift — serving cokes and busing tables in the darkwood-panelled depths of the Bear's Lair — into a regular, 25-hour-a-week job. My ongoing Saturday duties as an attendant at the Ashby Launderette, right on the Berkeley-Oakland town line, were certainly convenient enough, even fun, yet barely paid the rent; and I now needed to help finance my summer-school expenses since my parents could afford only half the out-of-state fees.

It had been a year of big changes, besides. The summer before that, I had definitively decided to scrap my major in pre-med and switch to English Lit. Oh, my science grades were fine, and I'd actually enjoyed those monster-sized Chemistry classes in which the professor was little more than a big speck on the horizon. But it somehow seemed as if every pre-med person I met, to a man, was in it just to make a million dollars. I remember my asking them — after lab, say, or in the dorm cafeteria — "What kind of medicine do you think you'll do?" and their promptly replying, "Whichever brings me the *most money*" or "the *biggest bucks*" or "the *quickest cash,* what else?" Then they'd ask me, too, and I'd mention my interest in becoming a psychiatrist and maybe helping people out — and they'd either chuckle or turn silent. I didn't much take to the idea of having guys like them as classmates for my next seven years and as colleagues forever after.

My initial thoughts of a shift in fields had a lot to do with the beginning of the end of life with Lisa, my old sweetheart from Highlands High, for whom, in part, I'd come here to Berkeley, following her just to be where she would be. (Owing to the difference in tuition costs, my parents would just as soon have seen me attend UNM, yet grudgingly conceded that, in my mother's words, "Love Conquers All.") I remember the Sunday morning at Lisa's place on Derby Street, when we awoke to the mingled sounds of a March rain outside and her two roommates and their boy friends puttering about in the kitchen. We kissed and hugged; I yawned, and eventually started telling her of my growing dissatisfaction with pre-med and my considering moving into English.

She sat up, apparently in shock. Her dark, bushy eyebrows frowned. Her large, red lips were folded inward; her first comment was, "And what about us, pray tell?"

"Well, we're together, aren't we? Don't we love each other? Remember W.H. Auden, 'We must love one another or die?' Or Matthew Arnold, 'Ah, love...'"

"Yes, of course," she interrupted, "but, I mean, look." She tossed back her long hair strands, grabbed a stray pillow. "If you dump pre-med to study lit, you're jeopardizing the entire future of our relationship. All those long-range plans for a shared life go by the wayside. Can't you see that?" There was anger and distress in her voice.

Things went downhill thereafter; we often bickered, and not just over the switch in majors. We'd already been having serious disputes over "those radicals" on campus and the thirty-thousand

GI's in South Vietnam, but my emerging plans were, for her, the last straw. Our 24-hour Greyhound bus ride back to Highlands early that June was mostly tense and silent, with few hugs or kisses; and the inevitable, weepy break-up occurred a week later at our local drive-in, where, with James Bond's escapades filling the big screen and the movie soundtrack squeaking at low volume in my father's old car, Lisa and I mulled over five years of past memories well past the midnight hour. Next day, at work, I stumbled over my set speeches, especially the new Spanish ones, and got a couple of phone messages wrong, too. Partly for distraction, partly to get started in my new field, I gobbled up lots of Dostoyevsky, and went on a poetry-reading binge, sneaking a peek at the Romantics or moderns at any spare moment, and, on evenings and weekends, devouring and sometimes memorizing lots of verse.

And then, as if further to complicate matters, my 80-year-old grandfather Rodríguez, a former sheepherder who had once taken me on many an outing, and taught me most of what I know about birds and trees and soils, had the effrontery and bad manners to keel over dead in our living room, beer in hand, immediately after an elaborate Fourth of July dinner with my parents, their siblings and nephews, and myself. It came as a shock to all of us, since his body and looks were of a man three decades younger.

And so a breather from my Park Service duties turned into a wake and funeral that spelled the end of another past tie.

The Christmas before that, *el abuelito* (as we used to call him) had bequeathed and ceremoniously handed to me five old notebooks filled with his wonderfully natural, spontaneous meditations and poems, penned in an archaic Castillian and ornate script during his long days tending sheep early in the century. My repeated browsing in that package over the next few months may well have spurred me on to study literature, to figure out how poetry works and why poets do what they do.

Still, my parents weren't exactly pleased with my switch in study plans either. Because the two of them did teach English

and Spanish in the Highlands school system, they weren't about
to pull out that old chestnut, "And what do you do with a B.A.
in English?" In fact they offered to help out with what would be
a fifth year toward my degree, while registering mild
bewilderment and displeasure. And so in September I took the
bus combination back to Berkeleyland, embarked on my new
life-path, riding into the sunset without Lisa's warm hand and
body at my side for the first time in years. I don't recall exactly
what I was feeling, though exhilaration it probably was not.

"Excuse me, could I have a large coke, please?" A short,
round-faced prof in a brown beard and gray suit shook me out
of the reverie I'd been lost in while wiping off the counter and
replenishing the ice cubes. I poured the dark, fizzy fluid into a
waxed cup, handed over to him his current object of desire, and
noticed that the next customer in line, a freckle-faced sorority
girl in yellow bangs, actually had the *Daily Cal* open to Zoltan
Jones's column, right on top of her Geology text. ("Hey, I know
that guy," I could've pointed and said to her, and it would've
been true.) From the far end of the Bear's Lair came the rippling
sounds of someone playing Chopin on the upright piano.

Vaguely under Zolly's inspiration, that summer Mitch and I
started going down once a week to check out recordings from the
public library a few blocks away on Shattuck, and there we'd ask
Annie-Lynn, the long-haired, lissome librarian for her advice on
different versions of this piece or that. Halfway into our first
visit I chanced to find out that she'd grown up outside of Santa
Fe, just an hour's drive from my own town of Highlands, which
gave us something more to talk about; and come July I was
dropping by more than once and alone, saying to her whatever
entered my mind at the slightest opportunity, hoping she couldn't
see through my smokescreen and into my little secret crush on
her. But alas, she lived on Northside, and I on South Campus,
and never could the twain meet, I then thought. Besides, I'd later
glimpsed her having lunch around the Terrace with her crowd of
music-type friends, and I was out of their league, having little to
offer in that department. Another of life's might-have-beens, and

all simply because I'd failed to listen to my parents.

Anyway, that first time Mitch checked out three renditions of the Brahms Fourth before he eventually got around to purchasing Toscanini's, and soon enough he owned the other three plus Tchaikovsky's *Pathétique* as well, crooning with them at dinner and sometimes stacking them when he'd have a date over for an evening or a night. As for me, seeking something newer, on Zolly's suggestion I eventually borrowed Robert Craft's complete Webern or the more way-out pieces by Boulez, only to find myself bewildered by it all, with little to latch onto. I rather envied Zolly's understanding of this music and wondered why I was missing out on so much.

Still, Zolly's articles made lively reading for me. They had what I now recognize as New York pizazz plus an occasional European touch, and his unique personality always came through in his prose. Mitch and I both got a real kick out of his twice-weekly offerings, each as erudite and witty as the last. From time to time I'd bump into the music man himself up on Telegraph, where we'd ignore the pedestrian and motor traffic and talk about his latest free batch of Nonesuch albums, or the simply incredible performance of *Das Lied von der Erde* he'd gone to in the city last night, or the "MAHLER GROOVES" bumper stickers you saw everywhere that year. His hair was getting longer, thicker, I noticed. And he smoked much more.

Meanwhile, as the school year started off I saw him several times with a cute, long-haired blonde whom I faintly recognized but couldn't quite place as yet. (These blondes, they all look alike sometimes.) The answer to the riddle came my way, so to speak, one night in October. I was sitting in the Heidelberg on a Tuesday evening, munching on their classic knockwurst and enjoying the background Mozart when in comes Zolly with his green-eyed blonde. "Hey, what's up, old man?" he says to me. "Mind if we disturb your peace for a moment?"

He introduced us. The name "Sally Simsby" rang some distant bell. She gave me a mechanical sort of nod and a "Hello."

They were soon back with their own sauerkraut-and-sausage

combos, and Zolly was identifying the Mozart divertimento being piped in amidst the food fragrances, even suggesting whose rendition it might be.

Then his friend remarked, "Mozart's real pretty, Zolly."

Something in me flashed as memory zeroed in on her Eastern voice and pat sentence. It was the distinctive set phrase and slightly frigid speech rhythms of the cute blonde who, last fall, had sat at my right in English 100. ("Shakespeare's real pretty," she once remarked as the discussion of *Othello* came to an end.) And I recalled that I'd thought of her back then as one of the silliest sorority girls I'd ever had the honor to share space with. ("The yellow peril," I liked to call her.) Among her most memorable contributions in class was her observation that, "Sure, Iago's real mean, but Othello's dense, too. He's just a fool to let Iago take advantage of him that way."

Early on that semester I'd casually asked her where she was from, and the smiling reply through her double row of large, even teeth was, "Suburban New York." By then I'd learned enough to construe that formula as a polite euphemism either for rich Scarsdale or well-heeled Long Island, the latter, apparently, the L.A. of the East. Several times thereafter I tried making conversation with her — part of my new need, in my lonely and unaccustomed celibacy, to meet girls — and she wouldn't register so much as a word in response. On one occasion, though, I was glancing at the bargain LP I'd just bought at Record City (Mozart's "Prague," I think), and, in an offhand way, recommended it to Miss Simsby. Without her facing me, the Eastern voice and automatic smile came back with, "Oh, I only like show tunes. I don't really care much for longhair music," as the classics were then known to some, before flowing locks became the rock musicians' trademark.

That fall she invariably dressed nicely for class, the wholesome, well-scrubbed look — plaid skirts, pink turtlenecks, penny loafers, even stacked heels a few times. In fact, one November afternoon, as I was subbing for a friend, busing dishes down at the Lair with Joan Baez's "Guantanamera" playing on the jukebox, I saw Miss Simsby seated in a booth with two of her sorority sisters, also blondes. She was talking excitedly about clothes — her latest purchases, the big sale at I. Magnin (whose name graced the rectangular white box at her side), memories of going to Bloomingdale's and Abercrombie and Fitch every week. Never in English class had I seen the girl gush forth with such passion and enthusiasm. As I ambled by with my cart during a lull in their conversation and picked up her and her friends' dirty coffee mugs, I bowed my head automatically, saying "Hi." She answered nothing in return and continued to look straight ahead at her companions. It was the first time I ever regretted having greeted someone.

And now here was this Sally Sorority turned pseudo-beat, with her huaraches and long hair, the whole "in" look. And claiming to like Wolfgang Amadeus to boot, which struck me either as an astounding metamorphosis or just plain phony with a capital F. What's she up to? I wondered. I played dumb and made no sign whatever of knowing Miss Simsby, the better to observe her at her game. (I could've bet hard cash she had no recollection of yours truly, this tan-skinned, part-Spanish grandchild of a deceased New Mexico sheepherder, and a real-live erstwhile classmate who had bused her dishes a year back.)

Only a bit less surprising was my abrupt discovery of a shift in Zolly's views. As the conversation went into full swing I found him slightly jaded with the old classics and what they stood for. "You know, it's amazing, though it gets discouraging, too," he started saying as he chomped on his sausage. "Mozart wrote forty-one symphonies in his thirty-five-year lifespan, and that's a hell of a lot. But hearing the same ones again and again wears you out, and I wish we had even *more* to choose from. If the guy had survived into his fifties there might be, like, eighty-five of them now. Who knows, maybe there's a lost manuscript someplace."

I seconded Zolly's notion. "The unknown and the unwritten Mozart. More of him to listen to. That's cool."

"Yeah, imagine it," he went on excitedly. "Bruno Walter

doing Mozart's Symphony number 66 in F-sharp minor, Koechel listing 847."

"You're so smart, Zols," said Sally Simsby as she touched his arm, causing him to smile appreciatively. Sally and Zolly. What a pair.

He lit a Salem. "Sometimes, though, I even wonder if the classics might not be simply passé. The whole thing may've run its course. Maybe rock-and-roll's the classical music of our time."

I can't say why, but there was something faintly calculating about Sally Simsby's grin as she interjected, "Well, Zols, that's what I've been telling you all along."

"Yeah, right," said Zolly after taking a long puff. "Beatles should supersede Schubert."

Sally hardly spoke during that encounter, and then it was mostly to agree with or praise "Zols." As I ambled back toward Dwight Way, perplexed, I pondered the change in her, and already sensed that it wasn't exactly real. All over Telegraph there were beats and hippies of every size and shape, from every conceivable background, but Sally had struck me as one of those bandwagon-jumpers you get in every crowd.

Just as I was passing alongside Cody's Books I saw Mitch stepping out, and we strolled on toward the apartment. With cautious irony in my voice I alluded to my chance meeting with Zolly and his blonde.

"Sally Simsby! Yeah, I should know," he remarked sheepishly. "I introduced 'em."

"Oh, boy. Let's hear about it."

For some reason the traffic on Dwight Way stretched down for a block.

"She was in my early-morning section last Spring. Not too smart, kind of your typical New York airhead debutante type. So-so as a student, but I thought she was trying to butter me up for a grade."

"So how'd they meet?" I was surprised how eager I felt to know.

At the corner of Dana, the two of us were interrupted by a long-haired brunette in a peasant skirt, earnestly berating her golden retriever, saying, "Strindberg! Stay!" Mitch and I looked at each other and laughed briefly.

"So anyway," he continued, "Sally and I are walking down from Wheeler after class one morning. Supposedly she needs clarification on some point in Descartes. When we reach the Terrace she invites herself to join me for coffee. Then Jones sees us and ends up sitting at our table outside — anything to meet a pretty chick, apparently. The rest is history."

Mitch liked these flourishes from time to time.

We speculated a lot that evening about Zolly's personality and his new amour. A few days later I was among the hordes routinely picking up the *Daily Cal* at the box by Sather Gate, and as I headed for Mr. Barish's Shakespeare class, turning to the Culture pages, I felt an odd sensation, as I read Zoltan Jones brooding on the very same doubts I'd heard him giving vent to that night at the Heidelberg. I realized our encounter had been a kind of practice session for him.

That was only the day's first, and milder, journalistic surprise. While reaching the door to Wheeler I finished Zolly's article, glanced at the facing page, and stopped in my tracks. I pulled aside to lean into a corner, oblivious to the dozens of passing voices, and stood there reading, knowing — as we all did — of Barish's famed custom of scolding and even kicking out anyone who dared to read the *Daily Cal* during his lectures.

There it was: a new feature, a personal essay, byline none other than that of Sally Simsby. Bearing the title "The Sorrows of Little Feefah," the premier piece dwelled on her Siamese housecat of the same name and told of the creature's daily sufferings, its loneliness, its fears. Among Sally's memorable quotes was her remark, "Oh, sure, I know there's lots of negative news these days about Asian peasants being bombed and Negroes being discriminated against, but it's not as if those were the only items in our big and beautiful country. What I do know for certain is that little Feefah mews so sadly every time I kiss her good-bye when I leave for morning classes. And that brings more tears to my eyes than does any talk of distant beatings or bombings." She ventured the theory that "if people only treated their cats especially nicely, there wouldn't be as many wars." And she ended with a reminiscence of her cuddling up with Feefah the other night and joyfully laughing through an "I Love Lucy" rerun, a program she solemnly adjudged "one of the great comedies of our time."

I read the thing twice, amazed, then realized that Mr. Barish was well into his lecture on Iago and Machiavellianism. So I grabbed the end seat in the very last row and proceeded to take some sketchy notes, my mind dwelling rather on ol' Sally and on how she'd gone about weaseling her way into Jones's life just to get a column in the *Daily Cal*. No doubt, the paper had its conservative voices, like Bill Buckley, or N.C. Brodin, a Swedish emigré who hated the welfare state in any form and made a practice of sniping at Civil-Rights activities in every article he could. Sally's musings, however, went beyond anything I'd seen so far in the *Daily Cal* or elsewhere.

Unable to control myself, I left class a few minutes early and headed for the Terrace, where the first lunch crowds were streaming in. I found Mitch seated inside near the entrance, munching on his burritos-and-meat-sauce, the lunch du jour.

"You read this?" I asked, passing him the item as I plopped down, still shaking my head in disbelief.

He tightened his tortoise-shell glasses, perused it in silence. "Jesus H. Christ."

"Can you conceive such crap?"

"No, but I can see it."

"I wonder if she could ever have gotten it into print on her own." Down the table from us, two short, thin, Chinese-speaking boys, probably freshmen, grabbed adjoining seats and dug into their own Mexican lunches.

Mitch just grinned at my comment, then said, "Well, look, what do you expect from Miss Suburbia in the flesh?" He cut up his burrito into regular, bite-sized chunks. All around us were

lunchers, some them caught up in their *Daily Cals,* and no doubt
a few were taking in Sally's feline thoughts at that very moment.
"You know," Mitch continued, "I had one of those all-time
classic experiences with her in Intro section. We're starting out
on Ethics and are about to do Aristotle, and I ask, 'So somebody
tell me, what is Ethics?' And good old Miss Simsby raises her
dainty hand and volunteers this gem: 'Well, its people doing
what they feel is right. If everybody does what he thinks is right,
that's all that matters.'" Mitch giggled. "It's the oldest of the old
chestnuts; every philosophy prof has heard it a hundred times.
Oh, and next class meeting she brings me a few religious
pamphlets. Looks like she's found herself another cause now,
though."

I grinned back. "Don't know about a cause. Helps her feel
important, I guess."

Over the next few months I'd see Zolly's and Sally's articles,
sometimes side by side or on opposing pages. She might touch
on local political goings-on and the latest rallies in Sproul Plaza,
yet somehow reduce it all to who's-been-seen-with-whom, and
what-was-so-and-so-wearing-that-fine-day, and how everybody's
"wonderful" speeches "addressed all our concerns," no matter
whether the given speech was pro-civil rights or against, dove on
Vietnam or hawk. When she commented on the big student strike
that fizzled out that fall, she managed to do so without discussing
any of the issues, as if it were simply another fraternity-sorority
bash. Zolly kept up his reviews of concerts and LPs while
wondering at greater length about the relevance of the old
classics and suggesting that, in the wake of the Rolling Stones,
Loading Zone, or Country Joe and the Fish, "the three B's may
have had their day."

Throughout the term I'd catch sight of the twosome around
town or campus. They'd be holding hands and looking like real
lovebirds. Zolly seemed less monkish, positively mellow, and I'll
even admit that Sally was good for him at the time, although I
still couldn't stand the sight of her. And again I would've bet on
her not recognizing me either from English class or the

Heidelberg.

It wouldn't last, Mitch and I both knew it. In fact one dreary day in January I happened to be walking behind them through Sproul Plaza, and it was obvious enough they were having a nasty spat over something or other. Sally was acting out the role of bitch, pushing his arm off from her shoulder. Zolly's hands in turn made a gesture in the shape of wounded pleas, even as his face showed anger.

The last time I saw them together was at La Fiesta, of all places — I vaguely recalled suggesting it to her in class once as the area's best for Mexican cuisine, especially their *flautas,* to which she'd replied with a brief, "Oh, I prefer American food." They were seated at a table for two, a happy relief for me as I didn't think I could take being around her for more than half a minute. Before settling into my booth near the door, I went to greet him.

"Well, Zolly, I can see you've got good tastes in food," I said and immediately regretted, worrying about such a statement being taken the wrong way.

He answered with his typical, "Hey, old man, what's up?"

I returned to my own booth, from whence I caught glimpses of a once-again starry-eyed couple holding hands even while eating. (I suppose she was left-handed.) As I watched, I noticed her reaching up and administering long, soft finger strokes on the back of his neck, though her red nails looked somewhat less loving than they felt to Zolly.

Berkeley in the winter is almost eternally gray, and that year's rains appeared to have no end. Through the forest of umbrellas and watery mists I managed a few mental snapshots of Zolly distant and alone, looking fairly desolate. Something no doubt had happened, though there wasn't as yet any way of determining exactly what. Mitch was spending long hours at his office, studying for his Master's oral, and at breakfast he talked mostly about the philosophers and the secondary stuff he'd boned up on the night before. As for me, my little jobs at the Ashby

Launderette and the Bear's Lair hardly paid the rent, and so I'd started part-time work at Moe's Bookstore, which had recently opened and fast become everybody's favorite spot for casual browsing and getting used reading fare on the cheap. I'd borrow poetry books from the store and go through them in my spare time. We were each of us quite busy; there wasn't much occasion to discuss Zolly Jones.

Around this time Zolly's reviews turned particularly troubled and sour, even strident. He was saying things like, "Listening to E. Power Biggs blow the pipes at Maybeck the other day, I couldn't help but ask myself why most organ music after Bach is such *trash.*" Or again, "Lyndon Strangelove keeps bombing the bejeesus out of Vietnamese peasants. I hear of B-52 flyboys who like obliterating villages and forests to the sound of the *Ride of the Valkyries.* And it's enough to make you reflect on the bankruptcy of an entire culture and its glorious legacy."

At the same time it was almost eerie to see, only inches away, Sally's sunny, smiling claims to the effect that everything was just right with our world. In her happy prose she mildly rebuked those "boring debunkers" who "feel so negative about everything," who "worry about things like nuclear war" and "don't realize it can't happen." In one article she relayed her own mother's memories of the Depression and the War, when "the dear lady was helping to organize charity balls for Manhattan's soup kitchens and even handling a few soup ladles herself. Well, friends, as old mom said to me last week, 'If we can survive *those* traumas, we can survive anything, and certainly some faraway little brush-fire war.' Anyway, folks, politics never saved anybody." Toward the end of the piece Sally recalled a prep-school teacher of hers who once started out class by reading "in a morbid voice" an unidentified lament for our times. "All doom and gloom, truly creepy. Then Mr. Hotchkiss looked up and told us the author's name: it was Plato! Things sure haven't changed, have they? Really, spare me the doomsayers (even though — alas — they will always be with us)."

II

Late in February Mitch passed his orals. I joined him and a couple of his philosophy buddies in celebration over beers at the Heidelberg. Several pitchers and much shoptalk about exam ordeals later, the two other guys started sharing their thoughts on an anti-war rally that they'd recently attended and that Mitch had had to miss.

I turned to Mitch and asked, "What's with Zolly and the blonde?"

"Haven't you heard? She dumped him for Dick Biddlesworth."

"Dick Biddlesworth..."

"Actually, Richard T. Biddlesworth III. You know, the guy who's involved with getting together the rock concerts at Provo Park."

All I could do was grunt and say, "'T figures."

He emptied out a pitcher into his beer glass and mine. "Biddlesworth. That's a *Mayflower* name."

"I didn't realize that," I said.

"There's Biddlesworths in high places all over the country. Even in rock and roll."

"So Sally found herself a Brahmin."

"I guess she did."

Over the next couple of months the magnolia trees began to sprout, bringing back some color to an otherwise grayish Sproul Plaza area. From time to time I'd bump into Zolly, alone or with fellow music-people, at the various places along Telegraph and South Campus. We'd stand, maybe sit around together for a while, chat about local happenings, music news, the unending war — but about Sally never. He apparently had decided to make absolutely no mention of the Blonde from Westchester, and neither Mitch nor I were about to bring it up.

In the interim he'd widened his activities and become more of a presence around town. Besides his *Daily Cal* columns he now wrote every week for the *Berkeley Barb* (where he used raunchier language, in keeping with the tone and style of that irreverent rag), did occasional sales work at Record City, and emerged as principal violinist for University Chamber Players. My roommate and I both reckoned that the guy was keeping busy in order to forget the whole Sally misadventure. Having passed his Master's exams a year ago, he was at least free from immediate school pressures and presumably could experiment with other stuff.

It was over ten months since I'd set eyes on Zolly's collection, but, in one of those chance encounters that can make life here so special, I got to sample a few more of Jones's thousands. I'd just come from seeing the movie *Blow-up,* and was on my first date with Annie-Lynn. A day earlier I'd been to the public library to check out records. With a minimum grin, she rubber-stamped and handed me my maximum half-dozen. There was no one else in the music section. Somehow I summoned up my courage, looked beyond those steel-frame glasses into her gray eyes, and stammered out an invitation to the flicks.

To my surprise she actually said, in her hushed tone of voice, "Well, that sounds like fun, why not?"

Before that I'd learned of her local reputation as a lutenist and had recently attended an early-music-ensemble concert where her two solos drew hefty applause. I'd also seen a love-sonnet of hers in *Spider* magazine that, as I recall, dealt tongue-in-cheek with the difficulties of writing a love sonnet. In sum she was arty and cute, brainy and funny and nice talking to, and besides, how many lute players with waist-length hair can a guy have a date with in his life?

We shuffled out of Cinema Guild and she remarked with enthusiasm on Herbie Hancock's lush soundtrack for the picture. "Or," she said with a mock-English accent, "'*Herbert* Hancock', as the opening credits put it."

Almost as if by reflex we crossed the street and headed for the Caffé Mediterraneum. While we queued up for espressos I heard the words "Hey, Rodríguez" descending from the second level. Raising my eyes, I saw Mitch and Zolly beckoning us, along with two girls whom I'd seen around and about the usual Berkeley spots. The smells of roast coffees coming from the front counter and of assorted Greek foods from the right rear were unusually sharp that Friday evening. Plates were clattering, voices bantering, puffs of smoke wafting, and recent book purchases from Moe's and Cody's were changing hands at this table or that. The narrow stairway called for careful navigation, for, coming down on the left side — mustachioed and stocky, tray in hand — was none other than bookstore man Fred Cody himself, who, as he customarily did, nodded and greeted me with a warm, gruff "Hi" through his Terry-Thomas teeth.

(He often ate his snacks there, holding forth in his West Virginia accent on the many books he had read, and with every sort of listener. My first exchange with the guy, I still remember, was in September 1963, when Lisa and I ventured into the store; and, approaching him directly at the front counter, I asked, "Do you have *The Conscience of a Conservative?*"

Cody gave us this wry, mock-offended look and said, "I don't have it personally, but we sure as heck carry the Goldwater title by that name." He rushed down the aisle and retrieved the 25-cent paperback, and, as he rang up the cash register, added, "I'm just a half-assed liberal myself." Lisa and I giggled while he bagged the purchase. Since then he had always said hello to me both at the store and outside, and a year later he even asked if Senator Goldwater had had any influence on my thinking.)

Meanwhile Annie-Lynn and I squeezed in to join the upstairs foursome; she and Zolly knew one another from music circles, and he introduced us to Phyllis, your classic curly-unkempt beatnik in black leotards from New York, and Val, short and willowy, with sandals, outlandishly reddish long hair, and that nondescript California accent. Both, as it turned out, were music majors. We talked about *Blow-up,* which they'd all seen and liked.

Phyllis knew the story on which the movie was based, by a South American guy called Cortázar.

"Wow," said Mitch.

"I'm impressed," said Zolly. "You read the thing in the original?"

"Sure did," said Phyllis, nodding vigorously.

"Wow," several of us hooted, and then laughed over the coincidence.

After a brief lull Zolly suggested, "Hey, how 'bout coming up to my place and blowin' a few? I've got some quality hash safely stashed away."

I looked at Annie-Lynn inquisitively.

"Well, yes, I'm game," she answered in her soft and proper speech.

Next thing I know, we were all starting our second joint and, variously sprawled about in Zolly's living room, we'd somehow heard at least half of Ravel's *La Valse*. Before that, if I recall correctly, it had been a Bach solo cello suite, with Annie-Lynn and Phyllis whistling and gesturing occasionally along with the music. In the wake of some roaring orchestral climax, Mitch exhaled audibly, and remarked casually on the extra shelf since grown by Zolly's collection.

I asked Zolly, who by then was flying high, about the new acquisitions.

"Yeah, Zolly, show us," Val seconded me.

The host arose from the floor and cleared his throat. "Introducing the two most recent additions to the Jones Collection. Two more Beethoven's Fifths. Another box of the six Brandenburgs. Some Bach arranged for jazz guitar." He placed his finger on the spine of each album while announcing it. "Et chettera, as they say in Rome. And for the moderns, there's Stockhausen over in the bedroom, and, ah yes, here's George Crumb." Suddenly all that could be heard from Ravel was the growling basses; Zolly's voice turned softer. "And what's it all for? Who knows? Meanwhile, let's have a party!" We applauded as he sat down again.

In fact we got quite a range of styles that night, from early Baroque to electronic. At one point a bleary-eyed Val even sat at the piano and played along with the solo part to a Bach concerto, and Zolly produced his fiddle from nowhere and added the orchestral part as Annie-Lynn sang along too. Musicians, I realized then, have fun, far more fun than us word-people do.

Zolly still had his special music stand next to the stereo, but he had made one concession and replaced the turntable with a changer, making it possible for him to stack several records that night while continuing to blow weed. As for me, when I inhale even basic grass I end up turning solipsistic, eyes closed, and feel myself hurtling through outer space, sort of like the light show that would serve as climax to *2001*. Last thing I could remember in the semi-darkness of that room was Zolly and Phyllis going through the exaggerated motions of Mozart's "*La ci darem la mano.*"

Next morning I was the first one awake, after maybe four hours' slumber, and I wondered momentarily where it was I had landed. There were sparrows singing and I could hear a finch doing its complex tune somewhere in the back yard. The bedroom door was shut, I noticed, and neither Zolly nor Phyllis were anywhere to be seen. On one end of the sofa was Mitch sitting sound asleep, on the other wholesome Val was curled up like a kitten. I was stretched out on the floor and to my astonishment so was Annie-Lynn, with the nape of her neck poised on my belly and her brown locks cascading down my left side, making me feel pretty sexual, though how much can a guy do on a first date with someone?

The four of us were beginning to stir. I sat up, grabbed a nearby cushion which I slid gently under Annie-Lynn's abundant mane, and arose slowly. In my stocking feet I tiptoed to the collection, plucked out a Brahms Fourth — Furtwängler's this time — and took the liberty of playing it, as softly as possible. I was amazed at the contrast with Toscanini's version — so much slower and darker, so languorously Romantic, so German, I thought. In some ways it sounded like a totally different piece, and I suddenly understood how a person such as Zolly might make a practice out of hearing and comparing new renditions.

The bedroom door squeaked on its hinges. A rumpled Zolly and Phyllis emerged; they were the last ones up for a quick morning's wash. The rest of us had been comparing last night's trips. Annie-Lynn recalled the feeling of having turned into a cat, and I whispered to her that there was already something catlike about the tilt of her head, to which she half-smiled and turned away. Meanwhile Zolly graciously warmed up some apple turnovers and prepared some French roast in his coffee pot. As he poured it into the mugs (which I recognized as vintage Bear's Lair), Brahms came to its end, whereupon the host announced mock-seriously, "And now for a sampling of Cage's *4' 33"*.

"What's that?" a puzzled Mitch inquired.

"Oh, yeah," said Phyllis, "right, that's the one where a pianist plays nothing for four minutes and thirty-three seconds and then splits."

"Got a better idea," said Val. "How 'bout a duo?"

"Be my guest," Zolly pointed at the piano bench, so they both slid in in front of the spinet and placed their hands absolutely still on the keyboard.

For a few moments the only sounds ruffling the stillness were the birds outside and the single honk of a passing car, after which our host queried, "Well, so how d'you like it so far?"

"Why, yes, I recognize it," Annie-Lynn remarked. "It's been transcribed for lute and guitar both."

"Haven't got that version in my collection yet," Zolly went on. "Hey, Annie-Lynn, you guys have it at the Library?"

Only then did we start catching on to the idea behind Cage's "piece" and speculating on analogous possibilities (orchestrations, unpainted canvases, whatever). Phyllis offered to perform a vocal adaptation for us then and there, apologizing for her weak sightreading skills, and Val wondered if the Cage piece might be too long.

"Or too short," said Annie-Lynn, and we held a discussion about changing the title to, say, *3' 16"*. Or *6' 52"*.

Before we knew it we were on to Minimal Art, via a clipping from *Life* magazine that Zolly had on the white oval table, and Val asked in all earnestness, "How do you tell which big black cube is better than any other one?"

Mitch's sarcastic voice said, "Probably if a world-famous artist makes a cube, all black or brown with pink polka-dots, his is automatically better."

Zolly took a final sip, raised an eyebrow. "Well, you know, Val, I've wondered about that, sitting and staring at these records. There's times when I can't say which Brahms is better, Toscanini's or anyone else's. Sure, for what it's worth, I'll say Brahms is great, it's no big issue, but, trouble is, someone's gotta play him."

Phyllis had remained seated at the piano, and now she played in its entirety what Zolly later identified as the slow movement from Beethoven's *Les Adieux* sonata. And finally, Zolly treated us to his latest recording of Debussy's very last composition, something for flute, viola, and harp, and it was wonderfully peaceful, the perfect sounds for a Saturday morning after a long night's tripping out on hash and the classics. Food for the mind and the lesser-understood senses.

The May morning was bright and dry. Zolly walked with us the whole five blocks down to Telegraph. "Need the fresh air," he said as we emerged out onto Etna. "Sometimes I feel hemmed in by all that vinyl." During much of the descent he and Phyllis were holding hands. But when we reached Dwight Way stop-light, they simply traded kisses, she joined Val, and the two girls waved in three directions, backing off toward Oakland. Zolly headed uphill. Mitch crossed the Avenue saying, "Gotta do this again someday." Annie-Lynn and I took our first steps toward Northside. Scattered "So long's" and "Bye-bye's" filled the quiet, early-Saturday air.

"Musicians do have more fun," I mused out loud.

"Yes, they do," an amused Annie-Lynn agreed.

The two of us walked slowly through Sather Gate and the still-silent, chiaroscuro slopes of the U.C. campus, yawning at times and commenting on the night's experiences. During a brief detour through Eucalyptus Grove she reflected on Zolly's thousands. "It's quite amazing. It seems he's having a conversation with those LP's. I do wonder where it'll lead him. I take it he's more involved with those records than with his own violin playing."

"Well, he told us he's not so hot a string player."

"Balderdash," she replied. "Poor Zolly, he is so self-deprecating. He's good enough to have taken violin solos in the star ensemble. And his viola playing is really quite wonderful! I've been to their concerts, and Zolly's no fake. Full of strange complexes, though, and rather notorious around the department because of them."

We glanced momentarily at the treetops and took in the delicious sweet fragrance of the eucalyptus. She pointed out the branches and their features; I noticed how deliciously desirable she looked in her bright green shawl-and-dress and little brown sandals. There was something enigmatic about her. As we approached her building on Euclid, just a few doors up from Northside Café, I lasciviously fantasized about what she might be like for some long nights of eros. But we were both sleepy, I couldn't figure her out, and it was still too early in the morning.

That July I went into seclusion, sweating over two summer-school courses in order to get my B.A. in English, much to the relief of my parents. It came as a surprise when I was accepted last minute into the graduate program, and I even got a job grading papers for Shakespeare classes, which took care of basic rent and food costs, allowing me to quit the Bear's Lair, though not the Ashby Launderette. And so I now daydreamed of PhD-ing and then passing on Keats, Yeats, and the rest to undergraduate Bohemians in verdant groves somewhere on this continent.

In a few months, however, I realized that graduate school in English was not what I'd had in mind, viz: reading lots of literature by every sort of writer — ranging from Chaucer to the Beats and even my own grandfather — and then just digging them while sitting around the Terrace; rather it was a job consisting mostly of studying countless critics and then spinning out one's own "reading" — actually one's abstract idea — of this poem or that. (About the only fun was in getting to know more of those classics.) Many an evening, moreover, I'd see and overhear the department's favorite sons and daughters, Eastern B.A.'s mostly, dining together in the cafeteria and talking and enthusing not over literature but about critics and criticism, about this "approach" or that "perspective." I'll even grant that they'd been better trained than I'd had the good fortune to be, though one of them did say to me after dinner once, as he donned his tweed coat, "I've never read a Russian novel, and never intend to, either" which allowed me the opportunity to recommend Dostoyevsky to him. Still, I found myself envying them their well-modulated, Ivy-inflected speech cadences and (in spite of my 20-20 eyesight) their perfectly round tortoise-shell spectacles.

By late December I realized how Zolly felt, dealing with the same few hundred names filtered through endless new reformattings that, in the grander scheme of things, hardly mattered, save making you wish Beethoven had composed eighteen symphonies or Shakespeare seventy-two plays, and that there were fewer critics and less criticism. I wondered how long I would stay with it, and certainly didn't like being one of the 500-plus graduate students in English, all of them aspiring to the literary-critical bureaucracy.

Annie-Lynn I'd see at the Library on occasion, though what with pressures both from attending seminars, grading papers, and working at Moe's Books I was borrowing few records lately, and the early-music group she belonged to was often on the road weekends. (I saw them in Maybeck again, and she looked radiant in her black dress.) Shortly after Zolly's hash bash, moreover, I'd heard through him and one of his music buddies out on the Terrace that, prim and proper as she was, the lute player also led a pretty wild life and even had a few intimate fans scattered about the West Coast. (Imagine that, the librarian and lutenist as swinger...) Well, if Annie-Lynn and I were to have something, I didn't want to be in a groupie line, however enjoyable it might be for a night. I remember reading somewhere that Sarah Bernhardt claimed a roster of three thousand lovers, which is the male population of many a small town in New Mexico, and I wonder how each of those guys felt. (We'll never know, probably.) Anyway, lonesome though graduate school was, this guy here wasn't ready for sex under any circumstances, especially after a relationship of five years. The world of fast bangs and one-night quickies was something I'd never quite understood, let alone been involved with.

Sally Simsby had also graduated, after having done a stint as Arts Editor! She took her public leave in a final silly column that June, and Mitch and I gladly bade her meditations good riddance and adieu. I caught sight of her walking up Telegraph once or twice that warm summer. The tall, blondish guy at her side — long face, angular features — I took to be Dick Biddlesworth.

Jones's articles kept coming out like clockwork in both the *Cal* and the *Barb*. Though no longer obsessing about it, he still expressed doubts about the Old Masters from time to time. The Monday after Thanksgiving I saw him stretched out at a big round table outside the Terrace, looking unusually fine. There was a chill in the air; most people were huddled inside, but his Salem seemed to keep him warm. I joined him with my stale coffee.

"What's up, old man?" he said. "You seem depressed."

"Well, Zolly, it's like this." I went into my growing misgivings about the great books. The established classics. The big names. The English department and what have you. Told him how I sympathized with what he'd been saying in his columns much of this past year.

"Yeah, it's a drag. Trouble is, the great works are still about the best we've got. Believe me, I've had to study Hummel and Spohr and plenty of other third-raters. To sum them up: *BOR*-ring." Boring. That's a New York word, I'd long realized. I felt the impulse to ask if he still thought of rock-and-roll as today's classical music, but held it back. "Anyway," he went on, "looks like I'll be teaching the stuff this coming February."

"Got a job?"

"Yeah, over in New Haven, Connecticut."

"Oh." I said nothing, for a moment, then asked. "Yale?"

He raised an eyebrow and smiled. "Nope. Albertus Magnus, a small Catholic college for girls. Kind of lookin' forward to it. None of this hifalutin, airy-fairy academic stuff."

"Well, Zolly, congratulations. We've gotta celebrate."

"Hey, right, man."

"We're going to miss your columns."

"Hey, I am too, you know, but I'll tell you, it was getting mechanical, too much like a routine. Need a change of venue. Different typeface maybe."

We never actually did get to celebrate, and in fact it was nearly six years before I saw Zolly Jones again. By then I'd picked up an M.A. and done a semester's work toward the Ph.D. before deciding to chuck it all and make Moe's Books a full-time job. So rather than hear smooth-spoken, well-groomed graduate students construing the old classics, or dream of new thoughts of my own to scribble and pronounce, I now helped keep the great books in circulation by buying or selling or trading them alongside the boxfuls of highbrow product and middlebrow schlock. (People went to Cody's if they wanted mint-condition printer's ink and book bindings; to Moe's if they preferred a shared artifact with red or yellow underlinings and the autograph of a mysterious stranger, all at just half price.) It was fun at Moe's; it felt meaningful in ways that had seldom been the case in the vast corridors of English Lit and Wheeler Hall. In a couple of years I rose to chief buyer and occasionally ran the place at nights, shooing out anxious browsers come 10:00 p.m., though wondering how long I'd last in this new phase of mine.

Meanwhile I managed to see my parents twice a year, which was about it for my travels thus far. Hadn't been to Europe yet. Hadn't even been back East. I'd more or less lost touch with old flame Lisa, though some time ago Mom had sent me a news item from the *Highlands Herald* reporting her marriage to a young Los Angeles brain surgeon. For a few years after our memorable, distant all-nighter, Phyllis, still looking the 1960's beatnik, would drop into Moe's, chit-chat a bit, and buy a book, though she and Zolly clearly hadn't continued as a couple, and at some point she just dropped out of the picture, probably returned to New York.

At least once a week I'd have a quiet lunch a few doors down at La Fiesta, a place I appreciated not only for its first-rate *huevos rancheros* but also for its traditional ambiance, ubiquitous blue tiles, and feeling of continuity. Since about 1963 the same orotund middle-aged man, Don Fernando, had patiently indulged my New Mexico Spanish as he'd take one of my three recurrent orders and thus allow me to relive dim childhood memories. Besides being a gourmet eatery, the place was something reliable at a time when, for me, things made increasingly less sense. Nixon's second electoral sweep more than a year ago had brought a palpable gloom to the human climate at Berkeley, and the sole consolation was the chance to see the nation's top butcher now reeling, bending in the wind over Watergate. Going to La Fiesta was a bit like returning to the other party that we'd all left behind in the sixties.

A piece of that party came back just last week when I headed for my customary booth. Sitting in it, mug of beer in hand, was none other than Zoltan Jones, his hair shorter now.

"Hey, Rodríguez, what's up?" he said. "Have a seat."

As I did I asked, "So what're you in town for?"

"Thesis defense, plus some final touches, like having the thing bound and delivered."

I almost felt envious. He'd stuck with it and finished. Maybe I should have too...

"So what else's been happening in your life?"

"Stayed with teaching, and I've been doing regular music stuff for a couple of Connecticut papers. Plus free-lancing for *High Fidelity* magazine. And I stopped smoking."

"Still at the Catholic school?"

"Yeah, haven't left, but just the other day I got this offer for an entry-level job at the local big U."

I didn't want to repeat our last encounter, so all I said was, "You mean..."

"Yeah. Yale."

"Think you'll take it?"

"Don't know, really. Albertus has been fun."

Mr. La Fiesta himself, decked out in a *guayabera* despite the chill and rains outside, came by our table. Zolly ordered *enchiladas*; that day I chose *flautas*.

"Hey, man," Zolly commented, "I didn't know you knew Spanish."

"What's left of it. Spoke it at home, after all. Anyway, Zolly, look, the three of us have got to get together and celebrate this time around. Doctor Jones. How about that?"

Zolly expressed mild surprise at Mitch and I still rooming together, although we probably wouldn't be much longer since he too was finally completing his thesis (Hegel, aesthetics) and travelling around doing the job-interview scene. When I remarked that Mitch now had seventy-some classical records of his own, Zolly seemed pleased.

That wet evening the three of us met at a round table by the Heidelberg's front window, with Mozart, as always, in the background. We slouched about and shamelessly guzzled pitcher after pitcher while watching the varieties of people filing by on Telegraph — long-haired kids in plastic ponchos, well-dressed couples huddled under large umbrellas, a sorority girl cradling a Pekingese in her arms, a bearded folk singer clutching his guitar case, radical faces still familiar to us from Sproul Plaza, two Indian women in ornate saris, Fred Cody in a gray trenchcoat — a show as entertaining as any French movie. And we reminisced about those years. The time Johnson quit. The troops on the Berkeley streets. The helicopter spraying of the U.C. campus. The big Cambodia uprising that we thought would end the war, the Panther rally in New Haven, the Christmas bombing over Hanoi.

And Zolly's job, Mitch's slightly depressed search for a job, and my job at Moe's. And, of course, Zolly's library.

Mitch raised the inevitable query. "Hey, Jones, how's the record collection?"

"Bigger and better."

We all laughed.

"How many now?" I asked.

"Maybe ten thousand. I lost count."

Mitch whistled. "How're you feelin' about the classics these days?"

"Well, I think they're going to be saved by quadraphonic sound," he said, raising an eyebrow. "Four speakers sound twice as good as two."

"So how's that help the classics?" I inquired.

"They'll have to be re-recorded. It's a sea-change. Starting all over, like the shift to LP's in the forties."

"Don't know what difference that really makes," said Mitch, with a slight wave of the hand. "Biggest beneficiaries'll be the stereo equipment manufacturers. Plus the record companies. They'll discontinue their existing regular LP's and drop 'em from their catalogs. We'll all have to buy quadraphonic, at higher prices. Same music; new packaging."

"Look, I don't dispute that," Zolly replied. "But it'll also provide better sound quality for everybody from Bach to George Crumb. Besides," he paused, and again raised that eyebrow, "it'll give me a whole new bunch of records to write reviews about. More assignments from glossies like *High Fidelity.*"

Mitch and I both giggled, nodded. "Yeah," I said, "I can see the appeal now."

Our fourth pitcher was inching down slowly. Outside the rain was letting up; some passersby were in no hurry and even strolled by unconcerned.

"What's your thesis topic?" Mitch asked.

"Pierre Boulez. Even interviewed him once. Man, is he an iceberg. Lucky for me he's stopped composing, so there wasn't much new stuff of his to bone up on. And then, I can feel like we're in the same boat, ol' Boulez and I. He conducts those established classics for his bread. I collect 'em, teach 'em, and review 'em."

Suddenly I wondered just how much of Zolly was for real and

how much an elaborate put-on. In fact I couldn't recall ever feeling certain or not as to whether he was being serious. For all I know that was just another cultural trait of New Yorkers. Someday, I thought, I'd spend time in New York and do field researches on their irony.

An ironic Mitch now punched him softly on the arm. "Hey, Zolly, with all those chicks around, you've probably had no trouble finding female company."

He made a kind of "ah, well" gesture with his hands and said, "Wouldn't know."

"Staying away from women?" I asked. The words "Sally Simsby" echoed resoundingly in my mind and probably in theirs, too.

"Let's say I'm looking into other orientations," he answered cryptically. "Somethin' closer to home. There's times when I think of women as creatures from another planet. Or at least American women."

An uncomfortable silence followed. That was the first time I'd heard anyone actually admit to such a preference, and so casually.

Soon after swilling down the last few drops of Lowenbrau we had our raincoats on and were stepping out onto the sidewalk. The rains had stopped but the air was misty. There were puddles on the Avenue, and we kept away from passing vehicles.

Mitch and I stood around wishing Zolly best of luck should he move up to "the big Y," while Jones on the other hand admitted that he still missed Berkeley.

"There's nothing in New Haven compares to Telegraph," he said wistfully, then reminisced a bit more before he shook hands with us, waved good-bye, and crossed to the other side.

As I watched, I raised and dismissed the thought that he might be headed up toward Etna Street again.

The March night felt damp all around. We started turning homeward, yet hadn't walked two steps when a short, slender woman in blue jeans and a peasant-style blouse also came out of the Heidelberg, did a double-take, and said to me, "Well, hello there." She made a little flourish with her small umbrella, then held it with both hands behind her long neck.

It was a few seconds before I recognized Annie-Lynn. She'd had her hair cut short, and the occasional snow-white streaks made her appear older.

"Mitch, this is Annie-Lynn, remember?"

"Sure I do. We all got high that night. One of my better trips, as I recall."

She and I hadn't crossed paths in three years, maybe more, and I suggested we all go for coffee at the Mediterraneum. Mitch walked our way but, like a good roommate who knows when three's too many, opted to go on home instead.

It being a rainy weekday night, the coffee clientele was sparse. Annie-Lynn and I went to sit upstairs at a table-for-two right by the bannister, from whence we could see the occasional night-hawks drifting in or out. Over a caffé bianco and a pastry I quickly summed up my uneventful past history and the evening's conversation, including Zolly's faith in quadraphonics.

She did her mysterious half-smile. "Ah, yes, I've heard the argument before."

And then, before I realized what was happening, Annie-Lynn was pouring out her soul to me, telling me about her disastrous and defunct two-year marriage with a gamba player who was also founder and director of their early-music group, Ian by name. To my growing amazement, she quietly recounted the relentless way in which he had abused her verbally, threatened her physically, addressed her as if she were a prostitute every night, and repeatedly suggested that she was utterly worthless as a person and as an instrumentalist.

Well, I thought to myself, musicians don't always have more fun. Or not necessarily.

It was all too much to absorb on such short notice, but I responded as comfortingly as I could. Her face looked tired and drawn as the story arrived at its end, and I raised the supposedly innocent question, "Still playing the lute?"

"Less than before, but they need me, so I perform with the

group for their sake, and Ian and I more or less ignore each other, except for business. I've also been working on jazz guitar, though. In fact that was just another apple of discord with Ian. He was always scorning my guitar lessons, dismissing them as 'rubbish.' Well, I think jazz is great stuff."

I couldn't help but query, "Were you by any chance getting bored with the early-music classics?"

"Well, yes, sort of. There is only so much you can do with Dowland's lute pieces, unless you're a Julian Bream. And I can't sing, so that limits my choices. But I'm getting tolerably good on guitar. It's not as if I'm Joe Pass yet, but there has been progress."

Annie-Lynn's way of talking was as distinctive and fresh as ever, and, in what I suppose is one of life's ironies, a bad marriage (or maybe it was getting out of a bad marriage) had made her sexier-looking.

At some point in our two-and-a-half hour chat and extra espressos I found out to my surprise that, back in the 'fifties, Annie-Lynn had attended a music camp in Highlands (where I might've actually passed her earlier incarnations on the sidewalk), that in 1971 we'd both happened to be taking in all of Jane Austen and also George Eliot and other old standards, and that we'd each of late been independently discovering Virginia Woolf's elusive lighthouse and Borges's "a-mazing games" (her pun); so now we could talk literature too, and I had something to offer in return. I pictured myself falling for this seasoned lute-and-guitar woman, and wondered if she entertained any like notions about me.

The last remaining Caffé employees had had to flick the lights and more or less kick us out at closing time, and reluctantly we emerged out onto the still-wet sidewalk, where Telegraph seemed almost as quiet as Christmas. As we approached the Bancroft Way entrance to the campus I saw tacked onto one of those free-standing bulletin boards some huge posters for a Stephane Grapelli concert, several weeks hence, in April. I suggested we attend; "Yes, why not," she nodded cryptically. I thought maybe putting my arm around her shoulder might be a friendly, consoling gesture, yet kept it as a thought, deferring it for after the concert.

Following her less-than-friendly divorce Annie-Lynn had chanced to find a basement apartment right next door to the second-floor place where I'd seen her off that night some years before. We approached the front steps; she climbed one, turned around and looked into my eyes as her mouth did its arch little smile. She came up close, briefly snuggled her round head onto my neck, then touched my lips with a more-than-split-second's soft kiss.

Reaching into her blue-jeans pocket, she produced and then flashed to me a brass key chain with a guitar motif.

She did an Italian-style handwave. "See you in two weeks," she said as she swung open the door.

Maturity Historical

The citizens of our island nation — the maturest and most advanced nation in history — lead their proud lives in uninterrupted silence. The silence has long been with us and is no doubt permanent. We may at times feel an atavistic desire to speak words or utter stray sounds. Yet the instinct goes unheeded, for the essence and indeed the very beauty of life amongst us islanders is our civilized though impregnable muteness.

That there was once an Era of Speech is a fact known to us all. Nor has it fully ended. Our talkative cousins on the mainland furnish a familiar enough instance. While their advances in space or weather technique may well rival ours, their daily customs remain stuck in a primitive and embarrassing volubility. However much we respect their gains in other realms, their *horror silentii* is repellent to us, and we customarily shun them. Their constant prattle brings to mind the ceaseless talk adorning the pages of several million novels, those now-dumb relics of a remote past when oral exchange was the chief link between individuals and society.

But by far the most striking souvenirs of the Era of Speech are the talking movies. These marriages of photography-cum-voice were in their time revolutionary. For us today their dependence on so bodily a medium as the vocal chord seems as quaint and old-fashioned as do an oakwood fortepiano or a Gregorian chant. Still it is unfortunate that film-production chanced to come late to us. Our neo-silent movies may be world classics, but talkies in our dialect were not many, and most of the ones in the museum are of foreign make. In fact the direct remnants of speech in our archipelago are few, and they date from the moment of terminal twilight and darkling obsolescence. I cite two of the noteworthier categories:

1) Some saturnine survivors, now withering away in their twelfth and thirteenth decades, who, having acknowledged the trend as inevitable, fell in with the forward march and took on a taciturnity as deep as ours. These residual characters, the living shards of an outmoded way of life, will speak privately to him who succeeds in gaining their confidence.

2) A handful of mysterious metal disks, made five generations ago by some of our ancestors (including a great-great-great-grandfather of mine), who, in order to satisfy the curious of aftertime, preserved for us the last embers of a human trait recognized by them as headed for nullification. The entire production can be listened to in less than ninety-five minutes: assorted combinations of twenty or thirty spoken words, most of them crude interjections, several of which were pronounced alike but spelled and employed differently. They can be listened to in our Museum of Antique Artifacts. I still remember my first attending as a boy and sensing within me an astonished chill upon hearing them, a sensation rivaled only by the vertigo I felt when, later that same day, I contemplated a conjectural replica of our yet-more-ancient simian forebears.

How this came about is a story mostly untold. The vast majority of my countrymen have no interest in learning about our past, and our younger citizens no longer read outside of the classroom, preferring instead to play with the latest bioelectrono conveyances that are unveiled every summer and fall. Everyone on these islands largely assumes that the move to silence was natural and foreordained. Our secondary-school histories ritually allude to and celebrate the great transformation while furnishing no explanatory background. There has not as yet been a single responsible attempt at describing the long process whereby the whole of this society — from Crown to humblest clerk — finally outgrew speech and achieved high silence.

Such is my aim and has been so since I began my labors as a low-level functionary at the Ministries, first of Conveyances, then of Archives and Collections. Somehow between the endless responsibilities of bureau and family I have been able to bring together on my desk the stages, the causes, and even the nuances of emotion that were bound up with the growth of untalkativeness. Thirty years of amateur archaeologizing have yielded the following modest results, which I believe to be truthful if not as yet complete. And inasmuch as few if any of my current compatriots will read me, these utterances are in all likelihood being penned for friendly readers located elsewhere and elsetime.

Let us begin with the physical aspects, leaving for later the other, more spiritual sorts of elements. Chronology demands this. As a sensible block of sound, our language had been flaking away long before modern developments quickened its demise. Despite stubborn claims to the contrary from entrenched priestly factions in several of the Ministries, it has been amply proved that geologic time can blunt the most massive crags and reduce them to gentle hills and flatland. In much the same way, even a language so rich as ours once was can and did stand subject to phonetic erosion. Sound law filed away at verb tenses, case endings, and expendable particles, leading to their disuse and disappearance. Syllables were imperceptibly simplified and then destroyed. Vowels were slurred into oblivion. Consonants went next. Pronounced carelessly, they all shared in the same fate, finally ending up somewhere in our library archives and the writings of philological sects long since dead.

Now it so happens that our island language, like our culture, qualifies as the oldest on planet Earth. In this I happily concur with the current high circle of His Majesty's councilors. (Previous circles had characterized our language as the youngest and hence most vital, though evidence points otherwise and to their discredit.) In so lengthy a history it stands to reason that sound and word erosion should have proceeded a good deal further than among humanity's more youthful speech products. Centuries earlier than elsewhere, case and tense suffixes vanished from our midst. (Certain mainland groups, by contrast, still cling stubbornly to their ablatives and accusatives.) But then our numbers system, with its fine distinctions between dual, triple, and duodecimal, was sliced down to differentiate between singular and plural, which in turn were reduced to solitary singular. Here perhaps lay the seeds for the disappearance of all nouns, for if the plurality of something is not worth mention, neither is that thing's singularity, and, it follows, neither is the thing itself.

Doubtless readers question this account of tense and number long lost. After all, my report rather bristles with pasts and plurals. (Indeed, that latter sentence makes use of and terminates with plurals.) Sometime in history, however, it happened that the *written* word ceased to develop as representational system. Royal and ministerial scribes simply gave up on updating the components, decided not to keep up with the relentless changes (syllable elimination, the new diphthongs, and the like) in our once-spoken language. So rather than write down sounds and sentences as he heard them, the man with his pen or other writing conveyances simply indicated how words *had been* pronounced, and sentences formed, at that very point in history in which writing innovations had come to their full halt.

The ever-widening gap finally led to a complete loss of connection between spoken sound and written symbol. To take a simple instance: Documentary sources strongly suggest that, just over three centuries ago, the sign *enough* was being pronounced, approximately, *nh*. There thus existed a total discrepancy between what writing purported to do and what it did in practice. Then, a century or so hence, the tenuous ties that linked written language to its source of existence were permanently snipped when spoken words vanished and the new biolectrono conveyances replaced them. But neither did this prevent the priests, the scriveners, and other groups from keeping the written word alive as a self-contained activity with values of its own. And so our written language, which had always lagged behind the spoken word, reached its fullest fruition in a kind of ontological self-sufficiency. Rather than lag behind, it simply pulled out of the race and set up shop for itself.

I have already suggested that the last words to disappear were the interjections. This completes the cycle since, according to a grand old theorist and former mentor of mine here at the Ministry, all languages once originated in the form of emotionally charged sounds, thence growing into fully-developed syntactic and semantic structures. An illuminating case in point is the archaic verb *phukyarss*. From scanty fragments dating back four millennia we infer that this word at one time carried a very specialized meaning, namely, "to perform sodomy in the month of May with a herd of young female goats, especially at sundown; said mainly of old men," an obvious reflection of the tribal, patriarchal, goat-herding economy whence it sprang. The word then expanded considerably its semantic field, and in documents dated another thousand years hence we find it apparently coming to signify, "to engage in sexual behavior of any kind, with anything, at any time."

This all-inclusive meaning inevitably left the word open to yet further extensions, interpretations, and abuse. What had been a verb appears to have undertaken a simultaneous career as all-purpose interjection, indeed became a veritable factotum in the employ of every whim and emotion from petty annoyance to cosmic malaise. Owing to repetition, the infinitive ending (*yarss*) was lost, the word being telescoped to *phuk,* and then — the logical step — as if it were some forgotten preposition from long-extinct Muscovite, to *phk.* (*Ph* indicated a bilabial, non-dental *f*, a sound resembling that which we produce when blowing out a candle.) One of these two consonants now faced imminent doom, but at this point there ensued a dialect split. Evidence from the north reveals that the northern region opted for *ph*, while the recorded discs of our ancestors, which are in southern dialect, show an unmistakable predilection for *k*.

Our interjection *phk>ph/k* seems to have been among the last, perhaps the very last, in disappearing. There is a rather fascinating fragment of a comic strip, its vintage set at approximately a decade-and-a-half after the pioneering bioelectrono conveyances had been introduced, and some five to ten years before the date when we can safely ascertain that the last words ever to be heard were enunciated. A sensational piece of sex and sadism, its extant initial frames tell of a ruthless and redheaded heroine, deceitfully demure but actually psychotic, who lives by using her boyfriends, bleeding them of their material and personal resources, and eventually discarding them with glee. In the concluding scene, by some less-than-believable coincidence, she and five of her ex-lovers converge within the ornate lobby of a sumptuous roadside inn, where, by an even more questionably spontaneous action, they seize her, defenestrate her, and plop her into the nearby river.

As she drowns, the traditional balloon floats over her, with the inscription:

PH !!!

— being the only spoken word to appear in some sixty-eight frames. If we can assume that the strip or at least the balloon reflects real conditions and not purely private fancies, then this is a clear indication that *ph/k* was an extremely isolated survival, arguably the only survival, of a human product literally at its last breath.

Needless to say, if someone today drew that frame, with that balloon, it would be looked upon as implausible, as fantasy or ancient folklore at best. It is true that our vocal chords, like our appendices, are with us still. Every newborn baby mewling in its nurse's arms unsettles us with its reminders of our primordial physiology. That someone over the age of two may talk, plead, or scream is a possibility, though so remote it remains inconceivable. For to emit any interjection, whatever one's distress, would be considered a breach of taste, a reversion to primitive ways well beneath the dignity of modern man. In my time I have heard no cries let out by any adult who is drowning or being beaten or assaulted, or who finds himself bereaved or abused. Were he to do so, we would recoil in horror at the atavism, and our day would be ruined. Some brave soul might venture to save the victim's life or soothe his woes. But the saved would survive only to be ostracized, standing out in our minds as the raw creature who, by lapsing into a barbarous and infantile past, had transgressed our civilized, mature mores.

Physical and moral pain are no doubt less than pleasant matters. And while it may be lamented that we've lost the childlike luxury of expressing them, such expression is now discouraged, nay, rejected, by our island nation's citizens. To us the acquired silence of our contemporary kingdom is what sets our humanity apart from the mindless cacophony of the animal world.

The other concurring factor that led to our transcending of talk was the velocity imperative, our merciless and uncompromising rhythm of change. For over a millennium now our life on this earth has been progressing at a speed so phenomenal that everything from home machines to priestly rituals goes quickly out of date. In its last centuries the waning culture of the spoken word also lived at this fast pace, not only in its rate of sound erosion but in that of verbal rephrasal as well.

It all began when the rules of good language were unlocked, revealed, and publicly codified. As a result the arts and sciences of words were put up for sale at every level of the marketplace. No one predicted it, though in retrospect it seems inevitable: Virtually every individual active in our society's speech-producing sectors became unprecedentedly wit-conscious. Absolute freshness and unrelenting innovation became the sole standard for what was deemed legitimate and acceptable speech. Formulas came and went, and great demands were made on all — whether the youngest of children, the humblest of servants, or the highest of priests — to bring together ever-new sets of words and phrases, much in the same way that most everyone then was all but required to combine ever-new shapes and colors in their daily attire.

In this dizzying quest for hitherto-unheard collocations, it often happened that an individual who had one day coined a *bon mot* would quite literally awake next morning and find it had become lifeless cliché. The necessary result: a pathological fear of repeating oneself, or — far worse — of plagiarizing another, howbeit unknowingly. The great fear was not unjustified, inasmuch as those unable to meet the high standard found themselves stunned into silence, and then despair. This horror of the has-been-said was terrifyingly exemplified in one of our few talking movies, which in the course of my investigations I watched at the Museum of Antique Artifacts. It begins with a man and his wife, happily married and ready for bed. He makes some topical comment, today undecipherable but clearly meant as a joke. She replies contemptuously, "Harry Fant said that yesterday on channel 191." The unintended platitude transforms him in her eyes into an irredeemable fool, which in turn sets off a whirl of events leading to marital disputes and several violent deaths.

As a result of such continual reshuffling of one's and everyone's words at every given opportunity, it came to be that all possible permutations were used up. Or, at least, people took to behaving as if all permutations were used up. Few if any would run the risk of reduplicating dead phrases. And so expediency won out: there emerged a lengthy interim period during which sign and gesture were revived. An ancestor of ours when shopping didn't say, "A loaf of bread, please." Rather they activated the bioelectronic conveyance of the moment and pointed at the loaf of their choosing.

It seems that uttering an old phrase would be favorably received only if it were obvious that one was voicing it with mockery or sarcasm, or was using it in some absurdly alien context, somewhat like our Anglo forebears might at times echo scriptural verse when wishing to be funny. I must confess that at this late date I too occasionally feel the desire to amuse myself with dead words, sometimes admittedly even to make myself better understood, humor or not. Reality, though, is merciless vis-à-vis personal desires, however legitimate certain desires may have been in our past. I know that, were I to employ so outmoded a conveyance, so dated a style as phonetic speech, I would appear as laughable, for example, as a California hawker in distant 1910 crying "Buy my wares, prithee," or as strangely false as that comic-strip heroine, with her gleaming smile, saying, "Thee I love."

The move toward muteness, it has been observed by my Ministry mentor, became definitive among the survivors of the last great missile clash of approximately a half millennium ago. In his view, such were the tasks of reconstruction that talk became superfluous and even suspect. Miraculously, during the time that followed, intercontinental wars came to be non-existent and even internal conflicts few. Speech too began seriously diminishing, though whether language shrinkage had anything to do with the fact of our long military peace is anybody's guess.

I do recall one military operation in my lifetime, when rural families in the north staged massive revolts against then-new agricorporate price policies on green beans, radishes, and lamb's wool. Shows of counterforce by royal troops did not suffice to quell the discontent. Suddenly, almost as if by magic, there occurred a broad amphibious assault by the armies and navies of the mainland. And how very strange it was! The invaders looked much like us, and yet *they talked,* an anomaly that shocked my preschool innocence and first sparked in my young mind a curiosity about accounting for our own superior difference.

For in the end it was a case of the mature conquered overtaking the benighted conqueror. I remember the foot soldiers, who spoke in their exotic, inflected ancestor to our own defunct language, punctuating it with strident laughs, all of which repelled us considerably. So they came, and they conquered; and the uprising ceased. But some of them stayed on, and over the years they found it necessary to rise to our own level. We observed with amusement as the onetime invaders gradually shed their old speech reflexes and eventually rivaled even us in their newly-adopted silence. With their blustering ways gone, they were in time accepted by the citizenry. A few went on to figure prominently in our small élite forces. Their children and grandchildren, growing up amidst our wordlessness, became silently active in everything from government to bioelectronics to sport.

Still, despite the high pride we take in our mute glories, I wonder at times if we haven't lost something, some more vital role in the theatre of Nature. Most Earthly beings, including many peoples, continue to emit patterned sounds. Clearly we've become a none-too-attentive congregation whereas in previous epochs our men and women added their counterpoints to a larger choir. It is good to be mature, civilized, and to avoid the primitive expression of now-useless passions, but I think we still sense within ourselves a vague impulse to show more for our states of mind than this equalizing silence. When I watch the old movies I can feel a strangely embarrassing nostalgia mingling with and qualifying my condescension. Those ancients, those ancients... While their hysterical sobs repel me, there is something delightful in their spontaneous laughter and bittersweet tears. With each step forward, I suppose, men lose as much as they gain.

More Satire

from

Amador Publishers

A NOVEL
OF COLLEGE LIFE
AND POLITICAL TERROR

THE CARLOS CHADWICK MYSTERY
A Novel of College Life
and Political Terror

by Gene H. Bell-Villada
ISBN: 0-938513-06-0   256 pp. $9.00

How and why does a college kid become
a radical, possibly a terrorist, in the early
1970's? The mystery is why the mainstream
media narrators fail to understand their own
story. This wild tale predicts the current
war in Peru and the pseudo-debate about
"political correctness." A marvelous spoof
of Gothics, Harlequins, college life and the
way the American mind works, or doesn't
work.

Gene H. Bell-Villada is a keen observer of the college scene, where he thrives
as professor, scholar, essayist and well-published literary critic and translator.
He has written for many national and international journals, and is author of
definitive books on Jorge Luís Borges and Gabriel García Márquez.   He
observed the American scene from a special perspective, having been reared in
the Caribbean area.

*"The central conceit -- the cult of 'balance' and centrism, and how that's
linked to various kinds of selective blindness -- is GREAT. The satire and the
aphorisms are mordant. Very funny, trenchant stuff."*
-- Carol McGuirk, FLORIDA ATLANTIC UNIVERSITY

*"Seductively readable, page by page. The portrait of the small New England
liberal arts college is wonderful, and Livie has to be the girl you love to hate."*
-- Mary Lusky Friedman, WAKE FOREST UNIVERSITY

*"Intriguing, and for those of us already disillusioned with the common
American ideologies, even fun."*   -- Mike Gunderloy, FACT SHEET FIVE

*"...A remarkable novel ... to be enjoyed and appreciated as part of a generally
muffled dialogue between different parts of the Americas."*
-- Paul Buhle, THE MINNESOTA REVIEW

*"The invisible ideology of journalistic objectivity serves as the all-purpose
whipping boy for this broadly comic tale... The author has done a fine job of
caricaturing those complacent collegians who don't realize the ideology is as
intertwined with college life as ivy to the walls."*
-- Jeff Reid, IN THESE TIMES

"For anybody who has lived through, or wondered about, the "culture wars" on U.S. campuses, THE CARLOS CHADWICK MYSTERY casts the debate in an entirely new light. Although the book is set in the 1970s, the issues that it deals with are as alive and relevant today as they were 20 years ago. The novel plays with the ideas of liberal objectivity and respect for different "perspectives" through the eyes of a student who sees the whole approach as a defense of moral and political alienation and paralysis.

"Raised in Latin America, in a family that would today be called "bi-racial" or "bi-cultural," Carlos comes to see the culture of intellectual detachment on his college campus as increasingly absurd in the face of U.S. actions in Vietnam. Both Latin American and U.S. culture and politics are presented in their brilliant diversity, and with wicked parody. The voices and the characters are disquietingly real, the satires drawn to a perfection that leaves the reader marvelling. The human portraits take each character just a shade beyond the people we all know and interact with every day. The book evokes its locations, which range from a quiet New England campus to Paris to Caracas, with vivid color and detail.

"Since I first read the book — and I have to confess to reading it seven or eight times by now — -I have been continually amazed at the way real-life events and people seem to have been taken "straight out of CARLOS CHADWICK." Life, politics, and academics will never look the same after you read this book."

— Avi Chomsky, Associate Professor of History
Salem State College, Massachusetts

VERMIN: HUMANITY AS AN ENDANGERED SPECIES
Harry Willson
ISBN: 0-938513-22-2 [192 pp. $10]

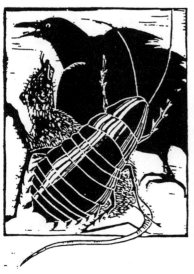

With dead aim and withering wit, Willson takes on plutonium, radioactive materials in the sewers, ozone depletion, government plans for the storage of nuclear waste, overpopulation and more personal follies like fundamentalism, free will, rituals, and even satire itself. In the title novella, VERMIN, rats, cockroaches and crows debate the use of scarce resources, while wondering what could have become of the humans. "The Extermination Game," remarks Ariel, the crow. "They were heavily into extermination."

"Willson is writing about ideas that can't just be digested over lunchbreak cheeseburgers and then forgotten in the scheduled hectic afternoon of 'normality.'"
— Ben G. Price, ANARCHY

"Harry Willson's previous novels showed his almost magical optimism about humanity. VERMIN, in contrast, is a group of cautionary tales and fables, some quite realistic, others quite absurd. Willson's dissection of human folly is necessarily painful, but he provides the appropriate general anaesthetic for the operation: a daring sense of humor. Definitely recommended."
— Bill Meyers, editor-in-chief, THE STAKE

"Spinning yarns and parables with spiritual and moral context, the author skillfully exercises a Socratic method of questions and conclusions, to expose the truths that the powers-that-be would rather keep hidden. What other author doggedly reminds us of how our civilization insists upon poisoning itself?"
— Jeff Radford, CORRALES COMMENT

"Throughout my reading of these stories and pithy comments, the words of Shakespeare's Puck resurfaced again and again: 'What fools these mortals be!'"
— Fred Gillette Sturm, Department of philosophy
University of New Mexico

THE GREAT TOBACCO WAR
The World's First Anti-Tobacco Novel
by Arthur L. Hoffman
ISBN: 0-938513-04-4 [157 pp. $8]

The fantasy of a public-health activist and his vendetta against the tobacco industry ranges from simple sabotage to outright guerrilla warfare. Genetic engineering, on top of tried and true tactics, lead to total annihilation of the product that now kills one thousand Americans per day.

Nationally recognized writer and educator, Arthur Hoffman has spent a lifetime crusading for a healthier world. Unconventional and imaginative, he dares his audience to think the impossible.

"...an impressive fable which stresses that if we wait for legislation and 2regulation to control the tobacco industry, millions more will die. A quick end to the entire industry is the best solution, and Hoffman offers handy, cost-effective tips for the activist health promoter. I heartily approve of the tactics!"
-- Michael Lippman, MD, Doctors Ought to Care [DOC], Seattle, WA

"Mr. Hoffman, an effective crusader for better health, has given us a unique, provocative and entertaining novel. It is a powerful new weapon in the fight against smoking, the most preventable cause of death in the United States." -- Victor W. Sidel, MD, Professor of Social Medicine
Past President, American Public Health Association

"...both easy reading and entertaining fiction which speculates how ordinary people can expedite the eradication of tobacco. It is a must addition to the arsenal of those who suspect that health is far too important a matter to be relegated to profiteer and politicians."
-- Thomas M. Goetzl, Professor of Law, Golden Gate University, San Francisco, CA

Order Blank

____PIANIST WHO LIKED AYN RAND @ $14   _____

____CARLOS CHADWICK MYSTERY @ $9   _____

____VERMIN @ $10   _____

____GREAT TOBACCO WAR @ $9   _____

Sub-Total: _____

Postage: __$2.00__

Total: _____

Send to:

Name _____

Address _____

City, State, Zip _____